TANGLED MAGIC

ONESONG: BOOK 1

DAWN BLAIR

MORNING STAR STUDIOS

Onesong

Tangled Magic

Sacred Knight

Quest for the Three Books

Manifest the Magic

To Birth a Destiny

History of a Dead Man (companion novella)

Prince of the Ruined Land

The Loki Adventures

1-800-Mischief

For Sale, Call Loki

For A Good Time, Call Loki

For More Information, Call Loki

For More Mischief, Call Loki

1-800-CallLoki (Omnibus of novellas 1-5)

1-800-IceBaby

Wells of the Onesong

Fractured Echo

Fall's Confession

The Doorway Prince

Stardust

Mystery of the Stardust Monk

Alexander's Den

Ninjas

By the Numbers

Space Ninjas Aren't Real

Other stories

The Last Ant

Broken Smiles

Oxygen

I'm With Cupid

Let's Make a Deal

Nonfiction

The Write Edit

Children's Picture Books

Eggs at Play

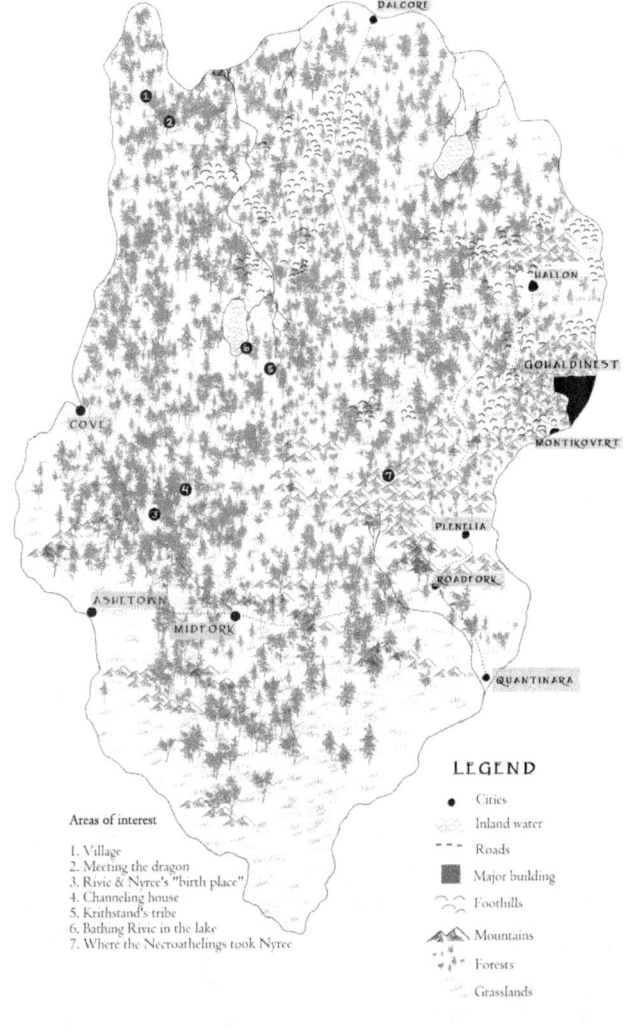

Areas of interest

1. Village
2. Meeting the dragon
3. Rivic & Nyree's "birth place"
4. Channeling house
5. Krithstand's tribe
6. Bathing Rivic in the lake
7. Where the Necroathelings took Nyree

LEGEND

- Cities
- Inland water
- Roads
- Major building
- Foothills
- Mountains
- Forests
- Grasslands

DALCORE

HALLON

GOHALDINEST

MONTIKOVERT

COVE

PLENELIA

ROADFORK

ASHETOWN

MIDFORK

QUANTINARA

Main Characters

Rivic – The hero of our tale, born with destructive magic
Nyree – Rivic's magicless twin sister

Early years

Ren – Rivic's aunt
Lyre – Rivic's uncle
Sontre' – Elderly woman responsible for training Rivic

Tribe

Krithstand – Tribe's chieftain
Ellonia – Daughter of Chief Krithstand and the tribal healer
Tovis – One of the tribe's border guards
Nex – One of the horserider guards for the tribe
Augina – Former healer for the tribe
Fronis – One of the tribal's council

Gohaldinest

Cirvel – Lord of Gohaldinest
Alityka – Acolyte who befriends Rivic
Lihn – Mistress to Lord Cirvel and Alityka's friend
Dragzel – Lihn's pet cahaster
Guardian – a dragon living in caves beneath Gohaldinest
Azote – A gaxlor working for Lord Cirvel
Kalt – One of Cirvel's Necroathelings
Madame Orcee – Owner of a local tea shop
Berrik – A very elderly Sapere under Cirvel's control
Melodin – An acolyte
Oren – An acolyte
Sempt – An acolyte

CHAPTER 1

"*N*yree," the young boy whispered. "Nyree, are you awake?"

The wind pushed against the leather skins which formed the walls of the longhouse. Or, in the darkness with the snapping of the tanned hides, it only seemed like wind blew from the outside. Rivic felt a rush of air against his cheeks as he crawled out from beneath his blankets toward where his twin sister, Nyree, slept. He tried not to think about how he could make out her sleeping form in the faint blue light coming from his hands. He shook the warm bundle of her blankets.

The temperature seemed to drop.

"Nyree," he pressed, rocking her harder back and forth.

"I am now, Rivic. What do you want?" she grunted as she rolled toward him.

"'Tis happening again." Rivic lifted his hands as Nyree rubbed fists against her face and sat up. Her eyes widened after she knocked the sleepy dust away and saw the vivid blue lines emanating from his skin. Her blue eyes reflected the light as if they were glowing as she drew nearer to him.

"What am I going to do?" Rivic asked, sounding helpless. "I need your help."

Nyree tossed the blankets off her legs and started to slide from her bed. "I'll get Aunt Ren. She'll know what to do."

"Nay," Rivic said, grabbing onto her nightclothes. "Stay here with me. I need your help."

"But the last time –" Nyree pulled hard trying to tug the cloth away from him.

Rivic didn't like her fear. He had to keep her close. How could he make her understand? "I know," he cried. "But I can't do this without you. No one else must know. Remember what they said?"

Nyree put her little hands on his cheeks, then leaned forward so their foreheads touched. "Don't be scared. 'Twill be fine. I won't leave."

She hugged him close and began to rock him as their mother had once done with them when they needed soothing. Rivic closed his eyes, pretending he couldn't see the glow extending up his arms. He wished his mother was here taking care of him, telling him how to handle this.

Aye, that's good, calm yourself. Hush now, child.

It wasn't helping. The bad thing would happen all over again.

Nyree tightened her hold on him.

"'Tis getting worse," Rivic whispered. His body began to tremble along with hers.

"What's going on?" Ren called out sleepily from the other room. "Children?"

Nyree's head lifted up to listen. "She's coming."

"I tied the flap," Rivic admitted, clinging to Nyree. "She can't get in."

"Did you do that before you woke me?"

"Nay, I did it just now."

As if to prove his point, Ren tried to pull the flap aside but it didn't open. "Children? What's going on in there? Untie the flap right now."

"Why did you do that?" Nyree pushed him away from her. "She can help. Let her in."

"Nay, I'll kill them, like I did the last time. We've got to run away."

Nyree shivered in the coldness again. "Stop, Rivic, please. We'll be all alone."

"We'll be alone either way." Rivic closed his eyes. "I can't let this happen. The bad thing. Nyree, make it stop."

"Stop." Her voice was nearly a shriek.

"Children!" Ren shouted. "Lyre, I can't get in."

Rivic heard footsteps approaching the flap. He opened his eyes, even though he didn't need to. He knew his uncle was coming toward the door, his dagger drawn. His uncle would cut the ties. They were coming in. They couldn't. It would be bad.

"Aunt Ren, get back," Rivic shouted. The words sounded foreign to him, as if they were garbled and hadn't come out right. They sounded like the first gurgling of a baby.

"Rivic, please stop," Nyree cried.

"Rivic, what are you doing to your sister? Leave her alone. Don't you hurt her!" Ren screamed.

"Ren, I told you we shouldn't have taken in the boy. His magic is wild. 'Tisn't natural, that demon child!"

"Cut the wall," Ren ordered.

Lyre's dagger sawed at the thick ties.

The whole room filled with blue light. Nay, it was the whole longhouse because Rivic could now see the silhouettes of his aunt and uncle behind the flap. He held onto Nyree, willing her to be safe.

A shout came from outside, followed shortly by another.

"When I get in there, boy, I'll kill you!" Lyre shouted.

"Cut through the wall," Ren yelled again.

"Lyre-Chief! Mistress Ren! Do you need help?" hollered someone outside. "What's going on in there?"

The blade of the dagger pressed against the hide wall, but it didn't cut through. "'Tis gone dull," their uncle said.

"Rivic!" Nyree screamed.

"Nyree, what's he doing?" their uncle shouted. "Is he hurting you?" Lyre's hands tried to pull the skins apart as if he could rip a hole, but it only made the knots of the ties tighter.

"Nyree, Rivic," their aunt screamed as she yanked and shoved at the skins as if sheer frustration would open them.

Every sound pounded in Rivic's ears. More villagers were coming. They were waking throughout the village. Someone whispered about the gargaxes hearing this commotion. The thought of the winged beasts descending upon them made Rivic's heart quicken. Nyree screamed. He and his sister had to get away. If they could squeeze out beneath the walls maybe where the hides weren't stretched too tightly, they might be able to run into the forest.

Rivic tried to move, but Nyree grabbed and clung onto him. Sticky wetness poured over his skin. He felt tangled in it. Nyree gagged.

"Can't breathe," she gasped.

The stickiness cocooned both of them.

A sword blade slashed through the leather wall, followed by a large man storming into the room and trailed by a slender lady with long, black hair.

"What 'tis going on here?" his uncle raged.

Rivic could barely see him through the webbing covering his face. Ren, with her hand over her mouth, appeared blurry at the edge of the glowing round strands.

"'Tis happening again... the bad thing," Rivic said. "Get back."

"Rivic! Nyree!" Ren ran for them and clawed at the webbing covering them.

"Stop!" Rivic found himself yelling in unison with Nyree. The word came out so rushed, so panicked. It seemed to surge from him with a will of its own. The cold temperature of the room broke away, evaporating in a sudden heat which Rivic felt pound from his chest.

Magic exploded.

Rivic and Nyree were slammed to the ground. Blue light radiated so brightly Rivic had to close his eyes, while a bold white lit the insides of his eyelids. As before, the bad thing brought a sudden and complete silence.

Rivic lay still, afraid to move, terrified to look. A moment later, Nyree shook him. He opened his eyes and saw his twin looking back at him. The sticky webbing dissolved from around them.

"Rivic?" Nyree said, her voice quaking and just a tad bit higher than normal.

He didn't want to look around. He knew the devastation around him. He could see it through her eyes.

"Aunt Ren? Uncle?" Nyree rasped.

Did he dare hope? Could they be alive? Was the tone of Nyree's voice hope or despair?

Rivic raised his head and looked around. His aunt and uncle were gone. As Rivic looked out further, he saw the longhouse gone, the village no more. The forest floor lay blackened in a wide circle out from their position.

The bad thing. It had happened again.

The entire village had been reduced to ashes, leaving only Rivic and Nyree at its heart.

"Rivic," Nyree asked with tears in her eyes, "what did you do?"

Rivic looked down at his hands, now back to their normal skin coloring.

"Rivic?" Nyree asked again.

Rivic wanted to run away, but how could he leave his sister here alone. He should have left when he'd first woken and run into the woods for the gargaxes to find. Why had he reached out for Nyree instead of leaving when he first saw the blue glow on his fingertips? He knew what it meant.

Nyree hugged him, clinging on. "There's no one else. We're alone again," she said. "Don't leave me."

It was too late for that. Rivic started to cry against her. "What are we going to do?" They were alone. Again.

Nyree began rocking him.

A cold breeze started to blow over them. If the gargaxes didn't find them, the season's chill would. Nyree shivered and Rivic wondered if she was already starting to freeze to death. Would it be that quick? Would it be just like falling asleep?

The wind picked up and Rivic felt Nyree reach up to brush her loose hair away from her face. The sound of her gasp made him look up.

"Nyree, run," he said, scrambling off the ground. He grabbed her hand, his gaze still looking upward as he pulled her along to scramble out from beneath a large, winged beast settling in for a landing.

"Is that a gargax?" Nyree screamed, pushing more hair out of her eyes with her little fingers.

"A large one!" Rivic wasn't really sure if it was a gargax or not, but from the stories he'd been told, this seemed close enough. He really didn't want to stick around to find out. At this moment, letting the cold take their souls seemed like a better idea. Even taking the chance of finding another village to take them in before they succumbed to the elements seemed like a fairer option than facing this gigantic beast.

The black monster landed as they hid behind a tree. "Children," it spoke. "Where are your parents?"

Rivic clasped his hand over Nyree's mouth as she did the same to him. They stared into each other's fear-filled eyes. Rivic slowly started to shake his head.

"Which one of you has the magic?" the beast asked. Between the branches of the tree, Rivic could see it stretching out onto its belly over the ground, moving more like a snake toward them than an animal with legs and wings. But its teeth were more frightening than that of a snake's. In the stories, gargaxes always had sharp, pointed teeth. This monster had to be a gargax. That's why it was asking which one of them had the magic.

"Though time is preciously short, I can wait," the monster said. "This is too important to rush." It closed its eyes.

After a few moments, Rivic saw steady puffs of smoke coming out its nostrils. He didn't remember any of the stories talking about gargaxes breathing out fire. Could this be the one beast more feared than the gargaxes? He tried desperately to think of what it was called, but most people had been too afraid to speak its name, referring to it as the primal god instead. He pried Nyree's hand away from his mouth. "I think it sleeps," he whispered.

He put his finger to his lips and breathed a small, "Shh," as they started to tiptoe out from behind the tree. Nyree pulled on his hand.

"Come on," Rivic mouthed to her. "We need to get away."

"Why are you going toward it?" she returned in a voice so slight he barely heard it.

Rivic looked around, realizing that they had come back into the ring of flattened trees and were indeed heading toward the creature instead of away. He tried to turn and step in the other direction, but his feet just moved in reverse so he was walking backwards toward the monster, whose breath he could feel like a hot breeze against his back.

"You cannot fight it, little one. Your magic wants me as

much as I want it." As the monster spoke, its words blew in puffs against him.

He reached for his sister. "Nyree," he wanted to scream, but the word barely came out.

She looked timidly at him, then back to the beast.

"Nyree." It came out a little stronger now.

The monster pushed up with its front legs and lifted itself off the ground. "Do not fear. You will be magnificent."

Nyree bolted from behind her tree and ran to Rivic. She grabbed his hand, trying to pull him out of the debris of the devastation he had caused and back toward the forest with her. Her bare feet slid in the dirt as she dug them in to keep them from moving toward the beast.

"Away from him, you magicless creature," the beast raged. "You do not belong with him."

Nyree threw her arms around Rivic. "I won't leave you, Rivic. No matter what happens, I won't leave you."

Rivic grabbed onto her too. He closed his eyes as he felt the huge, winged beast begin to circle them.

"Let him go!" the monster roared in Nyree's face. The breath was so hot Rivic wanted to flinch away from the heat. But Nyree didn't move.

"I am out of time and can no longer delay. I will take you both!"

Nyree's hold on Rivic strengthened. He squeezed his eyes as tightly shut as he could. A long warm blanket circled them.

Not seeing how that was possible, Rivic peeked open one eye. Nay, it wasn't a blanket.

It was the monster's tongue.

Rivic felt his feet lift from the ground. Nyree stayed with him, clinging tightly. He felt himself sliding, then coming to a rest.

His last thought before he fell into a dream was that the monster had swallowed them whole.

CHAPTER 2

More than 10 cycles later...
"Again!" Sontre' called out from the opposite river bank.

Rivic grimaced as he hoisted the log beam and set it behind his neck like a yoke before plunging back into the waist-deep water. As he took notice of his surroundings, he realized the elderly woman had already magically teleported him downstream. He tried to be grateful about not having to tread the loop through the creek again, but he knew what was coming.

Tightening his grip and adjusting the beam's weight across his shoulders, Rivic steeled himself. The cold water had made his legs go numb, making it hard to squeeze the muscles, but he had to. He pushed forward into the current and began to run. The rushing water cascaded against him, impeding his motion.

"Do you feel it coming?" Sontre' called out in her taunting way.

He couldn't let her distract him now. *Run*, he said, trying to focus his mind. Thrusting his legs forward, he sped against the river's flow. He felt like he was standing still. He needed to get his momentum up or it would catch him. *Faster*!

"Feel it."

"Rivic," Nyree called from the riverbank, "'tis to your left."

A breeze wafted on his face as the invisible monster swooped in front of him. He flinched. It was enough to let the water take him and he went under. The last surprised breath was all the air he got to hold in his lungs.

Vines whipped out from the log and lashed around his wrists, insuring that he couldn't use his hands to get out of the stream. The current swept him along, spinning him within the undertow.

The log hit a rock and sent pain jarring through his neck and shoulders. His knees dragged over the stones and pebbles at the bottom. He had to get his feet back beneath him. He needed to stand up soon so he could breathe. The water gave him another twirl.

At this rate, Sontre' would be fishing him out of the river again.

Again.

Nay, not again, he vowed. "Talcor dun," he said, expelling the remaining breath from his lungs. The words rose as a mass of bubbles in front of his face. Then he felt air on his skin. As the spell dropped him from several feet above the water, Rivic prepared himself to run in the flow of the river. His feet landed; he stumbled, but didn't fall, and then took off running.

His vision dimmed to black. Sontre' had foreseen what he was going to do and had handicapped him further.

Once he got back into the flow of the creek, he turned and started running blindly against the current. Only by feeling the shifting rocks beneath his feet did he know that he was actually making any progress. When the water started to rush against one side of him more than the other, he knew that he'd gotten off center and needed to correct his position.

Were Sontre' and Nyree still out there? Why wasn't Nyree telling him anything?

He had to get this blinding spell off him.

"Radin lukion." The magic remained. He should've known that Sontre' wouldn't make it that easy.

Nyree screamed.

"Sontre'!" Rivic shouted, hoping that Sontre' hadn't turned her magical beast on Nyree. His sister had no way to defend herself. "Attack me."

The beast thumped into Rivic's back, sending him face first into the water again. Except that it grabbed ahold of his hair and yanked him back up. Rivic felt himself lifted out of the river and thrown backwards. Water rushed up his nose and he ungracefully came floating up with his legs flailing for a useless grip. Harnessed like he was, he couldn't flip over.

Angry, he tipped his head forward and pushed the log upward. The wood pulled at his hair and scraped against his scalp. He no longer cared about the pain.

The beast seized the log. It gave a resisting jerk, which Rivic used to overturn himself and get his feet under him. He tried a second time to raise the log off his shoulders and over his head. Succeeding, he rammed the beast with the log. Satisfaction at landing the hit renewed his energy. Rivic screamed in rage as he plunged forward.

His foot kicked against a rock, sending discomfort through his toe and up his foot. Resisting the pain, he fell forward as the beast unhooked itself from the log and went flying by him. Rivic threw his hands out and the log still tied to his wrists caught on the rocky shore. Water splashed in his face, but he was glad it wasn't deep. Bringing a knee up, he managed to stand and turn. He thrashed back out in the river.

"Rokta toyia," he shouted, feeling the magic around him snap. With Sontre's spells broken, his vision returned, the vines retreated from around his wrists, and he heard a splash as the invisible beast transformed back into the rock it had once been. He looked to where Nyree had been standing to find her spot empty.

"Nyree!" he called out. "Where is she?"

Sontre' shrugged. "Another beast took her."

Even while he was certain that Sontre' would never let one of her magical beasts lethally hurt either one of them, she also wasn't known for pulling the punches. Lessons had to be learned and sometimes they were best acquired the hard way.

"Vochey," Rivic said, calling his sword to his hand. He pressed out of the river and rushed into the forest.

"You'll never catch them in time," Sontre' bellowed behind him.

Ignoring the taunt meant to slow him with worry, he dashed into the woods. Sontre's beasts were fast, but they were still magical. He swept his hand around in the air before him, feeling for the trail of magic. Finding it, he hurried on.

He wondered what magical protection Sontre' had put on his opponent today as he tried to recall the ones she's recently used: water, fire, earth, cold, warm... what else remained?

Snakes shot up out of the ground around him. Startled, he jumped backwards. A serpent slithered over his shoulder from the trees above him. Rivic jumped sideways, shoving the snake off him. It disappeared before it hit the ground. In the distance, he thought he heard Sontre' laugh.

So thought magic it was! Two could play at that game. Rivic knelt down and placed his palm flat against the ground. Sontre' wanted to play, so he'd play. "Shiba'lator ma kryias." That should do it.

He began running again.

After a moment, before he came upon Sontre's beast in the forest, he heard a shriek behind him and knew that his own startling thought had reached Sontre'. He couldn't help the smile knowing that for once he'd surprised her.

He sensed magic draw closer now as he neared Sontre's beast. He could feel Nyree with it. In fact, Nyree was currently petting her invisible capture. Rivic sighed with a relieved agitation. She'd charmed it, not magically of course, but with simple physical touch. It might as well be a dog at her feet lavishing in her attention. Rivic knew that would change the moment he entered the scene.

His ears filled with pressure and it suddenly became hard for him to hear. Of course. Sontre' had imbued this beast with sense magic. First he'd been blinded, now he couldn't hear. He didn't really care if he lost his sense of smell and taste or not; he'd never found smell the most useful of attributes to battle. But if he lost his sense of touch, he might be in trouble. He hoped the beast could only influence one sense at a time.

He tried to yawn and pop the pressure in his ears. It didn't help.

The compression continued along his skin. It seemed the beast was affecting the atmosphere and intended to crush him.

Nyree screamed. She felt it too. Had she lost control of her enthralled beast? Was that even possible?

Rivic ran, jumping over boulders and fallen logs. "Nyree, I'm coming," He shoved branches out of his way.

He found Nyree sitting at the base of a tree with the shimming body of Sontre's beast sitting on her lap. The creature growled, standing and rounding quickly from Nyree's hold as Rivic found them. It did indeed look like a small dog.

The weight against him deepened.

Sontre' appeared beside him and she raised her hand, dispelling her beast. The pressure remained.

"I was just about to finish it off," Rivic complained. "Why did you do that?"

"Because there is something else in our woods, someone not part of our training. Can you feel it?"

Rivic wondered if she was talking about the pressure all around him, but then he felt something else, something that didn't belong: chaos. "Aye."

"Go, find it," Sontre' urged. "I'll stay here with Nyree and keep her safe."

Rivic nodded, then started running in the direction of the tumultuous energies. He hurtled a fallen log and landed in a thick patch of grass. The presence of tracks indicated someone had moved through here earlier and left a trail behind. Instinct told him not to follow the trail, but rather to turn left. He followed his gut.

Beyond the trees ahead, Rivic saw two men standing in a clearing, each wearing robes so dark purple in color that Rivic almost thought they were black. He knew instantly what they were, who they were: Necroathelings. Sontre' had told him stories of the deadly maeges from Gohaldinest, but he'd never seen one. One of the Necroathelings sensed Rivic's magic and turned.

Rivic wished Sontre' were here. She'd know what to do. Her sparkling magic would fill the air. He didn't know how to deal with the Necroathelings. "Royka piryeian," was the only spell that came to his mind.

Vines grew up around the Necroathelings, trapping them.

Or so Rivic thought. His vines dissolved away, scattering in ashes around their feet.

"This is the one," a Necroathelings said to the other.

The second Necroatheling pulled two throwing knives off of a belt that looked loaded with the deadly weapons.

Without the belt, the two Necroathelings in their hooded, dark plum cloaks looked identical.

As much as Rivic wanted to flee, he knew if he turned he'd take the knives right in the expanse of his back. Better to face them and try to use magic as a shield. The Necroatheling looked startled that Rivic still stood to face him.

"Shakita," the Necroatheling said, raising his hands.

A branch above Rivic's head cracked and gave way. Rivic raised his hands and magically caught it. Then he shot it forward at the Necroatheling.

"Daurkin." The Necroatheling brushed his hand to the side and the branch exploded into millions of little shards.

Rivic acted quickly. "Shi'baten to'a helcord." The splinters all shot toward the Necroatheling, stabbing and impaling him repeatedly. The Necroatheling screamed, falling down.

The second Necroatheling had taken a few of the shards as well. He pulled a splinter from his leg before glaring at Rivic. "Malkibar."

The spell pushed Rivic backwards, flipping him uncontrollably a couple of times in the air before he hit the ground and rolled. He scarcely believed he hadn't slammed into a tree or something from the blow. A chill ran through him as he pushed to his hands and knees, then climbed to his feet. He wanted this done and over. Instinctively, he reached out to the Onesong for assistance. How best to end this?

One answer came and he spoke the word. "Shalish."

The ground beneath the Necroathelings softened and one fell right into the quicksand while the other one teleported out of it.

"Practa be," the sinking Necroatheling said.

"Paca'ta," Rivic said with a wave of his hand now to deflect the spell cast at him. The magic so near him almost made him miss the sensation of the uncaptured Necroatheling reappearing on the other side of him.

The sand-detained attacker unleased one more curse behind Rivic, "Shakalal."

The spell lashed across Rivic's back.

"Shakalal," the other Necroatheling called out.

Rivic saw the Necroatheling motion as if he were using a whip. The spell smacked across his chest and face, knocking him to his knees and leaving his vision blurred and stinging. Rivic angrily fought through it, blinking out the tears to clear his sight as he tried to get back to his feet.

Another tight compression wound around Rivic. The Necroathelings seemed unfazed by it, but the intense gravity held Rivic down on his knees.

"Now, before he is born," the Necroatheling being consumed by the ground yelled.

The Necroatheling with the daggers stalked forward and raised his blade. "Sha'tauk cril vashtadien cri'alk soona'ana-may. Oolalan ta."

The weapon slashed across Rivic's chest. A white flash opened up across him, lighting up the Necroatheling's broad smile beneath the dark hood. The Necroatheling reached into Rivic's chest. Rivic tried to move against the pressure as the Necroatheling's hand entered him. Resistance brought with it the terrifying solidity of the fingers moving within him. Rivic could now see his attackers brown eyes as his eyesight adjusted to the light. The Necroatheling's gaze danced with delight, mocking Rivic and his suffering, letting him endure a little longer until finally drawing out a long yellow thread. With mocking laughter, the Necroatheling lifted the thread, tilted back his head, and dangled it over his open mouth as if he were going to make to swallow it.

Though Rivic wasn't quite sure what was going on, he knew he had to get that thread back. He scrambled to get his feet under him and he lunged at the Necroatheling, who cupped the thread into his hand as Rivic caught him around the waist. The Necroatheling fell, nearly flipping in over backwards in an awkward somersault.

Rivic dove for the thread. The Necroatheling snatched it up before Rivic grabbed it. He pounced for the hand grasping the thread again, but the Necroatheling knocked him aside with a wave of magic. Once more, Rivic found himself on the ground, on his back staring up at the trees. He rolled his knees up to his chest, then arched his back hard, flipping himself up to his feet.

"Look at the pretty yellow thread," the one holding it said as he let it dangle from his fingers.

"Do it. Birth comes quickly now," the other shouted, now waist deep in the sand.

The Necroatheling's eyes widened with delight as he pulled his dagger and went to cut the thread. "First this, then I will have your life, boy. You will never see the light of day and my master will reward me greatly."

"We are not here to kill him." The Necroatheling twisted his hand and the yellow thread suddenly appeared in his fingers as if he'd snatched it from his partner. "Rok'shada tumay vakara."

The ground cracked beneath the feet of the Necroatheling who wielded the dagger. A swell of muddy earth bubbled up and swallowed the Necroatheling's legs. He dropped the weapon as he started to sink. Before the Necroatheling could say anything, the sludge pitched up over his head as if it were a living beast swallowing him whole.

Rivic stumbled backwards, toppling over as he tried to get away from the churning ground. The dagger rolled and slid along the earthen waves as if it also sought to get out of danger.

The buried Necroatheling reached a hand from the mud, struggling to get out.

"Wait, nay!" Rivic cried at seeing the ground mend right

over the top of the Necroatheling. He scrambled backwards away from the spot as the hand flailed for something to grab. Realizing the man was still alive, Rivic changed direction and rushed forward. He tried to dig into the ground, but quickly realizing his futility, he made to grab onto the Necroatheling's fingers. They clenched desperately onto Rivic. The ground burped and the hand sank beneath the gurgling surface, releasing Rivic right before pulling him in too. The Necroatheling was gone. Rivic felt sick to his stomach. Just as he thought he might retch, a voice came from nearby.

"Weep not. Some missions demand sacrifices."

As Rivic had been looking down, he realized that the slash across his chest was no longer there, nor was there a single drop of blood. Rivic lifted his head up to see the remaining sand-trapped Necroatheling giving him a puzzled expression.

"That doesn't stop you from feeling remorse over the Necroatheling?" the man asked.

Rivic wasn't certain why he should answer the odd question from a Necroatheling. "Aye, I do."

"Do not pity him any longer. There is not a soul to mourn."

"I have no quarrel with the Necroathelings. Why did you attack me?"

As soon as the question was out, Rivic wished he hadn't asked. The Necroatheling held the yellow string pinched between his fingers over his head and smiled up at it as if paying it reverence. "This is a thing of beauty, a rarity. Too bad I have to destroy it. Vochey dagger."

The weapon appeared in the sand-trapped Necroatheling's hand. He looped the thread and slid the dagger's blade into the center.

"Malkibar." At Rivic's push spell, the dagger slammed

against the Necroatheling's face, who grunted with surprised shock at the hit and dropped both the dagger and the thread.

"Malkibar!" Rivic shouted again. The dagger slid across the quicksand for a short distance before stopping and starting to sink. The thread, however, being lighter in weight, flew into the air and began to flutter back down to the ground. "Talcor dun!" Once on the other side of the trapping sand, Rivic snagged the thread floating in the air and began running through the forest as fast as he could.

"You may live for now, boy," the Necroatheling taunted behind him, "but we fulfilled our duty."

Rivic stopped, turned when he thought he might be far enough away, and looked back at the Necroatheling, who now stood buried up to his shoulders in the quicksand Rivic's spell had created.

"We will be rewarded in the afterlife," the Necroatheling screamed. He leaned forward and dove into the shifting sand, allowing it to swallow him. Only a small piece of his purple cloak remained on the surface. Soon, even that last remnant disappeared as well.

Numbly clutching the thread, Rivic began to walk. He wasn't even certain of his direction until he came back to the area where Sontre' and Nyree stood.

"What's wrong?" Sontre' asked.

"They were Necroathelings," Rivic responded. "We have never encountered anyone else."

"Someone was here?" Nyree looked at him, her eyes widened with surprise. "Sontre'?"

"Necroathelings here? Why would she do that?" Sontre' glanced toward the sky above them. "Why would you do that?"

Rivic wasn't certain who she was talking to or who she referred to, and it scared him knowing that even she was unsure why he'd seen the Necroathelings.

Sontre' looked at him. "What happened?"

"I fought them, but the Necroathelings took something from me," Rivic confessed. He found his hands quivering now and chills quickly growing up over his arms. He couldn't control the trembling.

Sontre' walked a couple of extra steps as if moving into the forest, then she turned to face him. "What did they take from you?"

"A yellow thread. Then Necroatheling fought over it, and one killed the other."

"Do you have it?" she asked hurriedly.

"Aye." He held it up, the string vibrating from his quaking fingers, and she took it from him.

"That is disappointing, but not the end of things." She examined it for a moment before handing it back. "They have taken an essence of your magic from you. What they believe they have done in service of their lord might be to our advantage yet."

"How do you mean?"

Sontre' held out her arms to put one around Rivic and the other around Nyree as they started to walk back to their cottage. "I need you both to listen very carefully. What I have to say is important. I do hope there is time for supper before you have to go."

"Go? Where are we going, Sontre'?" Rivic asked.

"You are going somewhere I cannot follow."

"We don't understand."

"As tangible as this realm has seemed, I have been training you. None of this is truly real. 'Tis a construct of the mind. Now, you must go back to the physical world. You are about to become novihomidraks."

"Novihomidraks?"

"You will be born from a dragon. Rivic, you were meant to be a champion, to help save this world. I can only hope that I have done adequate duty to prepare you both for your powers."

"Our powers?" Rivic asked.

Once more, a deep ache constricted around him. Nyree wrapped her arms around herself too. Only Sontre' seemed unaffected.

"Your dragon mother had to pick certain aspects to give each of you. Most of them, you will split, but some are individual to you. Rivic, you got the magic because your sister has none. Nyree, without magic, I could not train you as I did Rivic. I do not know what powers you each will receive; the taking of twins for novihomidraks should have never been considered and there is a penalty somewhere in the universe for that."

"'Tis that what the Necroathelings took from me? One of my dragon powers?"

"Aye, but I do not know which. Without it, you will be left vulnerable. You will have to learn to compensate for this weakness on your own." Her eyes grew wide as she turned again to Nyree. She reached out toward him. "Rivic, give here the thread."

He handed the thread to Sontre'.

"Maybe all is not lost." She beckoned Nyree. "Come close, child. Tip back your head and open your mouth, and let us hope this works though I do not know what effect 'twill have."

"Why can't you return it to me?" Rivic asked, nearly shrieking the question.

"'Tis better this way. In time, I suspect you will understand." Sontre' took out her dagger and cut the yellow thread on the blade over Nyree's face.

Several glittering sparkles sprinkled down onto Nyree, vaporizing as she breathed them in through her nose and open mouth. For a moment, Nyree glowed with a whitish-gold color. It condensed until it was like a single, glowing line situated from her throat to her stomach. Rivic felt sick at the sight of it. He'd lost something important; he just knew it.

After placing the dagger back in its sheath, Sonte' took Rivic's hand in hers. "Stay close to your sister. Whatever power the Necroathelings took from you, Nyree now possesses all of it." Sontre' touched Nyree's arm and a smile shared between them communicated something Rivic didn't comprehend.

Sontre' looked back at Rivic. "This world has been cut off from the Wells so I am unable to provide you with a mentor from the Onesong, Rivic, but know that you will not be the only champion. There is another who will help you, but be aware that she is high-spirited, sometimes even reckless and rash. You must be gentle with the champion who is already here because she is the guardian of this world and does not always see the bigger picture. She will need your guidance and temperance at times. You might be able to find others as well, an oracle or a Drifter if you are lucky, but do not count on it; the Onesong has forsaken this world."

"The Wells of the Onesong?" Rivic asked. He'd always imagined them as a metaphor rather than truth, but as he stood here holding Sontre's hands he could see them in his mind. Rivic knew that a world cut off from the Wells forgot the truth of the Onesong and began a long, slow death of war, disease, and famine until every person was fighting against another and the whole planet died. The only chance the world had was if a champion of the Onesong came to the world to save it and tried to waken others in the world to the truth. Now he knew that was real and more than just a story.

"There is another power you both will split, and because of that 'tis dangerous for both of you. When a novihomidrak leaves their pearl, the outer shell dissolves and becomes a protective layer on the novihomidrak, acting as armoring. Only the weapons of another novihomidrak can hurt the typical novihomidrak." Sontre' began to walk faster, her arms flapping slight as she spoke. "You held onto each other so tightly when the dragon came for him, little lost lambs that you were. She had no choice but to take you both. Because of that, you will have to split the protection of the shell and the dragon armor will be divided between the two of you, which means you will not be impervious to weapons as a true novi-homidrak would be. 'Twill take more to injure you, but you can be hurt or killed with normal weapons."

The ground shook beneath them and Sontre' looked scared. Rivic put his arms around her to steady her, but she shortly pushed him away.

She turned to Rivic and took his hands in hers. Tears welled up in her eyes. "We are not going to make it to supper. Time is short," she said. Sontre' released Rivic's hands and now went to Nyree. "You should not have clung to your brother so desperately when the dragon appeared. But you would not release him. I worry about what your lack of magic will cause."

Nyree looked like she might cry at Sontre's words.

"Take it not so hard now, girl. Let the worries be mine. Just be aware." Sontre' grabbed Nyree's arms and shook her. "The Onesong knew what it was doing when it forced you to stay with your brother. Continue to cling to your brother, keep him on the path. Now, you are the only one."

"The only one for what?" Nyree asked. Sontre' embraced Nyree hard. When the woman pulled away, she was crying and wiping the tears away furiously with her aged hands.

"The one who can keep him there and guide him," Sontre' said.

The earth shook beneath them once more.

"'Tis time for you both to go now. I will be watching from

a far," Sontre' said, stepping away from them. "I wish you both luck."

"Wait! You said there was a champion already on this world. How will I know this person?" he asked.

"Listen well to the Onesong. You will know."

The ground shook violently beneath them again.

"Do not fear," Sontre' said as she began to walk away from them. She yelled back over her shoulder. "Farewell, children."

Sontre' slowly grew further and further away from them, even though Rivic didn't see her walking. It seemed like the ground stretched out beneath their very feet to separate them with distance.

Once more, their world swayed violently and Rivic grabbed onto Nyree. He had to keep her on her feet as everything shook violently about them. He couldn't manage it. They both knelt down, protectively hugging each other.

He felt sticky wetness all around him and panicked as he thought his magic was going rogue on him again.

Rivic felt his chest tighten to the point he could barely breathe.

Nyree glanced up around them, a small grin on her face. "Rivic," she whispered, "watch as our world falls apart."

The sky began to crumble above them. Rivic wanted to flinch away, but there were no actual pieces coming down around them. Only the hitching breaths as he gasped for air. Black spots gathered above him. The ground gave way, but they did not plummet.

Nyree took Rivic's hand. "Let us fall away too."

With that, there was nothingness.

CHAPTER 3

*R*ivic opened his eyes to find himself curled up and surrounded by goo that had just the faintest glow to it. He couldn't move or stretch; his whole body felt stiff and tightly cramped. Something encased his mouth and nose and he couldn't breathe. He saw Nyree floating in the odd yellowish fluid also with her mouth and nose covered. Her eyes were still closed.

Rivic fought to free himself from the mess and, as he did so, found a hard wall beside him. He knew this was the pearl. He tried ramming himself against it and punching it. When that failed, he attempted straightening his legs and kicking it, but the wall still didn't give way. He struck it again, but could barely move without hitting his sister.

"Come on, come on," a muffled voice said. "You can do it."

He felt a thrashing and saw Nyree awaken beside him. She tried to claw the gooey mass from her nose and mouth. Panic covered the visible portion of her face and, in that moment, Rivic realized there was something wrong with her eyes. They weren't how he remembered them.

Rivic grabbed her wrists to gain her attention, then he

made a motion with his fingers to indicate they should attack the pearl together. She nodded her understanding.

Her eyes were indeed odd, all black except for a slender golden torch which ran from top to bottom. He wondered what exactly she was seeing.

They belted the shell in near perfect synchronization, Rivic's attack landed just before Nyree's. The pearl rocked.

They kicked again.

The shell broke around them. Fluid oozed out over the ground like a slow flood. The pearl collapsed on top of them. Rivic tried to roll over onto Nyree and cover her with his own body while shards rained down, but he found himself knocked away, partially by Nyree, but also by something much bigger beside them. He watched as the glistening pieces of their pearly husk absorbed into her skin, knowing the same must be happening to him.

When it stopped, Rivic pulled the yellow, gelatinous mass from his face, then helped to free Nyree from the one covering her mouth and nose.

"Nyree," he whispered. The word broke from his throat, leaving it sore where stale air cracked loose. Coughing, he curled back up into the familiar fetal position until he remembered that he needed to get on his feet. They weren't alone. He stretched out, wishing he could see what was going on around them, but it was a dark night in the forest. The trees overhead were so dense that it kept out all the moonlight.

Nyree's eyes opened and glowed in the darkness as if the torches at the center of her eyes were burning. She turned her head to look at something that moved in the night before Rivic heard the sounds of it stirring.

Rivic shoved backwards on legs that didn't quite want to function as he remembered. It was as if his muscles had gone soft.

The dragon watched them with black eyes and yellow slits. "You are alive. The Necroathelings did not harm you." The winged beast issued a grateful sigh. "Time is short and I must return. Let me be quick through the naming ceremony."

Naming ceremony, Rivic thought, but the words didn't come out. He picked his hand up out of the slime covering the ground and tried to figure out what was going on. *Before he is born*, the Necroatheling had said. Was it possible that he and Nyree had just been born?

"I have always called you by the names you gave to me when I found you. I name you Rivic and Nyree. Your faithful companions will be Honor and Submit," the dragon said.

Golden dragon writing floated in the air toward them, breaking and falling toward the twins. It landed on their skin, turning black and sinking in. Rivic felt a new magic course through him. He watched black lines race along his skin, up his arms, as the same happened to his sister.

"Honor and Submit, appear," the dragon commanded.

A sword appeared near Rivic, the word Honor blazing in gold over the blade, while a dagger with Submit on it glowed beside Nyree. Rivic reached out to touch the sword, but it faded away before his fingers landed on the metal. He looked to the dragon.

"Do not worry," she said. "'Twill come back to you when you have need of it. All you will need to do is call for it. Now, if you will, please provide you and your sister with some clothes."

Rivic looked down and realized for the first time that they were naked in the darkness. He grabbed a fallen branch. "Palixa jotal." He draped the cloak he'd made over Nyree, then searched in the darkness for something else to transform. All he found of any use was a rock, which he made into leggings for himself.

"My body doesn't work right," Rivic said, his hurting voice sounding even stranger to him and stinging him without compassion.

The dragon gave a rough laugh. "You've been in an egg for the last eleven cycles. What do you expect?"

"We've been in an egg?"

"Aye, but nay," the dragon said in a wish-washy way. "Pearl is really a much better term for it. You've been incubating. Did Sontre' not inform you?"

Rivic shivered. "She said we'd be novihomidraks."

"You are indeed new humans of a dragon. I am your novimather, your dragon mother." She lowered her large head closer to Rivic. "I found the two of you alone and lost in the woods. I came for you, but your sister refused to let you go so I took her as well."

Rivic was getting to the point where he could see the edges of the dragon even in the dark. "Why me?"

The dragon smiled, bearing several long, large, and sharp white teeth. "Dragons pick their humans for different reasons: because the human is pretty, the color of the hair, or maybe a smell reminds them of a long distant memory. But I chose you because I liked your magic."

"My magic?" Rivic remembered how his magic had been when he'd been younger: destructive.

"Aye, that lethalness is something that will be needed in the coming cycles. Do not fear what needs to be done to save this world."

At first, Rivic thought it was the dragon that had spoken, but as the words finished, Rivic realized that it had been Nyree to speak. "What needs done?"

The dragon gave him a look of concern. "Do you not know? Do you not hear it?"

"Hear what?" Rivic asked. As he shook his head, he looked

between Nyree and the dragon, hoping for an answer from one of them.

"The hum of this world and its events."

Rivic shook his head, glancing more pointedly at Nyree to see if she heard it. When she gave him no acknowledgement, he closed his eyes and listened harder. He caught nothing other than the sounds of the immediate forest around them.

"So it seems the Necroathelings have torn the Humline from you." The dragon looked crushed and defeated.

"The yellow thread," Rivic said, feeling the same devastation in his chest as he was certain his novimather experienced.

Nyree stared at the dragon, her face in a state of puzzlement. Rivic wished he could ask her what was wrong, but the dragon continued, "You had been my last hope. Now I find you have been born deaf. My work is undone."

"Might I possess it? Sontre said the abilities would be split between us," Nyree shouted.

"Your foreknowledge will always be limited because you hold no magic in your soul and cannot tap into the Onesong," the dragon snarled. "I have spent more than a decade incubating two worthless novihomidraks. The failure is mine."

"I do hear it though," Nyree said. "Even though I have no markers on the bloodwave, my brother still does, and blood is blood. We are twins and bound to each other. We share that connection too. Is there no way?"

"What you hear is the Humline of this world. The Onesong must be opened to you in another way. Without magic, I do not see how that is possible." The dragon stretched her large black wings and gave them a flap.

"Wait! Sontre' dispersed the magic of the yellow thread onto me. Won't that help?"

The dragon paused. "She gave you the essence of Rivic's thread?"

"Aye!"

"That imprudent old woman! She should have known better." The dragon tossed its head in frustration as it once again opened its wings to the sky. "Pray that you never manage to open communication to the Onesong. If you do, you will die. 'Tis more than you can handle."

"But Rivic still has the magic and abilities of a noviho-midrak. He can't rid himself of those powers. This world still needs a champion. Can't he do that?"

Rivic stared at Nyree, who seemed to know more about him than he knew about himself. Was that what had caused the secret, knowing look to pass between Sontre' and Nyree? Nyree had always been with Sontre' as the old woman trained Rivic. Had Sontre' been explaining to Nyree the whole time?

"You're right. This world does need a champion," the dragon called out as she rose to the top of the trees. "Only then can this world rejoin the Wells. But without the Humline, he will not even see his mission."

"What about me? Can't I see the mission?" Desperation made Nyree's voice elevate.

"I warn you again: you cannot hope to handle the Onesong without magic. Blood might be blood and, given time, it might even be enough to heal his connection to the Humline, but Sontre' gave you false hope. She was foolish to try."

Rivic watched as the dragon dipped, caught the air beneath her wings and soared high into the air. She circled once above them, then vanished from sight.

"What do we do now?" Nyree asked.

"We find shelter."

There wasn't much around. In the darkness of the thick

forest and with energy returning slowly to their weakened bodies, they curled up together beneath a bush just high enough off the ground to shelter them.

Morning came soon, and with it, Rivic felt stronger. The light mist that had formed along the ground right before sunrise now burned away as the air warmed. Rivic clipped along through the forest, jumping logs and trampling the high weeds to make the trek easier for Nyree.

He turned and found her sitting on a log a short distance behind.

"When will we rest?" she asked as he waded his way through the trees and brush back toward her.

"I want to keep going," he said, reaching out for her hand. He helped her back to her feet. She soon stumbled along the path that Rivic had made for her. He swept her up in his arms. "Rest," he commanded. "I will carry you a ways."

She put her head against his chest and soon she was asleep.

Rivic carried Nyree until it was almost dark, amazed that his body did not seem to weaken. Rather, the longer he carried her, the more strength he felt.

As the sun was about to set and he knew that he needed to find a place to stay for the night, he came upon an abandoned building. It wasn't quite large enough to be house, so he wasn't truly certain it was abandoned. Maybe there was just no one here at the moment.

He tried the door and found it unlocked. It only had one room inside, no furniture, but it would do for the night and allow for a place to rest.

Rivic lay Nyree down on the stone floor, wishing he had something to ease the hardness beneath her. He put his hand to the floor. "Palixa jotal."

The rocks of the floor turned to feather-filled pillows. It wasn't a great bed, but at least it was gentler than the stone.

He couldn't start a fire on the softened floor. Not that he was sure he wanted one burning in here under normal circumstances. There did seem to be some ventilation at the top of the sharply slanted roof and it looked like other people had once lit fires in here. He still wasn't sure he wanted to be one of them. At least the stone walls would keep the evening wind out.

Hunger rumbled his stomach and knew he'd have to go look for food. He wasn't sure if he should wake Nyree to eat or not. She seemed so tired. As much as he knew that she needed to keep up her strength, he knew she needed the rest too. Was the dragon right? Was the magic of the yellow thread too much for her?

Would it kill her?

He couldn't afford to think like that. They both needed time to heal. He tried not to ponder about the thread taken from him and his link to the Humline being destroyed. He'd known things, like the pearl when they had been inside; he had realized what it was called before the dragon had told them. Maybe his connection was merely as tired as Nyree's body was.

Rivic went outside leaving the door slightly ajar behind him. He didn't know what he'd find eat, but he'd look for something. He circled around the house, traveling in a spiral loop and moving outward. He could smell rabbits and mice, but by the time he located their burrows they had already fled. He was even too slow to catch any birds.

He came across a nest that had three little eggs in it. He took two, careful not to touch the third or the nest as he did so. He hoped the mother and father would forgive him and know how he appreciated the eggs for providing nourishment that would sustain him and his sister for another day.

Nature always produced a plentiful overabundance, Sontre' had often told him. The bush produced enough berries to feed the animals as well as to reproduce the plant. Enough fruit grew on a tree to take care of the creatures that could grab the fruit, propagate the tree again, and fertilize the ground beneath it. There was always enough as long as everything was kept in balance. That is why he left one egg. He and his sister only needed two.

He circled around back to the house, checking once more that no one else was in the area. This little building had a reason for being here. He just hoped they weren't in need of it tonight.

Before going inside, he silently hoped the owner of this building would not come around tonight. Then he sat down on the floor and cracked open one of the eggs. He tilted back his head and split the shells apart over his open mouth. The egg's contents spilled into his throat. He tried not to think about the slimy gooeyness of it and instead just forced himself to swallow. His hunger overcame the thoughts of how desperately primal this was. As he wiped the last remnants of egg white from his mouth and licked his fingers, not wanting to waste a precious drop of it, he hoped to never eat a raw meal again.

Yet as he looked at the other egg, his stomach growled once more. He had carried Nyree most of the day. His body needed the substance, but Nyree needed it too.

He struggled with in himself, knowing that come morning he could go back out and find her more food. Did he really want to subject her to the same meal that he just had? He'd already made the decision not to wake her. Why had he grabbed two eggs? He should've just taken the one for himself. Now, all it had done was make a battle within his mind.

Rivic felt selfish for wanting the egg and stingy for trying to justify it to himself. Had he honestly come to this point? What were they going to do? In his head, he could hear

Nyree asking him the question: *"Rivic, what are we going to do now?"*

"I don't know, Nyree," he whispered. What were they going to do?

He knew he should save the egg for his sister. A gentleman would do the proper thing.

He wasn't sure he was a good person anymore.

Something about him felt strange and alien, and he had no accord with his own skin. He had definitely changed and it, whatever had overtaken him, demanded his survival.

He reached out and closed his finger around the egg, then drew it slowly toward him. He would eat raw eggs and mice as long as his sister didn't have to. Aye, it might be justification, but he would take the unseemly aspects of their survival to provide better for her. He cracked the egg and drank it down, the second time being easier than the first.

His stomach stopped its growling.

Crushing the shells to dust between his palms, Rivic swiped his hands to clean away the evidence. Tomorrow, he'd find some berries or something he could cook for Nyree. He'd be more mindful of her needs. Hopefully, he wouldn't be carrying her through the day again, but if he was, he'd still be more attentive to what she needed. Tonight, she had unknowingly made another sacrifice for her brother. He swore that she would never do it again.

Rivic curled up beside Nyree and put his arm over her. He would now let her be warmed by his body heat. That was the least he could do for her tonight. He closed his eyes and let himself fall into sleep.

CHAPTER 4

*B*lue swirls of dancing magic woke him sometime later. Rivic had no idea how long he'd been asleep; only that the magic was coming for him again.

In the cobalt-colored light, he made out the edges of the stone making up the wall. For a moment, he forgot where he was. He jerked his head to look around and saw the slanting roof and the hole that opened up to sky above them. The memories of coming to the strange little building flooded back to him. They were safe here, or would be if not for the magic.

He glanced down at the blue threads running through his skin.

"Nyree," he said as he reached over and shook her. "Nyree, it's coming back. What do I do? Sontre' is not here."

Nyree rolled over, barely opening her eyes. "Rivic? Where are we? Are we in the forest?"

"Nay, we're in a little house. I thought we could shelter here for a bit."

Nyree's eyes widened as she sat up and looked around. "Rivic, what's going on? Even I can feel your magic."

Rivic drew back as she reached out to touch him. "Don't. We don't know what will happen if someone touches me."

Nyree blinked and when she opened her eyes once more, they were that odd black with the yellow torch-shaped slits. "You have come to a channeling house," she said in a voice much deeper than her own. "Great magicks are raised within inside here. They are meant to aid in the humans becoming more powerful. They were not meant for your magic."

Rivic jumped to his feet, forgetting that the floor had been softened. He wobbled, then caught his balance to steady himself. "Then I need to leave," Rivic said, not sure if it was a question or statement. Was he asking for confirmation, or did he already know?

"Expel the magic," Nyree responded. "That will give us several more hours of rest."

Rivic started for the door.

"Wait!" Nyree called out behind him. "You must do the magic in here for it to be properly released."

Rivic looked around the channeling house, then up toward the roof. He moved beneath the slanted roof and raised his hand toward the hole positioned above. "Elixe'ist praten karmiden val'orishem noctada raliest." Dozens of fiery stones burst from Rivic's palm. Several made it through the hole in the ceiling while others blasted through the roof. Wood and thatching pelted down on them until Rivic shouted, "Miex'calidori," to put a shield around them. He dispelled the bubble as soon as everything settled.

"Very good," Nyree said, already starting to sit down on the pliant floor once more. She swept aside some debris as she stretched out. "I'm tired. Let's get some more sleep."

Rivic watched the blue fade from his skin. He glanced to the roof and saw that the hole above had been enlarged significantly. The sky beyond seemed to glow as if his magic still burned in the air.

After he lay back down, it took him a long time to settle back to sleep. He watched the red sky, relaxing a bit as it began to fade back to darkness.

"I chose you because of your magic's destructiveness," Rivic remembered the dragon telling him. He hadn't needed to raise his power in order to decimate two villages as a child. Here, he'd left the sky on fire for nearly half the night. Imagine what he could do if he actively tried to do something destructive from here.

Rivic woke before Nyree to late morning sunlight coming through the hole in the ceiling and blazing right in his face. He jumped to his feet. "Wake up, Nyree. We need to be on our way." He dragged her sleepily to her feet and out from the channeling house.

"Let me have a moment to get my wits about me," Nyree protested, pulling away. She stumbled away from him and clutched onto a nearby tree. "What puts you in such a hurry? Where are we going?"

"I don't know, but we have to find somewhere. We can't stay here. You saw what I did last night. Surely someone else did to. They might come investigate."

They continued on shortly, picking berries for breakfast as they went. The fruit was a little sour and not quite ripe enough, but it was edible and filled their stomachs. Their midday meal consisted of two quickly cooked quails after Rivic downed them with a forceful blast of magic. He wished he could have taken more of them, but they had no way of keeping the meat from spoiling.

They walked through the night until exhaustion made Nyree stumble.

"I'm tired, Rivic, but I don't think I can sleep," she said as Rivic caught her and made her sit down on the ground. Her eyes had returned to normal. "I have too many thoughts going on in my mind. This world aches. The inhabitants are full of fear and pain. The gargaxes are only part of the problem. Are we truly doomed since you have no connection to the Humline?"

Rivic tried to shake his head. It came out more as an awkward wobble. "Nay, do not think on it anymore. Trust that the Onesong knows what has happened and will guide us. The dragon doesn't know what she's talking about. She's been long cut off from the Onesong too if the Wells of this world have been closed." The thought of it brought a terrible sting to him and he didn't want to think on it any longer, as if reflection only deepened the suffering of this world.

"But what if we don't know what to do?"

Rivic waved a hand in front of Nyree's face. "Mezzipalor." She sagged down into his arms and he rested her on the ground. "I am sorry, Nyree, but I can handle no more worrying right now. Making sure we are safe has to be my first priority."

Finding an area where there was a gap in the trees overhead, Rivic held his arms out away from his sides just a little. "Porta'mentay." His feet left the ground. He levitated straight up until he was higher than the treetops.

Even up here, the world looked dark. Two moons were on the far side of the sky, one higher than the other, while a third seemed partially hidden behind the distant horizon. Whether that moon was rising or setting, Rivic didn't know. The slight breeze in the air seemed colder and he got the sense that the weather was changing. It would snow here soon even though the night seemed clear. He closed his eyes and listened.

Aside from his magic, he felt empty. When they'd been with Sontre' he had a feeling of the entire world around them. Though they'd always been alone, just the three of them, he never felt that way. Energy had always surrounded them. That had to have been the dragon.

He extended his search, reaching for the dark mounds in the distance which he could only presume were mountains. Now the only energies he felt were pockets of magic. Rivic opened his eyes and looked to his right where he felt the greatest magicks now. That was the bearing they needed to head. There, they would find the source. He stretched out again with his magic in that direction. There was power there for certain. Maybe there he'd find out how to restore his connection to the Humline. The dragon had said it was possible if Nyree nurtured it back to health. He wondered what all that would entail.

Slowly, Rivic lowered himself back down.

"He knows we're here," Nyree muttered, still lying on the ground with her eyes closed.

Rivic knelt by her, knowing she couldn't have shaken off his spell on her own and doubting she'd woken up already. He confirmed she was still sleeping.

"Who?" he whispered, wondering if she would give him an answer while still remaining asleep.

"He knows we're here," she said again.

Rivic wasn't sure if it was her words or his own senses confirming them, but he felt a tingle over his arms. Someone had been sent out to search for them. They weren't coming very fast though.

He had to wonder if this was his weak connection growing stronger or just his own paranoia playing games with his head now. Rivic sat down against a tree and closed his eyes. He had time to get some sleep.

Afraid his thoughts would keep him awake, he didn't realize how quickly his tiredness pulled him under until Nyree's scream dragged Rivic from deep dreams. He'd been somewhere warm and soft. But hearing her wake brought the forest into sharp recollection. The skin of his back itched from leaning against the tree's rough bark for nearly the whole night.

"Rivic!" Nyree screamed out again.

He scrambled to his feet. "I'm here. Right here."

Daylight had just begun to touch the sky, beginning to coat everything with a grayish cast. It was enough that Rivic could make out where Nyree was and make his way to her.

She had her eyes open and the torch-shaped pupils burned yellow. Once she felt him nearby, she grabbed his hand. "Follow me, Rivic," she panted. "I will lead you there. I will show you the way to him, but you must pursue me."

"You're not going anywhere without me," he said.

"I am. You cannot stop it."

"'Tis a nightmare, Nyree."

"Nay, 'tis truth. He knows we're here. He's sent for us. We must go to him." She clutched onto his arm so tightly he thought her nails might break his skin. "You have much to learn before you can face him." Her voice came out raggedly deep.

"Who?"

"The Destroyer of Civilizations."

"Is he to the north-west?" Rivic asked. That had been the direction to his right last night.

"Aye. We should be there. We must go there. The Humline told me."

"Nyree, don't access the Humline. The novimather said 'twas too dangerous. Nyree?"

Nyree's body seemed to relax and her eyes slid closed. Rivic shook her. She blinked and opened her eyes, which now looked normal. "'Tis everything all right?" she asked, propping herself up on her arm and looking around.

"We were just talking. Don't you remember?" Rivic asked.

"Nay," she laughed. "That must have been some dream I was having. I must have been talking in my sleep."

He slung her arm around his neck and lifted her to her feet, not caring if she was ready to get up or not. The spooky feeling possessing him wouldn't leave until they got away from here. "Come on. We should be going."

"Already? Are we going to find something to eat along the way?"

Her words made him realize that he was hungry too. "Aye, we will," he said, though he wasn't sure how he was going to make that happen. He just needed to get moving.

They walked. Rivic shortly forgot about food, thought his mind fed him his fill of plaguing thoughts.

If their whole lives up until a few days ago had been a falsified realm, how would they survive now that they had been ejected into the real world? What if things were vastly different than they had been when they'd been in the pearl? Whatever dangers they had imagined while being incubated were lies. Now they had untold and unexpected dangers. What things were they not even aware of that they would have to face?

"I need to rest," Nyree complained, sinking down to the ground, though they had only been walking for far too short a time for Rivic's comfort. The sun hadn't even peaked above them yet. "I can't travel any longer. Face it, Rivic, we're lost." She stretched out over the mossy forest floor.

"We're not lost." To get his bearings once more, Rivic levitated above the trees and looked around. He saw a curl of gray smoke in the morning air. Someone had lit a fire. Coming back to the ground, Rivic took Nyree's arms and started to pull her up. "We must keep traveling."

"I'm tired, Rivic. Can't I sleep a bit more? You can go find us something to eat while I sleep?"

"Nay. If they extinguish the fire, I won't be able to find them."

"Find who?" She sat up and tried to stretch the tiredness

from her back and shoulders. Her eyes still didn't want to stay open and she kept blinking against the brightening morning light. Even here in the shade of the trees, she acted like the sun was too much for her.

"I don't know. But there's a fire…" He inhaled deeply. "… and I can smell someone cooking. We're close. We're going to have to ask for help."

Nyree got to her feet with Rivic's help. "Let's go." Her voice carried sadness in the words. He had to get her somewhere. She required more assistance than he knew how to provide. She needed a place to rest and recover, somewhere she would be safe. Taking her hand, Rivic began guiding her through the forest in the direction they needed to be moving.

"I thought you said this place was close by, that you could see it and smell it," she whined as the day pushed on.

"I could. I can still smell it, but the scent is fading. We've got to hurry." He hoped to encourage her, but at the same time he also thought they should have found the camp already. Had the people packed and migrated already? Or was he just traveling slower than he calculated because of Nyree?

As the day wore on, Nyree slowed with substantial drooping going through her shoulders until she could barely walk on her own. He carried her on his back for a while, and then when she was unable to hold onto him any longer, he lifted her up in his arms and held her close to his chest. It seemed like he was growing stronger as she weakened.

The scent of fire and cooking lured him as late afternoon began to streak pink light along the clouds. A moon touched on the opposite horizon like a rising beacon. He knew that even if the sun set before too long, this moon would give him good light for most of the night. He hoped he didn't need it. As much as he wanted to claim invincibility, he grew tired.

"Halt!" came a shout from the trees.

A person. A living person! Rivic dropped to his knees and released some of Nyree's weight to the ground. Her arms clung around his neck and he held her against his chest with so little effort compared to carrying her.

"Don't move," came a second warning. "Who are ya?"

Rivic felt himself wobble. "My name is Rivic and this is my sister, Nyree. She is in need of help. Can you aid us?"

A man appeared holding a spear in his hand above his shoulder as he inched closer to them. "What's wrong with her?"

"She's weak, lethargic," Rivic said, knowing a generalization of her symptoms would be so much easier than the truth.

"Has she been bitten?" the man asked, crouching a little bit as he inched closer. He looked Nyree over as he approached.

"What? Nay!" Rivic snapped, not quite sure what the man was talking about, but he could think of no bite that she had received, unless one counted being swallowed whole by a dragon as having been bitten. He certainly hoped that didn't count.

"One cannot be too careful with the gargaxes about. Don't want ya dragging her into our camp if the gargaxes are following ya."

That made sense to Rivic. "Nay, we've not seen any gargaxes. My sister has no magic for the gargaxes to eat."

The spear being held against him lowered slightly. The man gave him a sidelong look, the eye closest to Rivic which appeared to shrink as it scrutinized him. "She been sick long? We don't want illnesses here either."

"I don't know what's wrong with her, but she's not sick, not with anything contagious. I promise you that." It was a stretch. They hadn't been in this world long. For all he knew, now that they'd been exposed, they might be contaminated by everything.

"Our healer might be able to help ya." The man dropped his spear to his side as he straightened. "Might! She doesn't always help everyone. 'Tis her choice whether she helps ya or not. And don't try nothin'. She's the chieftain's youngest daughter. Ya now been warned, understand?"

"Aye," Rivic said. He rocked forward then back to give himself enough momentum to stand. He saw the man's eyes widen as Rivic brought himself to his feet with Nyree cradled in his arms.

"How did ya do that?" the man asked. "Ya didn't even wobble."

"Was I supposed to?" Rivic hoped his statement held enough caution in it to also learn what he'd done wrong. He'd need to be more human if he wanted to fit into this world. He wasn't sure how he knew that truth, only that he felt it on an instinctual level.

The man's eyes narrowed. "I don't know much, but I know a man getting up from their knees always favors their stronger side. Especially when they are carrying weight."

"I've worked hard to strengthen my weak side," Rivic covered. He wasn't sure which side was supposed to be more powerful, so his statement might not be false. Still, it would be something he'd have to consider. "Take me to your healer."

The man took the lead, suspiciously glancing back at Rivic every so often. When the camp came into view, Rivic wanted to turn and walk the other direction. It looked too much like his aunt and uncle's village with the hide-covered lodges and low fires burning outside of each one. People working outside at various tasks, tanning, drying meat, sewing, repairing lodges, turned to look at Rivic. Someone like him did not belong around so many innocent people. But Nyree needed help and he didn't know what else to do, so Rivic continued to follow. Finally, the man stopped before a domed hut and called out, "Healer, will you let us in?"

The man turned toward Rivic. "Now we wait for her answer."

As moments passed, Rivic was glad this wasn't an emergency. Maybe his impatience made the time lengthen.

The thick, tanned leather flap drew back and a woman with short bones tied in her light brown hair stood in the entrance. Her blue eyes widened as she looked at Rivic. "Bring her in." The man who had escorted them into camp seemed shocked to see her. "Tovis, you fool, I told you I was expecting someone." She reached out and smacked his head.

"That was days ago, Healer," he protested. "How was I to know today was the day?"

"That's why I told you," she snapped. She gave Tovis a slight push to keep him from entering with Rivic. She pointed toward the forest. "Back to duty with you."

The humidity inside the lodge nearly overwhelmed Rivic. A small fire lit the inside as smoke drifted slowly toward the cone-shaped ceiling and escaped through a hole in the top. Burned into the leather walls of the lodge were several different images of animals and symbols. A kettle of water sat on a tripod over the fire. Some of the stones around the edges steamed as if water had just been poured over them. Drying herbs hung upside-down from a tall rack on the other side.

Rivic turned toward the healer just as the flap closed behind her. He realized that she was near the age Nyree appeared to be. "My sister, she's been tired and lethargic for several days. Now she can barely remain conscious."

The healer looked him over, probably assessing him much in the same way he had her, then nodded. The bones in her hair clinked as she moved. "Put her down on the mat there," she said, pointing toward a small fur covering a pile of leaves. "What happened before? Did she do anything that could account for her state? Did she eat some unfamiliar berries, maybe some that you did not share?"

"Nay," Rivic said as he placed Nyree down. How could he say that his twin's condition had nothing to with anything she had done on this world, and that it had to do with being gestated within a dragon for more cycles than he knew? He wondered just how old he was. Had the time that passed when they were with Sontre' accurate?

"You are distressed too," the girl said. "Something has happened to both of you. Sit down." She pointed at a chair, then moved to a small table where she had several small pounded metal vessels sitting out. She pulled a piece of tattered cloth off a line that hung between two of the lodge poles and dipped it in one of the bowls. Ringing it out and folding it over a couple times, she handed it to him as she moved to another small table on the other side. "Put that on your forehead."

"My sister?" he asked.

The healer glanced over her shoulder. "Will get better with you. Now put that on your head." Picking up a pouch, she scattered the contents of small bones and rocks over the leather covering the table.

Rivic tried to put the cloth to his forehead, but as he got it close, he noticed a smell of greasy fat and strong herbs. He took another careful sniff. It was definitely coming from the rag. How was he supposed to put this stink on his head? He suppressed a gag.

"Do it," the woman snapped.

Rivic tilted back his head and set the cloth over his fore-head, still having a hard time ignoring the terrible odor. It made him a bit glad that he had nothing substantial on his stomach to come back up.

Meanwhile, he watched as she leaned over the small table

and studied the objects she'd strewn out. Occasionally, she flicked her finger against one of the bones to flip it. Her nails were short and though her fingers were clean, Rivic got the impression that she was use to digging in the dirt. This felt like a shadow influence, as if he could see her fingers currently blackened from pulling up roots buried deep in the ground. He smelled the earthy scent coming off her. She was currently wearing leggings and he felt like she normally didn't; she had been getting ready to go out foraging.

His vision began to waver before him. He blinked and tried to get everything right again, choosing to look up at the upside-down bundles of flowers and herbs tied to the poles above him. The smoke curled as it neared the top to exit the lodging. Over the hole, there were bones woven into a spiral pattern around in a circle and created a type of netting. Small stones hung from that.

"It keeps evil things from getting in," she explained. He thought she might be looking to see what he was staring at, but she remained hunched over the table. How did she know? Could she read his mind?

She laughed.

Rivic remembered watching Sontre' and Nyree baking little pastries, the way they would fold the rolled out dough over the berries and pinch the tops together. He felt like someone was bending his skin up around his thoughts and there came a new heaviness to his body as he went from being open and exposed to closed and contained, just like one of Sontre's tarts.

"You and your sister have been through a lot," the healer said, straightening her back. "'Tis no wonder she is so fatigued. Rest here. I must go have a word with my father." She scooped the bones and the rocks back into the bag and pulled the string to cinch it tight.

"He is the chieftain, right?" Rivic asked. He lifted his head and held the cloth in place at his forehead as he looked at her.

"He is. You have been informed correctly." Her leather shoes whisked against the compact dirt floor as she came over to him. "My name is Ellonia."

He looked at the hand she offered toward him, then glanced back to her face. He wanted to say that her name was the prettiest one he'd ever heard, but since he'd never known many people he wasn't certain he had a right to judge it. Tentatively, he reached up and placed his hand in hers. She shook it, but before she released it, she asked, "What is your name?"

"Rivic."

"And your sister's?"

"Nyree."

"Rivic and Nyree." She closed her eyes and bowed her head. "'Tis a blessing to meet you both. Please wait here. I'm sure my father will want to speak with you shortly."

"Will you do nothing for my sister now?"

She poked the cloth held against his head. "I am doing all I can do for her at the moment. I need you to do nothing for her right now too. Just keep yourself closed down. That's correct. Just like that." The firelight sparkled in her blue eyes and her lips looked so soft as she spoke. Rivic found it hard not to be entranced. The bones in her hair clinked as she turned and headed out of the lodge.

As soon as the flap closed behind her, a panic hit him. He dove out of his chair and, dropping down beside Nyree, shook his sister. "Nyree, wake up."

"Not now, Rivic," she whispered back. "I'm finally warm and not hearing your every thought."

Rivic sat back on his heels. Had that been what Ellonia meant in saying that Nyree would get better as Rivic did? Had he been the one overwhelming Nyree? Unsure and trying to contain his own panic, he returned to the chair, sat back down, and pressed the cool, but stinky compress back on his forehead. He wasn't certain what it meant to keep himself closed down as Ellonia had suggested, but he could gently relax in the warm lodge and let Nyree sleep until Ellonia returned. He wondered how long he had to wait.

The moist warmth of the lodging surrounded him as he continued to stare at the slanting of the ceiling and the little gray stones swinging gently in the shifting currents above. He began to feel tired himself. Soothed even. That was a good term for it. For the first time since meeting the dragon face-to-face, he felt calmed. Everything had been so terrifying, but here, he was safe. Feeling drowsy, he closed his eyes.

CHAPTER 5

A buzz woke Rivic from his sleep. He opened his eyes to see the lodging lit only by firelight. The hole where the poles converged above was showed darkness above. Every muscle tensed as he felt someone approaching. Rivic thought about calling Honor to him. He kept his hand curled shut. It wasn't time, yet.

The flap opened and Ellonia entered followed by several men draped in furs. Most had necklaces made of bones longer than the ones Ellonia wore which clinked as they moved. Many also had swords, daggers, and bows, not drawn and ready, but the men's hands flinched toward the weapons as they saw Rivic rise from the chair.

A man with graying blond hair came in. Bones were sewn in and tied to the fur capelet worn over his shoulders. His tunic and leggings seemed new and far better constructed than what most of his men were wearing. He had a necklace of thick stones around his neck and bracelets that matched. A band of pounded metal surrounded his muscular upper arm.

Rivic knew he should bow to this man before the other

men made him. He dropped to one bend knee and lowered his head.

"Good Father," Ellonia said, "this is Rivic, the man I was telling you about."

"Rise, Rivic," the chieftain spoke.

Rivic dared to get to his feet, helped by the fact that Ellonia came to stand by him. "Rivic, this is my father, Krithstand."

"Well met, Krithstand-chief."

Krithstand surveyed Rivic for a long while. Then he turned to his men and said, "Gather the council. We will meet at the rising of the second moon. If any should sleep, rouse them. We have important matters to discuss and we should have it done tonight."

Several of Krithstand's men left. The few that remained took positions by the flap, each facing toward each other. Rivic was pretty certain that he saw more standing outside of the lodging too.

The chief stepped further inside, his gaze going to Nyree sleeping on the mat on the other side. "My daughter has been foretelling your coming for many moon cycles. 'Twas the first double rising after the tri-lunar that she began to speak of your arrival as imminent."

Rivic knew he spoke of the parallel rising of two moons which occurred several nights after the evening where the three moons crested the horizon concomitantly. Sontre' had occasionally pointed out the cycles of the moons to him, but as like many things, he wasn't sure it correlated with this world exactly. Did the dragon mark time accurately for him or was Sontre's view of these phases different?

"She is very excited," Krithstand said. Even now, Ellonia bounced on her toes as she smiled happily. "I hope you are all she claims you will be."

"What does she claim I will be?" Rivic asked carefully.

"A key player in our tribe. We will discuss more later. For now, you and your twin need to rest."

Rivic knew he'd never mentioned to anyone that Nyree was his twin. Had Ellonia known that or was Krithstand guessing? Rivic nodded. "We've had an exhausting few days," he confirmed. "I appreciate you letting us rest here, Krith-stand-chief."

"Ellonia will be sheltered with me for the next few days," Krithstand said. "She will have unrestricted access to her lodging, but she will respect your privacy too."

Ellonia smiled. "Please make yourself at home here."

Rivic found himself grinning too, enjoying being welcomed somewhere. "Thank you."

"Ellonia, get a few things and let's leave him to some sleep." Krithstand turned and headed out of the lodging with his men following behind.

Ellonia moved quickly in gathering some of her belongings and set them on the table where she'd cast the bones. "I will bring you something to eat in the morning," she said. She motioned to the second mat in the room. "Please feel free to lie down and rest. There are more blankets over there if you need them." She pointed to a stand that was also covered by a leather hide.

"I am grateful for you taking us in," Rivic said, feeling useless as he stood near the fire watching her. He wanted to add that he didn't understand why she so readily trusted him, but he feared giving her a reason to be suspicious of them. "What matters does your father have to discuss with the council at this hour of night? It must have something to do with us. Should I not be there as well?"

"Do not concern yourself with it tonight. He is right; you need to rest. 'Tis my night to explain what has happened and prepare them."

"What about our arrival needs explaining?"

Ellonia moved over to him and raised her hand to touch her fingers against his cheek. "I have dreamt about you for many moons. 'Twas only recently though that I started to get a clearer picture of you." She stretched up on her toes and kissed his cheek.

Rivic wasn't quite sure what to make of it as she stepped back and looked up at him. His whole body felt tight, nervous. He didn't know what to say, or even what this meant.

"Rest tonight. We'll have plenty of time to talk." She smiled as she gazed down to the ground between them. Then she turned, grabbed her things, and headed for the door.

Rivic reached up and placed his fingers against his cheek where a tingle remained present. He stood there for long after she had left, then turned to the mat and lay down. Her scent wrapped around him as he closed his eyes and drifted back to sleep.

Nyree shook him awake sometime later. "Rivic," she whispered, "where are we?"

"We're safe, Nyree," he muttered as he rolled away from her.

"Are we, Rivic?" she asked, her voice laden with fear. "Have you looked at yourself?"

The words brought instant awareness to him. Rivic bolted upright and looked at his hands. They were streaked with blue just beneath the surface of the skin. "This can't be happening!" He swallowed hard. "I can't be magic spun again."

"Stop it," Nyree cried out.

The blue intensified with a pulse that lit the inside of the lodging. Rivic wondered if people outside were noticing.

"We shouldn't have come here," Nyree said, close at his heels as he got up and started toward the flap.

"Cut it out, boy!" someone outside shouted.

"Make him stop. Rivic!" He swore it was his aunt shouting at him. "Use your knife," Rivic's aunt continued. "We need to get in there."

The lodging's flap disappeared and in its place was just a hide wall. A blade sliced through the leather and tore downward.

Nyree stepped in front of Rivic. "They will never get to us in time. You should not be here. 'Tis dangerous for you to be around so many people."

Rivic stared at his hands, which were glowing blue and covered in a thick webbing of fine threads.

"Ellonia, you're going to kill her," Nyree continued, whispering the heckling words in his ear, "along with everyone else here." Her eyes were black with thin, vertical, golden torches.

"Nay, I can control this now." Rivic closed his fingers into fists and held them up in front of his chest while he breathed deeply.

"'Tis a demon child!" Rivic's uncle shouted, though his voice sounded wispy and ghostly ethereal.

"Get in there," his aunt screamed with that same unreal tone.

The tear in the leather had mended itself. "Demon child!"

"You will kill everyone here too," Nyree said. "The dragon took you because your magic is destructive."

"I can control it!" Rivic said, squeezing his eyes closed tightly to ignore the real evidence spinning away over his skin.

"You can't! Run, Rivic. Get away from here. Run!" Nyree screamed at him.

Rivic knew the words, the spell to take him far away from the village. He had to keep the people here safe. Ellonia. "Talcor—"

The world exploded out from him.

"Nay!" Rivic screamed, stretching out a hand before him. He sat up, seeing the lodging all dark save for low embers still trying to keep the fire alive. He stared at the hand he held extended before him, turning it over and over before him, and searching for the magical webbing. Panting, he looked around at the walls of the lodging, all intact and undamaged. Nyree still slept on her mat not far away.

Feeling the claws of the dream clinging to him, Rivic got to his feet and went to the flap. He lifted it back and stepped outside. The cool early morning air felt brisk against the sweat beaded on his face. Two guards standing watch looked at him warily. Rivic nodded to both of them in turn, then gave a sweeping glance around the village. All seemed fine, except the two sentries sharing a confused look. "'Tis all good," Rivic said as he ducked back inside.

He went to Nyree and knelt down beside her. Her breathing was deeper and more regular than it had been. When he touched her long black hair, she murmured softly and turned toward him. Her eyes fluttered open. "Rivic? Is everything all right?"

"I didn't mean to wake you."

"When you do, it always means there's trouble." She scooted back and sat up before wiping the sleep from her eyes. "Where are we?"

"We're in the village of Chief Krithstand. His daughter, Ellonia, is a healer. This is her lodge. We've been invited to stay, at least for a little while."

Nyree closed her eyes. Rivic felt her reaching out with her energy and touching upon something that was just beyond his reach. After a moment, she nodded and said, "We will be here awhile. During this time, you need to learn how to use your powers."

"My powers?" Rivic asked.

"Aye, your novihomidrak powers. Some you received

while we were in the pearl. Others will develop now that you are born."

The way she phrased it made chills run up his arm. What would happen to him? What would he become?

The dragon chose you because your magic was destructive.

"I can't do this, Nyree." The words burst from him with volatile force.

"What worries you, Rivic?"

Her question took him back a moment. She usually already knew what was on his mind and how he was feeling. For her to reflect a question back at him like this meant she had changed. Or had the dragon just simulated their twin connection in his mind while they had been in the pearl? How much of what he knew of Nyree was real and how much had been made up by the dragon? How much of his time in the pearl had just been a dream? Did any of it relate to what he'd need to know now?

All of those questions only deepened the one he now had on his mind: what if he couldn't control his magic? What if that had all been an illusion too? Had the dragon been suppressing it? His novimather had mentioned how sorry she was that she couldn't provide another mentor. He needed a guide; he felt that in his gut. "I'm sorry, Nyree," he said. "I'm worried because we've lost her, the old woman. What if I need another Sontre'?"

"Why would you need another teacher?"

"What if I can't handle the magic? I'm just not sure I can do it without her."

Nyree gave him a patient smile. "She explained it to you. You were magic spun. 'Twon't happen again."

But one look at her and Rivic knew she feared the same thing too. She'd felt it in him, the rising magic.

"I dreamt I was about to destroy this village too. What if 'tis dangerous for us to stay?"

"You've worked hard," she said, and the words momentarily soothed the panic surging through him. "You're trained to channel the power. You were a boy before and no one could have helped you."

"Aye," he muttered. "But what if that training was false, controlled by the dragon? What if I never really learned how to control being magic spun? What if I'm broken? Remember a few nights ago in the channeling house?"

Nyree reached over and touched his arm. She closed her eyes once again and he felt her energy dancing along his skin. When she opened them again, she said, "You are in control of your magic, but you have other powers you will learn to use. They might be unpredictable at first, but no one will be harmed as you experiment with these."

"How do you know this, Nyree?" he asked, feeling like she was looking beyond this present time into a future he couldn't see with certainty. Not the way she did.

She settled back on the mat, appearing tired once more. "You'll come to understand."

Rivic felt Ellonia approach the lodging. A bell chimed outside.

Rivic glanced over his shoulder as he expected the healer to enter, but no one came in. After a moment, the bell jingled again.

"You should answer that," Nyree said.

Rivic got to his feet and went to open the flap. Ellonia stood outside, a wooden tray with food on it in her hands.

"I wondered if you still might be sleeping. I hope I didn't wake you by ringing the bells," she said.

"Nay. I didn't realize I needed to answer." He admitted the last words with a blush warming on his cheeks. He didn't understand why he was telling her that, but he felt he needed to.

"How else will you know someone is outside?" she asked.

He had just felt her there. Much like he'd perceived when she'd arrived last night with her father. Maybe ordinary humans didn't have such an awareness, and this was one of the lessons he had to learn.

Ellonia moved by him with the tray and set it down on the table. She went to Nyree and knelt down beside her. "Bright blessings," Ellonia said as she introduced herself. "How are you feeling?"

Nyree nodded and took a deep breath. "Very tired."

Ellonia glanced back at Rivic. "I understand. I am acting as a doorway for your brother's emotions, trying to let you recover." She gave Nyree a soft smile. "When you are feeling stronger, we will work on opening that back up."

"Thank you," Nyree whispered back.

Ellonia patted Nyree's hand. "Most people don't under-stand what I do, but I know there is a lot I will learn from you. 'Tis good to meet someone with such a connection. We will be great friends."

Nyree closed her eyes and seemed to slip further down into the mat as she began to sleep again.

Rivic approached Ellonia. "What are you doing to her?"

Ellonia stood. "Letting her rest. That is all. You should eat." She pointed to the tray. "When you are done, I am hoping you will escort me into the forest."

"Why do we need to go there?"

"I need to go foraging," she informed him. "I was about to head out yesterday evening when you and your sister arrived. I thought you might like to get out and stretch your legs a bit."

Realizing she had no evil intent behind her words, Rivic said, "I would like to go."

"Then eat. We will leave shortly."

As Rivic ate, he tried to leave some for Nyree, but he hadn't realized how hungry he was. Ellonia noticed his hesitation. "Eat," she said. "We'll bring more for Nyree later. She's going to sleep while we're gone."

"How do you know this?" he asked.

"Because the world tells me she will sleep." She laughed at his confusion. "Once we are in the forest, maybe you will understand." She dipped her head as she turned around and started toward the flap. "Are you ready?"

Rivic looked around, wondering if there was anything he needed to take with him. He saw nothing that he required. "I am." He flapped his useless arms as if still feeling like there was something he should take with him. Then he followed her outside.

Several lodgings surrounded a central fire over which a large boar currently cooked on a spit being turned by a young boy while two women sat chopping vegetables. Three smaller girls also helped out. The women were chanting a song in low tones. Rivic wanted to draw closer, but Ellonia snapped her fingers to get his attention as she pulled further away.

"When you and your sister are feeling better, we will formally introduce you to the tribe. Until then, 'tis best you not interact with anyone lest they think you are an evil spirit."

"Why would they think I'm an evil spirit?"

She grinned, then tried to hide her amusement by looking at the ground as she walked along. She gave a little shake of her head. "We shall stop at the lake and you shall see."

A man entered the tribe on the back of a large beast. Rivic stared at the creature and rider who had it under control of ropes tied around its flailing head. "What is that?" Rivic asked as they drew nearer and the animal stomped and snorted.

"'Tis a horse," she answered, wariness coming into her humored look now.

"A horse? He has that horse under control?"

She forced a smile. "Aye. For the most part. Nex gets thrown off once every moon cycle or so." Ellonia touched his arm to get his attention back to her. "This way."

She pressed forward into the trees.

They hadn't gone far and Rivic began to notice that they weren't alone. Someone moved through the trees trailing slightly behind. Rivic moved up to Ellonia. "We're being followed."

"Try not to think about it."

"I don't think we'd be wise to ignore them."

Ellonia stopped to examine an umbrella of blossoms at the end of a long stem. She dug into her pouch and pulled out a flat stone tied to a stick. "I am the chieftain's daughter. They are here to protect me. I've told them that I don't want to be aware of their presence. 'Tis surprising that you have noticed them."

"I can feel them," he explained.

She nodded as she began to dig out the similar plants surrounding the one she had touched. "Pretend you are not aware of them." After she finished taking the plant from the ground, she pushed the earth back into place, patted it down, and bowed to the remaining plant. "Thank you, Grandmother Valerian." She stood and tucked the plants she'd harvested into a bag, then continued on.

"You said that once we were in the forest, I might understand how you knew that my sister would continue to sleep while we are gone. I still do not. Can you explain so I might recognize what I'm seeking?"

Ellonia stopped and held herself stationary, though she looked around at the trees. "Feel the stillness in the air around you. Can you hear the hum vibrating beneath it?"

Was she referring to the Humline the dragon had mentioned? Rivic tried. "Nay."

"Let the sound come to you."

He let himself remain quiet for another moment. Then, just as he was about to tell her that he didn't feel it and that it was mostly likely useless that he even try, he began to hear it, a faint zing of energy flowing all around him. "I sense it," he announced.

"Very good," she smiled. "I feared that you might be deaf to it, which would be nearly impossible. That is what I tune into when I look for information on the injured and sick. It gives me a feeling of what needs to be done."

Born deaf, that's what the dragon had said. He didn't want to divulge that to Ellonia.

She began digging in the earth once more, pulling up a stalk to the roots, shaking the dirt from it, patting the ground back down as she thanked it.

This continued on for several more plants.

"Why do you always leave the biggest plant and thank it as a grandmother?" Rivic asked.

"Because as the biggest and tallest, she has produced all the littler ones. She is their grandmother. I show gratitude for her efforts and respect what she has provided for me. Do you not honor what is given to you?"

"I haven't had much opportunity to," Rivic admitted.

"Do you thank the animals and the plants for the sacrifice they make for you in becoming your food?"

He felt the heat of shame entering his arms, chest, and legs. Sontre' had never made them give appreciation for their food, but then, that had all been an illusion. "Nay," he answered. "My life has been a little… complicated to explain."

She nodded and went back to foraging another plant she had selected as if she no longer wanted to look at him. After she replaced the ground and thanked the grandmother plant, she got to her feet and walked on. "The lake is over here," she said.

He stepped from the forest trees into the low valley grassland. The water of the lake looked so blue. He wanted to dip his fingers in, to see if it felt as cool as it looked. Giving into the urge, he knelt down on the bank and reached over. As he did, he caught sight of his reflection. His hair was all a tangled mess and it stuck out at odd clumping angles. The skin beneath his eyes looked blackened. This certainly wasn't how he remembered himself.

"You should take off your clothes and take a swim to clean up. I brought some grooming supplies for when you are finished." Ellonia said.

Rivic pulled off his tunic before she'd even turned away.

"Woah," she shouted, stopping him as he went to remove his leggings. "I'm going to go back to the forest and gather some plants. Why don't you wait until I'm gone before completely undressing?"

"Is there a problem with seeing me naked?"

Her cheeks went red and her gaze darted around as she blinked awkwardly. "Aye... aye," she puffed. Then she regained herself and dropped her shoulders back as she stood straight once again. "Let me guess: you and your sister were raised by an old man or woman out in the forest somewhere all alone."

"Aye," he answered, though he wondered how she had guessed.

"My father has told me about your kind."

He had a 'kind' now? "Really?" Maybe she meant other novihomidraks.

"Aye. Their families are so scared of the primal gods that they send their children out to live with someone in the middle of the forest, alone, so that hopefully they won't be found. From my visions and in first meeting you, I suspected you were one, but I couldn't be sure. My father tells me 'tis hard for the children after they grow up to assimilate back into a group culture. Let me guess, the elder you were living with passed from this world and 'tis why you and your sister were out wandering in the woods."

Coldness seeped through Rivic. "Something like that." Not exactly that, but close enough.

"My father says that because these children have never had to cooperate with anyone else, they do not know many of the customs necessary for survival."

"What does that have to do with me bathing? Or removing my clothes for a swim?"

Her cheeks reddened once more, but she smiled as she glanced away from him as if he continued to amuse her. "Boys just don't get undressed around girls and vice versa, not until they are coupled. Respect for each other's emotions, bodies, and spirits is vital to the survival of a tribe."

Rivic nodded as he took in this information and attempted to understand it completely. "I will try to be more mindful."

"Many people who come out of the wilderness to get taken in by a tribe don't make it." The playful tone fell out of her voice as she became more somber. "'Tis too hard for them to be part of the group and they don't find their place because they are too afraid to speak up for themselves."

He had no idea of how to respond.

She reached out and put her hand over his. "Please, don't be afraid. You can ask me anything."

Rivic turned his palm upward, then lay his other hand over the top to completely clasp hers. The gesture didn't feel nearly enough, didn't sufficiently bring her into understanding his sentiments, so he brought her hand to his bare chest, right where he felt the warm emotions coming over him, and placed her palm against his skin. He layered his hands on top of hers so she couldn't easily pull away. "I will," he pledged.

For a long moment, she kept her hand on his chest after he dropped his away. Not only were her cheeks still red, but her breathing had become quick and deep. Rivic felt the heat coming off her. Finally, she lifted her palm, pulling her fingertips away last, and curled her fingers into a fist. "Aye, good." She turned and looked down at her hand as she walked away, rubbing her hand as she went.

Rivic watched her disappear into the forest trees just a short distance away. One of her guards standing nearby gave him a disapproving look before he turned to follow Ellonia back into the forest.

CHAPTER 6

*L*ooking at his reflection in the water, Rivic understood why Ellonia had said that others in the tribe would think him an evil spirit. Matted hair and a dirty face revealed a savage rather than a person. Any spot not covered in filth looked pale in comparison and made his eyes appear even darker and scarier.

Rivic washed, dunking himself, shaking his head, and tussling his fingers through his hair to comb it. In between breaths, he worked at loosening up the mass of knots in his hair under the water. As it untangled, he realized the length hung nearly down to his waist. When had it gotten so long? Cleaned up now, his reflection started to look like a human once more.

He heard a rustle in the branches behind him as if something came through the reeds toward him. He turned, his feet sinking in the mud nearly up to his ankles, and raised his hand up with curled fingers. His heart pounded.

A bird took flight, chased out by one that was slightly larger.

After a moment, all grew silent again. Rivic lowered his

hand and found himself breathing deeply. Several strange sensations went through him. His ears seemed ultra-focused on the noise all around him, as if the whole forest was humming.

A fish splashed behind him and he could hear it swimming around. He looked down as it circled his waist. Not only was the sound of its movement through the water like a smooth song in his ears, but he could feel the pulse of the water under the thrust of its strong tail. Instinctively, he reached down and grabbed the fish.

His fingers slashed right through it.

He brought up the fish, its body ripped in half and hanging in shreds, bloody water running through his fingers. In trying to figure out what had happened, he saw his fingers, or what he thought was his fingers. He dropped the remains of the fish into the water and twisted his hands around to look at them. Curved, white claws had extended right out from beneath his normal fingernails. He tried to snap one off and pain flared through him. He examined the flesh around it, bloodless, but it had definitely come from him.

"Are you done yet?" Ellonia called out from just outside the woods.

Water splashed up around him as Rivic doused his hands into the lake behind his back. He was pretty sure that she couldn't see his claws from the distance where she stood, but putting them behind him made him feel more protected. "Nay!" he shouted back. "A little longer, please."

Ellonia waved and turned around, going back into the woods.

So much for feeling human.

A part of him knew his mind should be asking what he was going to do about this, but he knew it would be all right. He didn't know how, but his body remained calm. After a moment, the curved claws shrank back down under his nails. The skin sealed right over the top of them. He turned his hands over as he looked at them.

How could he duplicate this? He had to know. He didn't want those things to pop out uncontrollably. He searched for another fish, then, upon finding one, tried to grab it. He caught the fish in his hands. Its muscular body squirmed back and forth, thrashing to escape. He let it go and looked at his hands. Nothing.

Rivic tried again without success. He knew the main difference was that he had been startled when he went for the fish that first time. How could he replicate that scared feeling?

The thought of Ellonia coming out of the forest again rose in his head. He felt his heart quicken as he fought the urge to look. He imagined her calling out his name behind him.

Claws popped out.

He shrieked.

As he bit down on the sound, he did look to see if Ellonia was behind him. He thrust his hands under the surface of the water just in case he saw her standing there. She was nowhere to be seen.

Rivic breathed deeply to get himself to relax. The claws retracted. He shivered, finding the water around him growing suddenly cold. But it was also more than that. Nyree's warnings whispered in his ears: he had to learn his powers. This was obviously one of them. Wondering how many others would adapt him physically, he wished Sontre' had warned him about this.

Rivic got out and pulled his clothes on. A moment later, Ellonia called out to him and he responded that he was presentable. She came out of the trees once more, her guards behind her flanking her steps.

When she got there, she lowered a bucket down into the water and scooped so deeply that the sleeves of her tunic dipped into the water. She hefted the bucket from the water and set it aside. "The mud here has great healing properties," she said, wringing water from the loose ends of her sleeves. Then she pulled what looked like a claw from her pouch, but he quickly saw that it was actually a wooden base with long animal claws attached to it. She pointed at the bucket. "'Twill take a moment for the mud to settle. Sit down in front of me and let's see if we can take care of your hair."

He still wasn't sure what she was going to do with the instrument in her hand, yet he settled down uneasily in front of her on the bank. His skin tingled as she touched his head and began to run her fingers through his hair.

"Hold still," she laughed, when he jerked his head to see what she was doing with the claws. She started near the ends of the long strands and pulled the comb through his hair. "I think we should cut this." She put a finger on his back about his shoulder blades. "Would you like this length?"

He really had no clue what she was asking him about, so he just nodded.

She pulled her knife from her belt.

Rivic spun away from her and put up his hands. "Woah. What are you doing with that?"

She gave the knife and him a strange look as she held the weapon loosely on the flat of her palm. "I'm going to cut your hair with it. Have you never had your hair cut before? Is that why it is so long?"

"I've never had my hair cut before." He felt silly for saying it. Feeling the wild beating of his heart, he curled his fingers into fists out of her sight, afraid that the claws would come out once again. "Will it hurt?"

"Nay," she smiled

He once again sat back down before her. "All right."

She held onto a length of his hair and pressed against it with the knife. It pulled on his scalp.

"What?" she asked, confused. She sliced the knife across the hair. Taking a smaller section, she tried again. "Why 'tis it not cutting?" Only a few strands fell away from her fingers as she released his hair.

"What's happening?" he asked.

"My knife, 'twon't cut through your hair."

He turned in time to see her cutting a section of her own hair. "Ow!" she said.

"It does hurt!"

"Nay," she denied. "My blade has gone dull. I sharpened it only this morning." She ran the knife across her finger.

"Don't do that," he said, reaching for her weapon.

A thin line of blood emerged from the wound. "'Tis not completely dull," she announced. She tried again to cut his hair, but it wouldn't.

A vague memory of what the dragon had said to him floated through his mind. "Let me see your knife."

After she'd handed him the knife, he wondered at the wisdom of what he was about to do. He pressed the blade against his fingertip, but in dragging the blade across it, he found that it would not cut him.

"What?" she panted.

He pricked his fingertip with the point and a spot of blood appeared.

"At least you bleed," she said. "I can't believe my knife has gone completely dull. Most of the roots I dug up this morning didn't require cutting."

"Don't blame your blade yet," Rivic said. He switched the knife to his other hand. "Vochey Submit." Nyree's dagger appeared across his palm.

Ellonia gasped.

"Try this," he said, handing the dagger to her. "I think you'll find it much easier."

She tentatively reached out and took it from him.

"Be careful," he said as she tried to handle the weapon, which had more weight to it than her knife.

She took several slices of his hair before it was obvious that she was comfortable again. "You can call weapons to you?" she asked.

"A couple," he said.

"You must have some special magic then." She continued to comb his hair with the claw. "How did you come by it?"

"I was born with it." That was the simplest answer he could think of.

Ellonia turned at the sound of sharp whistle behind her. She handed his dagger back to him. "We should be going."

"Is there something wrong?" he asked as he got up.

She tipped the bucket to let the water that had risen to the top drain off the mud that had settled to the bottom. "Not yet. But let's keep it that way."

Rivic trailed up the short hill after her while she carried the bucket. "So your guards signal you when you've stayed in one spot to long?" It was the only thing that made sense.

"Aye."

"Let me take that."

He reached for the bucket, but she pulled it out of his reach.

"I must carry it," she affirmed. "I cannot have someone else's magic tainting it."

Rivic felt there was more to it, but he didn't press the point.

Ellonia made a point of staying ahead of Rivic as they went back to camp. "I have been a fool," he heard her mutter as they strode along. "Way to go, Ellonia. This is exactly why the oracle told you to control your emotions."

He wanted to catch up and ask for an explanation behind her rantings, but he suspected he'd frighten her even further for overhearing what she'd said.

Once they were back at her lodging, she set the bucket by the door, then went to check on Nyree. "She still sleeps," Ellonia said, kneeling down beside Nyree as Rivic entered and came to stand behind her. She didn't even look at him as she stood up, then went to a bag. "My father asked me if I'd done this already. I should have done it right when I first took you in."

She held out a stone in her hand. "Take this."

Rivic reached out and took the stone from her. The weight of it surprised him. Worse, as he held it, it got heavier.

"Hold it up," she commanded. "Let me see it."

It took both hands for Rivic to be able to flip it over in his hand, then to hold it up as he uncurled his fingers from around it to show her. It blazed a bright reddish gold.

Ellonia took a couple steps back as tears filled her eyes. "You're like *him*, aren't you? Please tell me you haven't come here to destroy my village. Please?"

Rivic let go of the stone, the light winking out of it right before it hit the floor. "I don't know who you are referring to. I haven't come here to hurt anyone." Or he hoped he wouldn't. He looked back over his shoulder at Nyree. "I just wanted to make my sister better. We needed shelter."

"Swear to me that your words are the truth."

"Ellonia, I have no need to lie to you. You have been nothing but kind to me."

"Yet you can call weapons to you and your magic is powerful. Until now, only *he* could do those things." She took a sharp intake of breath as she glanced at the stone on the ground, then back to him. "I was told in my vision that only you would be able to stop him. It makes sense though; you would need matching strength to defeat him." Her last sentence held a tone of growing hope.

He wanted her to slow down, to explain things better to him. Instead, she rushed over to him, took his face in her hands, and stretched up on her toes as she gave him a quick kiss which left him stunned.

She picked the stone up off the ground and tucked it away. "I must tell my father. I'm sure he will want to speak with you over evening meal tonight. You should probably get some rest before then." The next instant, she was out of the lodge, leaving him alone with his confusion.

CHAPTER 7

*E*llonia slipped into the hut sometime later. Rivic raised his head from the mat where he'd been trying unsuccessfully to get some sleep.

"I'm sorry if I woke you," she said, placing a bowl of water on the table.

He rolled over on his side and propped his head up on his bent arm so he could better watch her. "I think my sister is sleeping for both of us right now."

Ellonia went to check on Nyree, crouching down beside her. "She needs it. Poor thing. Her body just wasn't ready for what she went through." Ellonia brushed a strand of hair away from Nyree's face.

"Do you know what happened to us?" Rivic asked.

Ellonia looked back over her shoulder at him. "I know it was traumatic. I know it has changed both of you. But I do not see the specific details of the event. Do you care to share them?"

"Nay."

"I thought not." Ellonia stood up and came over to him.

"About earlier," he started, unsure of where he was really

going after that. Her caresses, it had meant something, but what was she expecting from it. Maybe he just needed to be forthright. "I don't know why you kissed me or, well, what any of it meant. I'm sorry. I just don't understand any of this. It's all very new to me."

"Remember what I told you earlier, by the lake?"

"About not having the skills needed to fit into a tribe? That I could talk to you about anything?"

"Aye, that." She sat down on the floor beside his mat then reached out and took his hand. "I did not mean to push or confuse you earlier when I kissed you. I forget that this is all new for you. I have dreamed about your arrival for many cycles. You are exactly as you have been in my visions. I feel like I am on the road ahead of you waiting for you to catch up."

Rivic sat up, pulling his legs in so he sat cross-legged before her. "I feel like you're trying to tell me something and I should be understanding, but I don't. Do you see something between us?"

She reached out, closing the gap between them as she took his hands in hers. "I do. I've seen it in many different ways. Every one of them depends on the choices we decide to make along the way."

He felt his breath deepening and his pulse quickening, especially as he glanced down to their joined hands as she spoke.

"Forgive me if I already feel like my heart belongs to you, even though you don't know me. You've been in my dreams and visions so often that I am already in love with you." Ellonia squeezed as if willing him to understand. "Augina says I should fight it, that I shouldn't tell you, but I can't help myself."

"Who is Augina?"

"She is the oracle that I trained with until our village had to split four cycles ago. She stayed with the original tribe and I moved with my father to become his seer and tribal healer. Two cycles before that I started seeing you."

Her words began to settle into him. "So you've been waiting six cycles for me?" Fear that Augina had been right tiptoed in, unnerving him.

She met his gaze and gave a small smile. "At least. But the visions of you have increased in these last few moon phases."

Rivic withdrew his hand from hers. "I'm sorry. I don't know what to say to that. I know I'm on a dangerous path and I don't want to put you in harm's way."

Ellonia put her head down, her blond hair falling around her face to shield her and make sure he couldn't read the expression on her face. "I know. You have to help my sister. She has to come first."

"Your sister?"

When she looked back up, she pushed aside the misery that was plainly written on her face and replaced it with a broad smile. "We'll talk about it later. Father is waiting for us to meet him for dinner. You should go wash up now." She pointed to the bowl of water on the table before she got to her feet and went to take something out of one of her wooden boxes pushed off to one side.

Little, fern-like leaves and tiny, white yarrow flowers floated on the surface. Folded over the side of the bowl and with one end dangling into the water, was a cloth which Rivic dampened and used to wash his face.

"I made this," Ellonia said behind him. "I had to guess at the size, but I think I got it right. I'd be honored if you'd wear it."

Rivic turned and found Ellonia holding up a black leather tunic. Pieces of rounded bones had been dyed yellow and woven onto the leather in little overlapping waves. It reminded him of his novimather's scales. He found himself drawn to it even while he knew that he ought to turn it away. She'd put too much work into this. Regardless of what she said about all her visions of them, he knew some day, probably soon, he'd have to leave to fulfill his mission. He wasn't certain he was coming back from it.

But for the moment, the gift summoned him. "I'd be honored to be allowed to wear it," he said, taking it from her.

"I'll be right outside," she said as she left him to change.

Shortly, he raised the leather flap to find her standing in the fading sunlight waiting for him as she had said she would. At first, he thought she might say something, but she didn't. She just came over and took his hand, then led him off toward the lodging in the center of the village.

A woman stood hunched over a fire pit around the longer side. The scent of cooking meat and spices brought a growl from Rivic's stomach. He wondered how much formality there would be before dinner was actually served.

Two guardsmen at the door didn't look at Ellonia as they approached, but Rivic noticed one of the men secure his grip on his weapon.

Ellonia lifted the hide cover and entered. She bowed once she was inside. "Good Father," she said. "I present to you Rivic."

Rivic felt a need to bow. "Krithstand-chief."

Ellonia's father sat behind a small fire centered in his lodge with a brown fur cape over his shoulders. "Cleans up well, doesn't he? His eyes are brighter now, clear. That is good. Come, sit."

Animal hides lay stretched out with the fur-side up on the floor near the fire. The smoke drifted toward a small cone in the ceiling with a hole at the top.

Krithstand kept his hand raised toward the furs until they were seated. He added, "The remaining council will be here soon."

Council? Rivic didn't know they were expecting others.

"Has he been tested?" Chief Krithstand asked.

"Aye," Ellonia said. "His power is strong, just as foretold."

Rivic had thought they would have spoken about this earlier when Ellonia went to her father. If not the subject of the strength of Rivic's magical abilities, then what else had they talked about?

Krithstand's gaze went from his daughter, to Rivic, then back to Ellonia again. "Does he pose a danger to the tribe?"

Rivic wanted to tell Krithstand that he was in the room, but something whispered at him not to speak, so he didn't.

"Aye, he does. We are beyond the limit with him. I haven't even had a chance to test his sister yet." Ellonia shifted slightly, uncomfortable about telling this to her father. She cast a shy look to Rivic with a wane smile as if asking him to endure this just a little longer and that she would make it all right. How strange that she could communicate all that to him with merely a glance.

"She has not awoken?" Krithstand asked abruptly.

Ellonia slowly pulled her gaze away from Rivic to her father. "Nay, she still sleeps. Her trauma was great. She walks in the land of dreams to heal herself."

Krithstand nodded.

A chime rang outside. "Come," Krithstand called out and then the flap lifted and several people entered. The first was an elderly man, walking bent over a thick branch nearly as twisted as his back. Behind him was a woman several cycles older than Ellonia, then two more men close to Krithstand in age. They approached the fire and sat down where they could see Rivic.

Krithstand quickly filled the council members in on what Ellonia had just told him. The leather rose again and several more people entered with trenchers filled with sliced meat and potatoes, a wooden tray of fruit, and another tray with several cups. Krithstand stood as the trays were set down on short tables nearby and he raised his hands toward the ceiling of his lodging.

"Spirits of the ground, thank you for the bounty," he said. "Spirits of the air, thank you for the harvest. Spirits of the water, thank you for the nourishment. We share this meal knowing we are part of the cycle. Beginning to end to beginning. All is connected. Blessed be."

"Blessed be," the council and Ellonia repeated. Rivic muttered the words, but a moment behind the other, feeling stupid for needing to follow in their example.

Krithstand sat down again. The people who had brought in the trays now began to serve the food to the council.

"I find it hard to believe this boy could be the one we are waiting for," said one of the councilmen shortly after taking his first bite.

Rivic accepted his trencher of meat and potatoes. The bread felt warm in his hands. Thin, brown gravy clung to the tops of the meat and diced potatoes, but most of it had soaked into the bread. Rivic followed the others and began to eat with his fingers. The smoke in the lodging as well as the sharp scents the other council members had brought in with them stung at his eyes and nose, making it so he had to fight to keep from wincing. He blinked several times, trying futilely to clear the soreness from his eyes.

"The signs are clear," Ellonia protested, failing to keep signs of irritation from her voice. "He is the one."

"So says you," the other man scowled.

Ellonia's eyes sharpened on the councilman and her mouth opened. Rivic swore that he could see the knife-sharp retort on her tongue, but her father interceded. "None of this matters now. He still bears too much trauma over what has happened to him."

Rivic wondered what it was about him that the chief

could sense that. Was Krithstand just that intuitive with people that he knew when his men were too worn to go to battle?

Krithstand nodded at Rivic as if silently telling Rivic that it would be all right, that the chief hadn't meant any slight against him. Rivic tipped his head in acknowledgement, finding himself truly respecting the chief.

"Right now, we are only assessing our safety in having him and his sister with us. The healer says that he has significant magic and there is cause for our concern."

Rivic wished he wasn't holding the trencher because he wanted to shrink and wring his hands together as if he could contain the magic within him. He found himself nearly apologizing.

"We just had a Split. We barely have enough people to handle all the tasks as it is. If we Split again, neither village will make it on their own," the councilwoman protested.

"Fronis is right," the first man spoke. "If this boy alone puts us over the limit, then we have to send him away. Take him to another village, let him be their problem."

"But he is the one," Ellonia claimed.

Rivic heard the hitch in her breath as she felt herself losing this battle. But he could also see the fear held in the eyes of each of the council members, except Chief Krithstand, who seemed to be legitimately torn. Rivic set his gaze on the chief, knowing that the final decision would rest with him.

"Child," Fronis said to Ellonia in much the same way a mother would admonish a toddler, "we cannot let feelings dictate how we rule. We must think of the greater good."

"And the greater good is Rivic and his sister feeling like they are part of our tribe. If they don't help us—"

Fronis cut across Ellonia's words, "Augina told me about your visions. She feared what you might tell your *chosen one* when he showed up. How much has she already told you?" Fronis turned her hawkish stare to Rivic.

Now he felt completely uncomfortable and started to rise. Ellonia made a grab for him, but he was already on his feet. He set a hand on her shoulder. "Clearly, this whole land is in great peril. Ellonia has said only that she believes I am the one who can help. I cannot do that from here, nor do I wish to stay where I am not wanted. I understand your concerns and the fears for your safety. My sister and I shall leave straight away."

"But—" Ellonia said, her words faltering.

Rivic handed the remains of his trencher to one of the servers as he headed toward the door.

He never made it out. Two guardsmen pushed their way inside, one knocking Rivic on the shoulder without apology as he passed.

"Krithstand-chief, Nex returned from outer patrol. The beasts have been spotted. We have incoming," the first man said.

"All ready?" Krithstand turned to Ellonia. "How much over does he put us?"

Ellonia looked to the ground, sounding regretful as she answered. "More than double. He has enough power to be his own tribe."

Fronis stammered for a moment as she got her words in order. "What? He should have been made to leave straight away. Why was he--?"

"'Tis done already," Krithstand snapped as he got to his feet. "So even if we sent him away, they would just track him down?"

Ellonia nodded. "Aye, Good Father."

"We must send him away, now," Fronis said. "Get him a horse. Make him run fast."

Rivic whirled around. "I will not leave without my sister. She is in no state to ride."

"If his sister is as powerful as he is and she stays, they might not go after Rivic, but would still attack us anyway." Ellonia spoke the words to her father knowing she had but one rushed chance to convince him. "If we sent them both away, the beasts would hunt them down. They'd be slaughtered."

Rivic opened his mouth to say that Nyree was his twin and would have no magic. Ellonia and Krithstand knew this. Had they not shared the information with the council? They hadn't, for tonight they kept speaking of Nyree as his sister. He got the sense that Ellonia hoped the council would have compassion for Nyree in her state and let her stay.

"Let me fight with you," Rivic said. He had no idea what he'd do, but being alone in the forest scared him even more than facing unknown beasts.

"We need a vote," Krithstand said. He turned toward the council with his arms out, spreading the furs that spanned his back. It made him seem like a much larger man.

"I say we send him away," Fronis said.

The first councilman stepped beside Fronis. "I second that."

"He stays," Ellonia shouted as if fearing that she was quickly being outvoted.

The second councilman lowered his head. "He's here. He should stay with us. There is no guarantee that they will go after the boy if he leaves; we would still face attack. His power might be helpful. If he fights with us and dies, then we know he has no right to be here."

Rivic couldn't help looking at Krithstand, knowing his fate now rested with the chief. He found Krithstand inspecting him.

"He stays," Krithstand said.

Under the chief's scrutiny, Rivic felt magic ripple through him as if coming awake and raising its head. "Thank you. You will not regret your decision," he said. His voice came out deeper than he'd ever heard from himself before.

"I suspect we won't," Krithstand said, patting Rivic's shoulder as he started for the leather flap. Then to the guardsman, he said, "Inform the lines. Let's be ready for the beasts."

The guardsman left. Rivic made way for the chief, then followed him outside. The guards had hurried off so quickly that Rivic didn't know which direction they had gone. Krithstand, forgetting that Rivic was behind him, turned and nearly stepped into Rivic. The chief dodged around Rivic back to Ellonia.

"Get yourself to safety," Krithstand said.

"I have a convalescent," she protested.

Krithstand didn't look pleased.

Rivic came to stand beside the chief. "Go back to your lodge and stay with my sister. I swear no harm will come to either of you. I won't let it," Rivic said to Ellonia. Then, to the chief, he added, "Which direction are the beasts coming from? I will head out and make sure they never get this far."

"That'd be as foolish as you heading out on your own," Ellonia insisted.

"I've made a promise to keep this tribe safe," Rivic declared. "I intend on keeping it."

Fronis walked by him. "You'd do us all better by leaving."

Krithstand pointed toward the central bonfire. "If Nex was reporting this, then they must be coming in from that bearing."

Rivic nodded and, without another word, started running in that direction.

CHAPTER 8

*R*ivic dashed through Krithstand's village and jumped fallen logs which circled the outskirts. As he ran, he found himself crouching lower and lower. The hair at the base of his neck began to tingle and he knew he grew closer to the enemy. His breathing deepened.

His nose itched as he picked up the scent of pungent, earthy magic. Fear ticked into his chest, followed by an ignition of fury and he surged forward. His eyes narrowed and his vision sharpened. Saliva poured into his mouth. Rivic felt hungry and ready to attack.

Yet the first assault wasn't his. The beast swooped in on him, diving at him with a scream. He didn't even see it, just heard the leathery creak of its opening wings as it pulled up to keep from hitting the ground.

Claws extended from Rivic's fingers. He snatched out his arms, encircling the beast even before he knew what it was. It squirmed and fought against him as the white, curving extensions from his fingers pressed through flesh and took a deep hold.

It tried to bite into him. Rivic tore through the beast,

ripping it open as he moved just as quickly to keep it from nipping him. The animal screamed more from rage than pain.

It feels nothing, Rivic thought as he seized the creature's throat and slashed downward. As he reached its chest, he saw no blood pouring over him. *It doesn't bleed.*

It lashed out with its talons and tried to stab the sharp, bony point of its tail through Rivic's back. The beast's natural weapons all bounced off him.

The demon stopped and stared at Rivic, who smiled, showing the creature a mouthful of elongated teeth. It made to shriek in terror, but Rivic had already sliced its throat wide open and it had no way to create the sound.

"Cazidor palikiem," Rivic said and the demon burst into flames in his hands. As the magical fire burned around him, Rivic wanted to pull away, but he didn't. He held the beast as it quickly withered and turned to ash. The death of the monster in his hands launched a thrilling ripple through Rivic and he desired to do it again. He wanted to feel all the beasts melt away and delightedly sensed more rushing toward him.

A man on horseback charged up behind Rivic and slid to a halt. Rivic whipped around, mindful that he had a mouthful of additional teeth and these long, curved white claws on his hands. He tried to obscure them from Nex, not wanting to terrify the man.

"More gargaxes are coming," Nex shouted at Rivic as if he needed to be told. The scout's gaze held toward the tops of the trees rather than on Rivic.

As if on cue, several of the demons cried out overhead.

"Here they come," Nex yelled, kicking his horse in the sides as he turned it and started galloping away. "Take cover."

"Elixe'ist praten karmiden val'orishem cazidor noctada

raliest," Rivic shouted. The night sky filled with streaks of light and the gargaxes began to fall.

Nex fought to turn his panicked horse as he looked back at Rivic, who was calmly walking through the fiery hailstorm.

A dying gargax barreled through the treetops and thumped on the ground beside Rivic. It made a final vicious attack, trying to take Rivic down with a slash of its talons.

"Pit'ta cazidor rhona," Rivic spat and he pointed at the beast, which exploded with a thunderous boom. Rivic glanced up to see the scout staring slack-jawed at him.

"Any others?" Rivic asked. With the back of his arm, he wiped away the saliva that spat from his misshapen and unfamiliar mouth.

Nex shook his head, still unable to close his jaw.

"Good," Rivic said as he walked right by the scout. He honestly didn't know who was more scared of what had just happened: Rivic himself, or Nex. Rivic trembled. He'd saved Krithstand's tribe as he said he would, but what had it cost him?

As he got closer to the village, he noticed the warriors on horseback staring at him. Rivic knew someone else had witnessed what he'd done and he saw the trepidation in their eyes. As he walked, his face shifted back to normal and he moved his chin and neck as if assuring himself that they were his own again. The white claws at his fingertips slowly receded. The more he felt himself returning to his usual state, the more he began to shiver.

People, mostly men, sidled out his way, their eyes wide as he moved through the village.

He kept his feet moving steadily beneath him, focused, until he got to Ellonia's lodging. Inside Ellonia sat beside Nyree and looked up when Rivic came in. Ellonia rose. "Are we in danger? Are the gargaxes coming?"

Rivic ignored Ellonia as he went over to Nyree and slid his arms beneath her. He felt Ellonia move, turning toward him as he began to lift Nyree. "Rivic?"

"The dragon was right. My magic is destructive." Rivic shifted his legs so he sat on one bent knee. Then he pushed himself to his feet carrying Nyree with him. "I didn't have control of it. I felt savage."

"Rivic, what happened out there? Is it over already?" Ellonia put her hand on his arm as though she could stop him if she wanted to, if he let her. "Rivic, talk to me."

"I can't stay here. If I do, bad things are going to happen." Rivic turned the opposite direction so that her hand fell off his arm.

Ellonia wasn't about to give up without a fight. She grabbed his tunic and held it in a tight fist. "Your sister can't leave yet. She's not well."

Rivic turned sideways as he went through the doorway with his sister. "I know, but we can't remain here. It's way too dangerous for your village, Ellonia. It took control of me. I had no choice. I wasn't acting under my own will. I can't cause more destruction. Innocent people will die." As he got outside, he saw a ring of warriors surrounding Ellonia's lodgings. They knew. The warriors had come for him. They were scared of him too.

He stopped, realizing that he held his sister before him, like a shield and just as defenseless.

Krithstand stepped in front of his warriors. The movement felt odd; it made more sense for a ruler ordering his men to stay back rather than coming to the forefront. Rivic felt that truth ripple through him. There was more going on than what he could see. What exactly was about to happen? Rivic wondered if the chief meant to take him into custody by himself. Maybe the chief was trying to let him save face.

Rivic knew he still couldn't go willingly into captivity. He and his sister had to get out of here before something bad happened. Yet he couldn't bring himself to feel the urge to fight. Instead, he felt strangely calm. When he knew in his brain that he needed to get away, why did he stand here so serenely? He didn't understand these feelings which seemed so different than what his head was telling him. He swallowed hard, a movement that worked his jaw in the action. He and Krithstand stood there staring at each other.

"I hear you decimated the gargaxes by yourself," Krithstand said.

Rivic tried to discern what he heard in the chief's tone. He didn't want a battle. "Fronis is correct; we should leave. Let me depart without a fight. My sister and I will go far, far away from your tribe and not bother you again."

Krithstand gave a smile and strode toward them with an open hand. "You think I'd let a power like you just leave?"

Rivic moved warily away. So, the chief meant to keep him prisoner and use his powers when beasts came around.

"Do not fear," Krithstand said. "Anyone who can destroy the gargaxes like that is someone we want on our side. Tonight, you have saved many lives in our village. We all owe you a great debt. Please stay as a member of our tribe."

Rivic could scarcely believe what he was hearing. It felt unreal.

It felt dangerous.

How could anyone want him around after seeing what he was capable of doing. Did they realize it could've just as easily been them rather than the gargaxes? Rivic started to make his way through the warriors.

Krithstand moved to intercept. "You would still leave us?"

"If you value your lives, you will let me go. Don't you understand how vicious and untamed my magic is? Who is to say I won't kill you next, not because I want to, because I can't control this."

At the threat of Rivic killing the chief, the warriors swarmed in around him, closing off his way out. Rivic felt the magic rear inside him and he constricted it before it struck out. He turned to face the chief, wondering how terrifying he must look when Krithstand motioned to his warriors to step back without any words being spoken.

Rivic continued on.

"We really wish you would remain here. We need you to stay." Krithstand grabbed his daughter and yanked her through the crowd, aiming her toward Rivic. "Ellonia, do you foresee any dangers? Does he pose any threat to us?"

Rivic stopped and looked back. So desperately in his heart he wanted Ellonia to confess how dangerous Rivic was, and yet he didn't know if he could stand to hear the words from her lips. He steeled himself, prepared for the worst.

Ellonia's eyes grew wide as she realized that the fate of her village rested upon her now. She licked her lips, and then gradually started to nod slowly with her gaze down. But as she got more confidant with her beliefs, she shook her head faster and raised her gaze to Krithstand. "Good Father, Rivic poses no threat to us." She looked to Rivic now, her eyes fiercely pleading. "He is meant to be with us."

Krithstand threw his arms wide. "'Tis decided then. Rivic stays with us."

Several of the guardsmen raised bows and staffs into the air, giving a triumphant shout as they did so. Even Fronis stood nearby, clapping together her thin hands.

Ellonia rushed up beside Rivic and touched his arm motioning with her head for him to start back toward her lodgings. Rivic saw that he would not be allowed to leave the tribe. They would follow him if he tried. Acquiescing, he followed Ellonia.

"Come first light, we begin to build Rivic's lodgings," Krithstand shouted to the village.

As Rivic stepped inside Ellonia's hut with her close behind him, he said, "I should not remain. I am too dangerous."

"I know." Ellonia circled around him and went to lift the fur hide on Nyree's mat. After Rivic had lay his sister back down to sleep and Ellonia covered her with the blanket, Ellonia took Rivic's hand. "But we are in much more peril without you."

She slid closer to him, her hand caressing his cheek as she came up against him. For a moment, he thought she might kiss him, but she moved on by him and hurried toward the door. "Blessed dreams, my love." The flap dropped closed behind her, leaving him to wonder if they really were in more jeopardy without him.

As the moon cycle progressed, Rivic's hut was built. Nyree, who after a week of sleeping nearly all the time, was still weak. She had recovered enough to walk, with his help, as he moved her to his lodgings.

Rivic spend every moment with Ellonia that he could. It took a while, but life began to settle in and Rivic found himself enjoying his days with the village. He had never imagined that his life could be like this, so calm and peaceful and yet so exciting to wake up every day knowing that he was surrounded by people. People who weren't threatened by him.

Rivic waved to Ellonia as the hunting party he went out with had left that morning. Now he returned to her carrying a large wastile tucked under his arm. He smiled when he saw her.

Ellonia sat at her table outside, waiting for the men's return. She currently busied herself by grinding dried herbs in a bowl with a rock as he set the bird down beside where she worked. The wastile's head hung limply off the edge of the table, dangling on its long, thin neck.

She turned, looking first at the bird, then to Rivic. "Oh, 'tis beautiful. Will you save me the long feathers?"

"Of course." Rivic leaned in and kissed her cheek. "Whatever you wish. I brought the whole bird for you."

"For me?"

"For taking care of me and Nyree," Rivic said.

The softness in her eyes hardened with pain. "I don't want payment. I did it because it was the right thing to do."

Rivic dropped down to his knees beside her and grasped her hand. "Nay, please don't think of it that way. 'Twas certainly not my intention. I just wanted you to know that I appreciate what you've done for us." He pressed her hand to his lips, squeezing his fingers around hers.

"Do we have a proposal going on?" laughed one of Krithstand's guards as he sauntered by.

Rivic suddenly realized what this must look like, but before he stood up to correct the situation, he saw Ellonia's face redden with a blush. That's what she wanted: a proposal. Nerves rolled around in Rivic's stomach. Now was certainly not the time for that. There was a protocol.

Rivic stretched up on his legs and kissed Ellonia, this time on the mouth. As he backed away from her, he whispered, "Patience."

She pulled the pain from her eyes and forced a smile.

The guard, Tovis, came running in the camp. "Rivic, I'm glad to find you. Gargaxes have been spotted coming in from the east."

This had become such an occurrence that Rivic was getting quite used to it.

He gave Ellonia departing smile, then followed Tovis. As soon as they were outside of the boundary of the tribe, Rivic and Tovis began to jog through the forest. Several other men, including Krithstand, caught up to them matching them in their stride and pace.

"These attacks, they are becoming ridiculous." Krithstand shook his head as he spoke to Rivic. "Lord Cirvel of Gohaldinest keeps trying to reign through terror and subjugation. I wonder if you are the kind of man who would stand with me to change all that."

Rivic had felt this coming. Krithstand's own ambition was growing on the pedestal of Rivic's power. At first, Krithstand had only wanted Rivic around to destroy the gargaxes and keep the tribe safe. Now he spoke of engaging in larger battle. "I find that things that stick their heads out of the ground usually wind up headless. Do you really wish to endanger your daughter and the tribe like that?"

Krithstand slowed his pace to match Rivic's, who only now realized that he had dropped his speed. "I have another daughter who left us. I am already exposed and at risk. If anything happened to Ellonia, if these attacks Cirvel sends out upon us were to harm her, there would be no holding me back."

The chief's words goaded him. Rivic knew that if anything happened to Ellonia, her father would have to take a position behind him for razing Gohaldinest down to stone in order to take revenge upon Cirvel. He wasn't ready to say those words to the chief yet, nor was he sure that Krithstand was ready to hear them. Either way, Rivic had no right to speak them.

He spun all the anger stirred up by his imagination back into himself; it wouldn't do any good if the gargaxes sensed his location through these heated emotions. Yet it did give him an idea.

Deep in the forest now, Rivic came to a stop and closed his eyes. He reached out with his magic, feeling the gargaxes. "There are two of them, flying low and from the east."

"Only two?" Krithstand asked.

"Maybe they had hoped by keeping their numbers small,

they could scout ahead and find out what kept destroying the gargaxes sent out earlier. Aye, that was exactly what they had planned. They still wouldn't get the chance." Rivic nodded to the scouts that were with him and he whispered the spell that would lift him up above the trees. Once above the branches, Rivic spotted the gargaxes. As they drew closer, the up and down bob of their flight became more and more apparent.

"Cazidor palikiem."

The gargaxes erupted into fire. Rivic wished he was closer, so that he could hear their ashes sprinkling down among the leaves of the trees of the forest below. It almost didn't seem fair, him being able to destroy them from such a distance or before they could even look eye to eye at each other. It certainly had taken all the fun out of it.

More gargaxes would come. Rivic would be waiting. Let them wonder where their comrades had gone. Though Rivic did wonder that since they were a magical race, did they feel when one of their species had been snuffed out?

Rivic slowly lowered himself back to the ground. The scouts eyed him with wonder and curiosity. "Another two gone," Rivic stated in a matter of fact tone. "It appears they are sending new ones trying to see what has happened to the others. More will come in search of these two."

Krithstand nodded his understanding at the underlying threat held in Rivic's words, but tonight, the scouts didn't care. They brought Rivic back to the tribe in victory, rejoiced in their safety, and reveled in Rivic's magic which allowed the gargaxes to be dispatched before harm came to anyone. And that night, as many other nights of the past few weeks, a feast was held in Rivic's honor. His mood to dance and cheer had waned for he now felt something, a much bigger threat coming on the horizon. He sensed that it might be happening soon. Maybe they were already being watched.

Rivic saw the flap to his lodging draw back and Nyree,

with Ellonia's help, came outside. Sitting on a simple crafted chair across from the fire, Nyree watched him now. It was only the second time she'd been able to get out to enjoy the festivities. Her smile showed renewing strength.

That gave Rivic cause to celebrate. He danced with Ellonia and enjoyed feeling her move beside him, wishing that this time would never end and knowing, just knowing, that he wasn't going to get his wish.

CHAPTER 9

"Oh 'tis just too cute!" Rivic heard a woman squeal somewhere within Krithstand's village early the next morning. Several other feminine cries of delight followed. He got up and started to go outside to see what the commotion was within the tribe.

Nyree called out behind him from her bedding. "Be careful, Rivic. Do stay safe."

He pulled the tie on the flap and put his hand against the leather. "I will," he responded, not really sure what her words meant to begin with, but feeling the air of caution around them. He stepped out into the brisk sunrise air which carried the scent of fires being rekindled for the day.

"I wouldn't try to grab it," said one of the older women a short distance away. "'Tis probably too wild. He might bite you."

Several of the younger women were trying to entice a tiny creature with food. Rivic wasn't sure what he was looking at it first: was it a lizard or maybe a baby dragon, though its size seemed too big for the first and too small for the latter. It appeared to be more the dimension of a squirrel, except that it had scales rather than fur.

The creature came out from behind a tree, its long tail flickering. As one of the women approached with a piece of meat in her outstretched hand, it shrank back and flattened its ears against its head as its blue-green eyes looked between the womenfolk surrounding it. The animal tried to growl with a sound that only made the females giggle. That seemed to make the creature mad.

Rivic stepped forward, putting himself between the villagers and the creature. "She is correct. It might be rabid. You ladies best get back." As he forced the women apart, the creature ran through the first opening it found and dashed further in the camp. Rivic shook his head with a curse. He had to get the thing out of camp before it really did get nasty.

He ran after it, seeing it just as it slipped inside Ellonia's hut. A panic took him. What if she got bitten by the creature? Knowing that Ellonia was usually an early riser, he hoped that she'd already untied the flap for the morning. He tried to press inside and felt the tie still knotted. He drew his dagger and cut through the opening.

Inside Ellonia's lodgings, she'd already lit a candle and, in the sparse light it provided, Rivic saw Ellonia sitting with the creature in her lap. The scale-covered squirrel looked back over its shoulder, panic in its luminous eyes, and then it darted behind Ellonia where she tried to conceal it even further behind her arms.

"You all right in here?" Rivic asked warily.

I'm fine."

Rivic took a step closer, inching to see around Ellonia and saw the beast peering back at him. Rivic considered the unlikely question and had to ask. "Do you know that animal?"

Ellonia reached back and put her hand around the tiny creature, pulling it back into her lap. "I do."

Rivic sensed there was something more, something she didn't want to tell him. He wondered just how far he should intrude, but it didn't seem to be his place. As he turned and started back toward the flap, he pointed to the cut ties. "I'll have someone come by and fix that later today."

"Don't bother. I'll fix it myself."

He truly was the trespasser here, not the creature sitting with Ellonia. "I'm sorry," he said again. He started to pull back the leather.

"Necroathelings have been sent out from Gohaldinest," she called out after him. "They'll be here in a few days."

Necroathelings. So that was what was coming. Rivic turned back to her. "What's taking them so long? Why aren't they here already?"

The creature looked up at Ellonia. Rivic saw a small canister attached around its neck.

She shook her head. "The order has just been given."

"Who gives you this information? Does it come via that beast?"

Again, the strange, little animal looked up at Ellonia and even gave a shake of his head as if to tell her no. Ellonia frowned as she looked back up at Rivic. "In a fashion. My sister sends word of the attack." Strangely enough, Rivic thought he saw a look of relief pass the creature's face.

"Where is your sister?"

"She's an acolyte in Gohaldinest"

"What makes her privy to this sort of information?"

"In order to help her tribe," Ellonia said looking down toward the creature as she nervously pinched her fingers over its scales, "she is an acolyte in Gohaldinest."

Rivic felt his knees weaken. "Your sister is training to become a Necroatheling? And she's doing this to help the tribe? What could she possibly hope to gain by putting your-self in such danger?"

Ellonia glanced back up to him. "She dispatches information to let us know when danger is coming, when the
gargaxes are about to go out cull the herds."

Cull the herds. Rivic understood; separate all the human
tribes that were getting to be too strong and that were beginning to become a threat to Lord Cirvel. With him and his
sister in the village, this tribe had become Cirvel's number
one threat. The gargaxes had been sent and none have
returned. Now, Necroathelings would be arriving.

"We must inform Krithstand-chief." He barely had the
words out when a tingle went through Rivic, making him fall
silent. The Necroathelings weren't just coming; they were
here.

He felt the flash of magic, then another right as an explosion sounded in the middle of camp. The Necroathelings
were arriving and fully prepared to take everyone down
before there could even be a fight.

"I should have known. He's never come to me in the
daytime," Ellonia said, putting the animal down on the
ground.

Screams erupted. Ellonia was on her feet in an instant
and followed Rivic to the entrance of the hut. "Stay here and
get down," he commanded.

She tried to rush by Rivic, but he stopped her. "People
might be injured. They need my help," she protested at
having her way barred.

"Let me take care of the Necroathelings first. You can help
whoever still alive when I'm done."

Ellonia's eyes narrowed on him. "'Tis kind of harsh, don't
you think."

"As harsh as I need to be if it keeps you alive."

She stared right back at him, but he stood firm against
her seething gaze. He would not back down from this. "Stay,"
he entreated once more.

"I can't. I'm the healer. You're wasting time. Mine and the tribe's. I will not stand by here and see who remains standing after this battle." She ducked low enough that she avoided his arm as she went to exit the lodging. "I will not stand idly by."

Having no choice but to follow her, Rivic seriously considered using magic to get her away. He could do it without her consent, but he knew just how angry she would be. Plus, the spell would instantly pinpoint him to the Necroathelings, denying him a sneak attack. As Ellonia had already reached someone who had fallen in the first attack, he continued on to hunt the Necroathelings.

Rivic ran low through the encampment, crouching as close to the ground as he could. He saw the Necroathelings with their dark purple hoods pulled way up over their heads. They stood back to back, three of them making a good defense in all directions. Not only did they have eyes on the situation around them, but they were encased in their own magical shell of protection. He wasn't sure he'd be able to breach their defenses. Could his magic take out their three combined magicks together? This would definitely be a lot harder than taking out the gargaxes. Not to mention that they were also human lives. Hadn't he taken enough of those already?

A familiar presence moved up beside him and curled her hand around his arm. "They are here because of us," Nyree said. "We must go."

"This is our home, Nyree," Rivic said firmly as his gaze went to find Ellonia and make sure she was still safe. Around them, people fled. Within the screaming chaos, he and his sister seemed like an island of calm. Rivic didn't even really feel like moving either to attack the Necroathelings or to flee from them. Time felt like it had slowed.

"Nay, 'tis not. 'Tis been our temporary reprieve while we

both adjusted to our new selves. If we don't leave this village now, all will perish."

Rivic looked at Nyree and saw her eyes were black with the thin yellow torch running vertical through each of them. He hadn't seen her like that in such awhile and had nearly forgotten. "If we leave, will they follow our magic?"

"Follow your magic? Aye."

Rivic put his hand over Nyree's as if securing her hold on him. "Talcor dun."

Once the world returned to focus around them and Rivic saw they were outside of camp, he bent down and put his hand on the ground and grabbed a handful of the mossy undergrowth. "Salick'ne."

The plants expanded within his fingers until he could no longer hold his hand closed around it. As he straightened and backed away with Nyree staying at his side, a circle of magic surrounded the plants until it looked like a glowing green orb levitating slightly off the ground. He took Nyree's hand as the orb continued to expand. "Talcor dun."

They had arrived on a particularly steep slope of the mountainside and their feet slipped beneath them for a moment. Still sensing the orb growing in the forest below, Rivic turned his feet outward to stop his slide as he glanced up at the much steeper cliff above them. He squeezed onto his twin to keep her from falling. She had lost weight in her sickness and he felt like her slight body would glide from his embrace.

Nyree's looked back in the direction of their tribe. "They have picked up your magic."

"Are we far enough away?" he asked.

"From the tribe? Aye." She twitched as an explosion vibrated through the trees. "Your orb worked, but now you've just made them angry. Do you plan on surrendering?"

Rivic began to walk with his sister alongside him, helping

her over the rocky ground as they continued downhill. "I ensnared them in plants which exploded with enough force to kill someone without magic and you think I plan on surrendering?"

"'Tis the easier of the options at this point."

Rivic scoffed. "Options? The only option is to lead the Necroathelings far enough away from the village and destroy them so they can't return to Gohaldinest."

"I told you 'twas time to leave the tribe."

"I don't want to," Rivic protested. "I'm beginning to feel at home there."

"Nay," Nyree said. "You are having feelings for Ellonia. But she cannot delay your destiny any longer."

Rivic skid over a scattering of loose rocks and it was his sister's hand that caught him. As he regained his balance, he noticed Nyree staring off into the distance. He turned to look, yet he saw nothing but the forest treetops below them.

"You can't let them know what you have become," she stated. "You must control these new aspects of yourself, the ones you have used to so easily defeat the gargaxes. You can let no one and nothing in connection to the magic of Gohaldinest discover what you are. Do you understand?"

Rivic felt his mouth go dry. "I can't always stop it, Nyree. I've never been good with containing the magic. It always takes over."

She turned to face him, her strange black eyes locking with his. "You must fight to reign it then, because if the Lord of Gohaldinest finds out about you, he will overpower you, torture you, and break your mind long before your body gives out. He has experience which will make you seem insignificant."

"I know." Rivic felt the usual terror rising within him. The Lord of Gohaldinest had rested a tainted layer of fear over this world, which prickled Rivic's awareness much in the same way he could sense the gargaxes. "He feels me too. I perceive it. I know I'm supposed to challenge him, but how can I, for exactly the reasons you stated?"

"Which is why you must hide what you are for now. The day will come when you can reveal the true extent of your power."

He didn't know how he was supposed to do that. She didn't understand how little he controlled the magic when it came over him. "Come on," Rivic said, reaching out for Nyree's hand, "we've stayed here for too long. We need to move."

Rivic heard a swarm of crisp wings land on rocks above them. "Gargaxes," Rivic whispered. But there was something more.

"Remember to control those new aspects of yourself," Nyree warned gently.

Amongst the many smaller, gray, winged gargaxes paused a much larger beast. A tingle of terror rippled through Rivic as if he were witnessing the most disturbing of ancient magicks. While the gargaxes all hunched over with their wings curled partially around them, this one stood tall and straight on two legs, its wings folded erect behind it. The rock-solid, gray beast was old indeed. Rivic had never seen one before, but he suspected he knew exactly what it was, though its name had failed to come to him many times in the past: a gaxlor.

"Don't challenge it," Nyree issued in forewarning again.

The gaxlor tilted back its head and roared.

Heeding Nyree's portents, Rivic slid on the incline and dragged Nyree with him. "Talcor dun," he yelled. They landed on much flatter land, Rivic noted as he glanced around. He saw the gargaxes and the leading gaxlor soaring toward them. "Run!" Rivic shouted at Nyree.

The line of gargaxes surged toward them. He realized all

too late that he'd given the gargaxes exactly what they wanted: a chase.

He might not be able to attack with his new abilities, but they expected him to use magic. Maybe he could slow them down. "Shi'baten to'a helcord." He held out his hands, feeling a forceful magic shove from his palms. The trunks of the trees nearby exploded, leaving the trees to fall like badly stacked wood.

Rivic turned and ran. He pushed faster, but he knew their speed was quicker than his. He caught up to Nyree and grabbed her wrist. "Talcor dun!"

A tight grove was in their path as they reappeared. While sprinting, Rivic pushed Nyree to the side but he didn't duck soon enough to keep himself from hitting the tree. His shoulder slammed into the rough bark and sent him spinning. A branch snagged at his head, poking into his scalp and tearing at his hair. His knee twisted beneath him and he fell into the dirt. Scrambling up, he ignored the stinging pain and tried to run it off. Nyree had kept going, but her pace had slowed.

Behind them, gargaxes cried out with excitement. The hunt was on.

Magic charged into Rivic's hands. His whole body felt on fire. Rivic grabbed Nyree. "Talcor dun."

Shivers ran through him again. The magic. It felt so... he couldn't define it. Nay, he could. Wild. Aye, the magic felt wild. It felt hot and cold running through him, almost as if it were fighting inside him.

He wanted to release it.

He wanted to contain it.

He wanted to explode and take the gargaxes with him.

Nyree shrieked and stopped short. Rivic ran into her back and he had to grab onto her to keep her from falling.

Seeing what had scared her, he yanked Nyree tighter against him.

The gaxlor glided down before them, settling on its huge, clawed feet. The statuesque beast held its wings open. The sheer size of it, its pure muscular bulk which backed up its forceful magic, froze Rivic where he stood. He couldn't acquire any words to summon magic. His mind felt blank.

As the gaxlor reached for Nyree, she ducked and circled around behind her brother. Rivic noticed that the gaxlor never looked at her as he made the grab. Then the gaxlor's arm stretched just a little bit and seized Rivic around the neck.

Gargaxes landed in trees overhead, high-pitched sounds belting from them as they cheered the gaxlor toward victory.

Rivic closed his eyes as the rock-solid, cold fingers closed on his neck. In the darkness of his own mind, the words he needed found him. "Rok'shada tu-may vakara."

The ground beneath the gaxlor began to shake. In the effort to keep its balance on the dirt rising beneath its feet, the gaxlor dropped Rivic, who skid and fell on the moist undergrowth of short ferns.

Barely noting that Nyree had slipped away, he tumbled backward, tripping and falling on the roots and vines. The ground continued to swell up around the gaxlor and devoured the beast. Earth and rocks jolted by Rivic as he scrambled to get out of the zone of trundling soil as it rolled on top of the gaxlor. Rivic's claws came out as he dug into the dark brown loam for balance.

Nyree escaped the ring of churning land and reached back for Rivic. She seized his hand and pulled weakly on him.

The gargaxes shrieked, taking wing from the tree branches where they had landed. Rivic put more effort in not pulling Nyree back in than she did toward dragging him out, but as he got his footing beneath him again, the terrain began to settle.

"Are they gone?" Nyree asked. "'Twas that their leader?"

"I don't know, but I don't think we should stay here," Rivic answered. He put his arm around her again. "Talcor dun."

He flashed them twice more and found himself in territory further out than he'd gone hunting with the tribesmen. All he could do was hope that the knowledge of the planet he had learned from Sontre' actually referenced this planet. He'd hate it if he knew the geography of an irrelevant world.

"I'm tired, Rivic," she said and he noticed that her eyes had gone back to their normal coloring.

Rivic looked around for immediate danger and found none. As much as he didn't want to stay in one place for too long, he also didn't want his sister getting weakened and sick again. Whatever the dragon had done to her, the magic took its toll on Nyree and she needed rest. "Mezzipalor." At his spell, she dropped into his waiting arms and he lowered her to the ground. "Sleep well, sister," he said. As she slept, he paced around and tried to feel for flashes of magic nearby in case the Necroathelings got close. After a while, Rivic picked Nyree up and carried her in his arms through the forest until she woke up.

They continued to travel throughout the day. This area of the forest was abundant in little frosty-blue berries on small shrubs. The holly-shaped leaves pricked their fingers as they took fruit, which had a sour taste to them, but were edible. He wasn't convinced that they were worth eating for the pain one had to go through in getting the food, but it did ease the aching of his stomach so he wouldn't complain too much. Toward nightfall, he set a trap for a rabbit, but none came along.

"'Tis getting cold." Nyree wrapped her arms around herself and rubbed up and down with her hands.

Rivic agreed. It might even snow tonight and he'd like to be in shelter. Maybe waiting for the Necroathelings wasn't a good idea. Maybe he should be concentrating on finding a town.

"Like Gohaldinest," Nyree said.

"What?" Rivic asked, turning to look at Nyree.

For just an instant, he caught her eyes glowing with those unnatural torches, but she blinked when he spoke and her normal eyes returned.

"I didn't say anything," she said.

"Sorry. I thought you did."

He sat down with his back against a tree and closed his eyes as if that would make him forget the hunger gnawing in his stomach. Nyree dropped down beside him and curled up against him. He put his arm around her to keep her warm.

He wasn't really certain that he'd fall asleep, especially with his stomach growling so painfully, but soon he relaxed into dreams.

Nyree nudged him awake in the morning. As he looked at her, she shifted her gaze to look toward the forest.

"Is something wrong?" he whispered, quickly coming completely awake.

"Rivic, they sense us," Nyree whispered. She looked at him, her black eyes glowing brightly around the yellow torch-shaped pupils. "The Necroathelings."

Rivic grabbed onto Nyree's wrist. "Talcor dun." He didn't care what direction they went or where they landed. Away from the Necroathelings would have to be good enough. They landed on ground thickly covered with stones and sticks uncomfortably beneath their legs.

"Are we far enough away?" he asked, shifting to slide some of the pebbles from beneath him.

She looked around in the air with her strange eyes. "Walking to the ends of the world would not be far enough away. They are coming. Better them than the weather, right?"

She was correct. They were Necroathelings and there was no running from that power.

"I'm hungry," she complained with her hands over her stomach.

Not only would they require food, but water and additional clothing as well. Rivic started searching for what they needed. He found a stream trickling down out of the mountains and gathered some of the water in his hands to taste. Then he plucked an aspen leaf, enlarged it, and collected some of the cool, clean liquid in it to take to Nyree.

"Thank you," she said, taking the leaf from him and drinking deeply.

He wasn't certain how much attention simple transformation spells would attract, so he decided to be fast about it now that he'd started. He changed a rock into a dress for her and another into a shirt for himself. He transformed a pinecone into a cloak and a branch into a walking stick for Nyree.

"We thought we felt magic," said a Necroatheling as he stepped forward from the trees. Two other Necroathelings followed shortly behind him.

Nyree began to scream. She sat on the ground with her knees now drawn up to her chest, hands over her mouth, and she continued to shriek.

"Shut her up," the Necroatheling yelled at Rivic.

Rivic knelt by his sister, trying to peel her hands away from her face.

"Nyree!"

Her eyes were so wide they were practically bulging. But Rivic noted that they hadn't changed.

"Nyree, I need you to stop, please."

The Necroatheling grabbed her long black hair and lifted her up. She tried to draw back, but he didn't release her. He struck her across the face and her scream instantly stopped. Raising her chin, she glared at him.

"Kalt," the Necroatheling said to the other, "come look at her eyes."

The second Necroatheling, Kalt, came over and took Nyree's face in his hand to force her to look at him. "Open your eyes," Kalt demanded.

"Please don't hurt her," Rivic begged.

"Oh, I don't want to hurt either one of you, so don't make me." Kalt turned his attention back to Nyree. "Open your eyes, girl."

She must have done so, because Rivic heard the Necroatheling gasp. "Lord Cirvel will want to know," Kalt said. He turned to the third Necroatheling who had yet to say a word. "Go inform him." The third Necroatheling nodded before he took a couple steps away and disappeared in a sweep of magic.

"What are you going to do with us?"

"What happens depends on your choices and if she remains a good little girl." The Necroatheling released Nyree's hair.

"My choices? Like I get a decision in any of this?" Rivic asked.

The Necroatheling crossed his arms over his chest. "What decision would you like to make?"

"If I had my choice, you and your friend would go now and leave us in peace."

"Well, that's not one of your choices."

"Then what option do I have?"

"You have enormous power within you. You could be a great Necroatheling."

"Or you could be a splendid hunt for a Necroatheling,"

Kalt said. "With your power, one of us could keep you alive for days by just draining you slowly."

A small, undistinguishable sound came from Nyree.

"Let me take my sister some place where she's safe first," Rivic argued, hoping to let them know that this point was not negotiable.

"With those eyes, your sister has great value to Lord Cirvel as well," the first Necroatheling said. "Only extraordinary magic could do that."

The third Necroatheling returned and stepped up to the others. "Lord Cirvel wants the girl. We shall see if the boy is worthy."

"You have a reprieve, boy," the first Necroatheling growled. "Nothing more. Lord Cirvel will most likely destroy you."

Rivic dared to look away from the Necroathelings and over his shoulder to Nyree. She met his gaze with equal amounts of fear and bravery as she gave a miniscule nod. He turned back to the Necroathelings "Very well," Rivic said. "We will go to Gohaldinest."

"You never really had an alternative, except that your sister gets an automatic pass," Kalt said as he disappeared. He rematerialized beside Nyree and wrapped her up inside his purple cloak. Before Rivic could move, Kalt added, "You must prove you belong in Gohaldinest."

The Necroatheling with Nyree vanished.

CHAPTER 10

*R*ivic stared at the spot where his sister had disappeared, his hatred of the Necroathelings growing. His breath, though deep and even, felt wrathfully hot within his chest and seemed to burn as it came in and out of his nose. His whole body heated.

As if the forest themselves knew of Rivic's anger, the trees began to shake. Leaves rustled and dried pine needles sifted to the ground with a rattle in warning. He felt all the energy of the trees surging toward him, offering him their calm power. He would destroy these Necroathelings and then he'd get Nyree back. All of Gohaldinest would quake in fear.

Yet Nyree's warning lingered close to his thoughts and echoed that he could only fight with magic, nothing more.

One of the two remaining Necroathelings thrust at hand at Rivic. "Shakalal."

Rivic raised his arms. "Miex'balish." As his shield spell raised, the Necroatheling's spell cracked against it.

"Very good, grasshopper," a Necroatheling said. "Let's see what else you've got. Malkibar."

When Rivic felt his feet lift off the ground and he was thrust backwards, he realized that these Necroathelings wouldn't be as easy to defeat at the ones he'd faced while he'd been tutored by Sontre' inside the pearl. These were different. Besides, he couldn't go on trading blows with these Necroathelings. He had to get to his sister. The Necroathelings holding her were the ones he wanted to challenge. "Talcor dun."

The landing was not smooth when he reappeared and he went tumbling backwards, then started to roll. He finally came to a stop on his stomach. Leaves and dirt in his mouth, he gave a quick spit, but didn't bother to get up. He wasn't sure how far from the Necroatheling he'd traveled. "Talcor dun."

He knew the Necroatheling would be tracking his magic. Of course, he could also follow the Necroatheling's power and he desired to use that to his advantage. He levitated onto a branch of a tree and crouched down. The Necroatheling would be led here by the spell, but how long would it take before he actually looked up? Rivic waited.

Shortly, the Necroatheling appeared in the clearing.

"Oh, grasshopper, where are you?" the Necroatheling called out.

Rivic watched patiently as the Necroatheling walked around the area searching behind trees. Every so often, the Necroatheling would stop and close his eyes, then he'd resume his hunt. He knew the Necroatheling was checking to see if Rivic was still here or not by seeking for the magic. It seemed to perplex the Necroatheling.

"Vochey," he whispered. Rivic held out his hand as he leapt out of the tree and came down on the Necroatheling, smashing him to the ground. His fingers curled around the metal hilt arriving in his hand. He rolled as his hit toppled over the Necroatheling and Rivic came up holding his sword.

Rivic swung Honor with as much force as he could put behind it and cut through the Necroatheling's neck. He closed his eyes, knowing he'd forever hear the thud of the head bouncing off the ground and rolling. He heard the body slump, coming to final rest.

The other Necroatheling who had remained behind stepped out of the shadows of the trees. "We knew you had it in you. Lord Cirvel will be pleased."

Rivic firmed his grip on his sword, but as the Necroatheling stepped closer, Rivic took one hand off his sword and held up defensively in front of him in case he needed to cast a spell.

The Necroatheling knelt down beside the body of the other and put his hand on it. Rivic felt a curling spin of magic rush around him and the head of the Necroatheling rolled back over to the body and seemed to reattach itself. A moment later, the once beheaded Necroatheling rose to his feet. He shook out his shoulders and rotated his head. As much as Rivic wanted to cast another spell or make a charging attack, the reality of the horror he had just witnessed held him. The dead had been brought back to life.

"Gohaldinest has many protective charms," the last Necroatheling said as his friend continued rolling his head from side to side as if trying to get the adjustment just right. "Your next task is to get there, if you can. Make your peace with your world here and prepare to leave it behind. But mind you, the longer you take, the more fun we'll have with your sister."

That brought the rage right back to overcome any fear that Rivic might have. He raised his sword and charged. But when he got to the spot where the Necroathelings had been, they were gone.

Rivic spun around, but he saw nothing. He listened. The birds soon resumed their songs. He reached out for other magic in the area and found none. Once he was certain that he was alone and the Necroathelings weren't coming back, he teleported back to the tribe where he found the villagers finishing with the cleanup.

He glanced around for Ellonia, but figured if she had anyone that she needed to help, she'd probably have them in her hut. He headed in that direction. When he got there, he opened up the flap and indeed found her treating a few of those too injured to return back to their lodgings. He ducked inside.

"How bad was it?" he asked Ellonia as he came up beside her.

"Thankfully, no one is dead or severely injured. Mostly just scrapes. We got off lucky." She gave him an appraising glance then turned back to dab at the wound she was treating. "How are you and Nyree? I worried when you didn't return last night."

He touched Ellonia's arm near her elbow. "We should talk. I need to leave."

Ellonia looked at person she was treating pressed the cloth against his four head. "Here, hold this there." She took his hand and guided it to the cloth. "Pressed softly."

Ellonia turned and began to follow Rivic out of the hut. "You're leaving?" she asked.

"I have to. The Necroathelings took Nyree."

She looked confused. "They took Nyree? So you're going to go to Gohaldinest to see if you can find your sister."

"Yes."

"She's probably already dead. You know that, don't you?"

Terror jumped upon Rivic's heart. "Why do you say that?"

"Because you are the magical twin. They have no interest in people without magic. She serves no purpose."

"Except to draw me in." He looked toward the edge of the

village, knowing he should be leaving already. He'd stayed too long. "They know I'll come for her."

Ellonia grabbed onto his forearm and squeezed it tightly. "She's still weak. I'm not sure she'll ever recover."

"They said her eyes would interest Cirvel."

"Rivic, please! We need you here. I hate to say this, to be the one to tell you this, but your sister can't live with the magic. Whatever happened to you two, whatever she went through, 'twasn't supposed to happen to her. Her body can't handle it."

"Nay." Rivic denied her words. "She just needs time."

"Either the magic will kill her or they will. She's the magicless twin."

"I have to try. She's the only family I have left."

A look of irritation flashed across Ellonia's face. "If you go, you're walking right into their hands. Please talk to Father and take some of the warriors with you. You can't go in there alone."

"I think I can. They want me for some reason. They're willing to use my sister to get to me. They'll keep her alive, and as long as she lives, they think I'll do what they want. Your sister is there training be a Necroatheling. I will already have someone on the inside."

She didn't look pleased. Her face had gone pale. "Wait here a moment," she requested. "I'll be right back." She lifted the flap and disappeared inside.

Ellonia returned a moment later with a thick blue cloth over her arm, but she first held out her hand toward him. "Here, take this. She'll know it's for me." She opened her fingers and showed him a small, blue, teardrop-shaped gemstone.

He didn't want to take it. As if sensing that from him, she grabbed his hand and smacked it into his palm.

"'Tis said that she was born with it in her mouth, that she would not cry out for air until the birthing woman fished it from her mouth," Ellonia told him. "She gave it to me so that I would still have a piece of her with me always. She'll know that I trust you when she sees it."

Reluctantly, he placed it in his pouch for safekeeping.

"Take this too," she said, pulling the cloth off her arm. "I've been working on it for you and finished it a few nights ago." She held it up before her and Rivic realized that it was a dark blue traveling cloak trimmed in gold. She thrust it toward him.

"'Tis beautiful," he said, taking it.

"I didn't know I'd be giving it to you just in time for you to leave. I'd rather hoped it would be a present for a more special occasion."

He wanted to tell her that he'd hoped for just such an event too. "I better…" he began, but he just couldn't finish his words.

"I know," she whispered. "Nyree is waiting for you."

He couldn't bring himself to leave her. He'd rather stand here and look in her eyes for as long as she'd keep looking back at him. There were so many things he wanted to say. He didn't know where to begin or how to overcome the fear of what the words would bring if they did escape his throat. Would he be able to come back here and continue living a normal life after all this was done? Assuming he was still alive after facing the Lord of Gohaldinest.

He took her cheeks in his hands and leaned forward to press a kiss against her forehead. He didn't want to let go. Her fingers curled into his tunic as he felt her soft, gasping breath against his neck.

Rivic didn't want to leave her with thoughts of him going to his death. Nor did he want to put that out to the universe lest it come true by him merely thinking it.

He pushed himself backwards with all the effort he could collect.

"Talcor dun," he said before she could say anything further.

He appeared in his own lodgings, gathered a few things, including a sword he'd hidden away. He'd been working on it during days when he had not much else to do. Now, as he held it by the hilt, and thought the metalwork was done, he knew he wouldn't be able to finish the spell work. He'd wrapped it in all the enchantments he could muster as he had worked the metal with his own hands and had intended on it being a present. Since that day when he first realized that Ellonia waited for his proposal, the sword had been meant as a gift for her father. But now, rather than an exchange for giving up his daughter, Rivic would give it to Krithstand to keep her safe.

He flashed to Krithstand's lodging, finding the man in council with many of the other warriors. Rivic bowed, holding the sword flat across his palms while the traveling cloak hung over his arm. "Krithstand-chief, I must follow the Necroathelings. They have my sister and she is my responsibility. I wish for you to have this weapon and with it keep Ellonia safe." At the thought of her, he realized he could still feel her hand against his arm as if she stood there right beside him. Rivic rushed forward and handed the sword to Krithstand. "Use it well for I feel it will serve you ably."

As soon as Krithstand took the sword, Rivic didn't stay for the chief to examine it. "Talcor dun."

He repeated the incantation several more times until he began to feel Ellonia's touch fading from his skin. As he stood there in the forest, he took his bearings.

He had no idea where he was. He couldn't even fool himself and pretend that he knew.

A shadow passed over the ground and Rivic looked up to see a gargax circling overhead.

"Talcor dun," Rivic shouted over the sounds of flapping leather wings. He didn't know what direction he was going in, or even which way he should be going. He knew Gohaldinest was north-west of Plenelia, but how far? Or was that just an imaginary land where the dragon had been training his mind? How was he to know that any of that knowledge was valid? What signs did he need to look for? How long did he have to go before escaping the gargaxes?

"Talcor dun," he said again as he barely appeared back in the forest. Did he really understand enough about his tele-portation to know how to control the direction? Short distances weren't hard because he either knew the terrain or had line of sight. But this…

After he reappeared for the third time, Rivic stopped and listened. He couldn't hear anything around him. That didn't mean he was safe. He just had a moment's reprieve. He leaned against a tree and closed his eyes. As he waited and listened to the magic within him, he felt himself grow calm. Everything would be all right. He knew it with the utmost sincerity through to his bones. He would take care of this.

Strengthened with a new resolve, Rivic got his bearings. Aye, the gargaxes were after him, but they obviously couldn't teleport. Let them chase him all the way back to Gohaldinest if they wished. They wouldn't catch him.

"Talcor dun." Upon reappearing, he took note of the sun's position again. Now knowing what direction he had been going in, he made the corrections he needed and started toward Gohaldinest.

After teleporting three more times, Rivic dropped to the ground exhausted. He stretched out over the leaves and ferns and breathed deeply. The magic replenished, but his body was another matter.

"'Twould take a miracle for you to get into Gohaldinest, especially at this rate," a high voice said near him.

Rivic raised his head and saw two blue-green eyes glowing at him. The creature he'd seen with Ellonia came out from beneath a bush. "What are you? Who are you? How can you speak?" Rivic asked.

"Aye, a mind filled with questions. Not the ones you need answers to either! How about, *how am I going to get into Gohaldinest? Or what am I going to do once I get there? How will I get out? Will I even survive?*"

"You know so much, you tell me. What are the answers?"

The creature eyed him as if giving him another assessment. "Lord Cirvel will make sure you get into Gohaldinest. Then you will entertain him. If you impress him, he may ask you to become an acolyte. If you do not, you won't survive. Either way, I suspect you will not leave Gohaldinest once you are in."

"I already knew that much. Tell me something I don't expect."

"I'm here to make sure you survive," it chuckled.

Rivic stared at it and wondered if the creature spoke the truth or not. "Why? What 'tis the advantage for you?"

"I have been asked to do this for you. Because I love the one who asked, I accepted."

"Who asked you?"

"'Tis not for me to tell. Now, will you allow me to aid you safely into Gohaldinest?"

Rivic thought on it for a moment. Could this creature be trusted? Probably not. He had to remember that this could be a spell which either made the animal look as if it were speaking or someone transformed into animal form. He wasn't certain that either were really possible, but he knew enough magic to know that anything could be possible.

"What repercussions befall you if I don't make it there safely?"

The beast slid around Rivic's legs, weaving between his feet. "My mistress has not had an easy time of late. I do not seek to bring her any more unhappiness."

Well, that told Rivic a little. Like most people, this creature just wanted to be loved and accepted. "Very well."

"Then you come willingly with me to Gohaldinest?"

Rivic nodded his acceptance. "But I need to know what to call you."

The beast's blue-green eyes looked him over. "Names have power and you want mine. 'Tis true, aye?"

"'Tis true. But if you don't want me to call you by your name, then let me call you by what you are. If you choose to not give me some way to identify you, I'll call you Squirrel."

"Squirrel!" The creature sat back on its haunches and put its front paws on its hips as if highly offended. "Do you not recognize a cahaster when you see one?"

"I've never met a cahaster before, nor any tiny creature capable of speaking."

The cahaster shook its head as it dropped back down to all four legs. "You're never going to survive against the Necroathelings."

Rivic knew the animal meant it as a soft jab to indicate that he was a village simpleton, but the comment hit deeper. "Don't you think I know that?" he muttered.

"Then why are you even going?"

"Because they took my sister." He raised his gaze from the ground to the cahaster. "Would they really hurt her if I didn't show up? Might they just let her go?"

"Ah, the twin without magic as I've heard." The cahaster's eyes grew sad. "Aye, they would hurt her, probably even kill her eventually. Without magic, only her lifeforce matters to them. Other than that, she is completely useless."

"Then I have no choice but to go to Gohaldinest and face the Necroathelings and this Lord Cirvel."

"I'll be there with you."

Something about those words made Rivic feel like he'd found a friend and it gave him comfort. "Let's be on to Gohaldinest then."

CHAPTER 11

From the road, Gohaldinest looked like a dark fortress looming over the trees. Gray clouds emphasized the massive block shaped castle with all sorts of high towers and arching walkways. From here, Rivic could see a couple balconies and curtains blowing lightly in the mountain breeze. The air had grown colder. A light covering of snow dusted the sides of the road.

Tingles of magic ran over his arms with feather-light touches. Rivic shivered, unsure if it was the power he felt or random snowflakes landing on him as both pricked at his skin about the same. He had never sensed so much magic in one spot and even as it terrified him, it called and beckoned him in. Yet, if the snow thickened, he might not be able to get out.

"A little closer," he whispered to himself. If he just took it slowly without overloading himself with magic, he'd be fine. He felt the new aspects of himself, the teeth and the claws, lurking just beyond his touch. It would be so easy if he could just let the abilities consume him and take the direct charge.

The enormous stone walls before them blocked the view

of the city as they neared the closed gates. Magic spilled over like crashing waves, getting higher and deeper the closer they got to Gohaldinest. Rivic fought to suppress his every instinct.

The cahaster sighed deeply beside him. "If you don't start acting like you are in control of your power and your life, the guards will eat you for lunch even before you get to the Necroathelings."

"Easy for you to say." Even after three days of traveling together, the creature made Rivic edgy. Or was it his growing struggle with the magic? "You're the one who told me at the base of the mountain that I couldn't use magic anymore. That the gargaxes would come and eat us if I did."

"I did," the cahaster snapped tersely, "and I meant every word of it. I have no need to lead you astray nor do I want to be eaten by gargaxes." It seemed to calm a bit. "I am merely saying that you need to have some courage. Gohaldinest and its inhabitants know fear when they smell it. They are all too willing to prey upon the weakness."

"This from the small creature that spits fire."

"If you think these guys are nice to *small creatures*, boy, do you have another thing coming. We've all come to a simple understanding."

"That would be…?"

"You'll see." The cahaster dashed up Rivic's leggings and tunic up to his chest. "Grab me."

With sharp claws so close to his skin and a little muzzle of spikey teeth next to his neck, Rivic wasn't certain he wanted anything to do with the animal. Rivic put his hands around the cahaster as if he were holding it close to him.

"Nay, like I'm a prisoner," the cahaster said. "You are bringing me home after capturing me."

Rivic tightened his grip.

"'Tis better, I guess," the cahaster said. "Now knock on the gatehouse door."

Rivic wasn't sure what a gatehouse was, but he saw the entrance beside the massive gates and figured that if there was to be a house somewhere, it must be behind the door. What a gate needed with a house was yet another question. He rapped on the wood.

Magic lashed out at his arm like a slashing claw. Rivic jumped back and battled with the transformation which threatened to instinctively overcome him.

A hatch slid open and two light blue eyes peered out at him. "What do you want?" the gruff man asked.

Rivic held up the cahaster. "I'm bringing him back again."

"Dragzel! Ah, get that demon spawn out of here. Couldn't you have left him lost?" The man let a good amount of silence follow his words while Rivic stood there unsure of what else to say. Then the man continued, "Ah, his mistress will unfortunately want him back. Take him back to her and tell her to get a thicker chain for the damn thing." The hatch slid closed and a moment later the large gate creaked open.

Rivic slipped through as soon as he had enough room, then the gates began to close behind him. The guard wearing thick plates of red armor motioned him forward. They entered a small, rather dark wooden structure which had some sleeping cots, a couple of chairs around a table, and weapons racks filled with swords and bows on both sides of the gate. The door at the back stood open, allowing some sunlight to filter inside what Rivic supposed could be called a house.

"Remember to hold him away from you," the gate guardsman shouted after them. "He'll bite your nose or pee on you, both if he gets a chance."

The cahaster hissed and spit a spark over Rivic's shoulder toward the guard.

"Aye, go on, Dragzel," the guard yelled. "Maybe this guy'll drown you before he gets you to the castle. Or better yet, maybe he'll send your sorry behind over the cliffs. A good dropkick'll do you!"

Rivic headed on out into the streets beyond, clutching to the cahaster even harder as he tried to quit trembling. He was inside Gohaldinest now. He had to take his mind off that thought.

The door slammed shut behind them.

"He really doesn't like you, does he?" Rivic asked.

"Aye, and he doesn't know I speak either. He thinks I'm just a dumb cahaster who can't understand what he's saying."

"Dragzel, is it?"

The cahaster growled, a rumble of lightning sparks behind his teeth.

"'Tis a good name," Rivic said quickly.

"Aye, but now you know it."

"I won't use it against you," Rivic promised. "So where to now?"

"Straight down the street," Dragzel said. "We've just entered the city's outer curtain. We still have to get into the inner castle and it just gets more fortified from here."

The space between buildings was little more than a rocky footpath. Sunlight barely reached the bottom.

A maiden with a basket came running along down the street toward them. She kept her eyes down as she approached, daring only to raise them as she passed by. "Good day," she uttered.

"Good day," Rivic said, turning to watch her hurry on down the slope. She opened a doorway and disappeared inside.

Dragzel took a side alley between buildings. Lines of clothes stretched between windows high above them. Sharp odors of rot and stink filled Rivic's senses. Rancid water ran down the alley and spilled into a grated pipe.

A door ahead of him opened and a large, gruff looking man stepped out into the alley with a wave of spent magic rolling with him. He stretched his arms, which magnified the muscles on his shirtless chest. Sweat poured off his olive colored skin and plastered his curly black hair to his head. He huffed as he took in and exhaled an expansive breath.

Rivic threw up some mental walls to keep from internalizing the magicks that washed over him. They wouldn't be able to continue on until the man moved from their path.

"So the devil returns, eh, Dragzel?" the man said, before giving Rivic a hard, unfriendly stare.

Dragzel rubbed up against the man's leg. At first, he started to smile, but then he crossed his arms over his chest and continued to glower at Rivic. "Look what the cahaster dragged in," the man said. "Don't let the cahaster fool you, boy. He's no lost kitten."

Dragzel zipped into the room, leaving Rivic to follow.

At first glance, Rivic wasn't sure he wanted to pursue the cahaster. Inside were all sorts of weapons on the wall and a sleeping mat. A bloodied man lay panting on the mat and gave a soft groan as he moved slightly. An arm lay twisted at an odd angle which certainly indicated it was broken. The remnant traces of spells pressed against Rivic, making him shiver.

As Rivic continued on, he met the shirtless man's gaze. "Don't let the cahaster fool you. He speaks perfectly well and only pretends to be silent."

The man looked confused. Rivic chuckled to himself as he locked that image in his mind in order to get him through the room which smelled of metal, blood, and magic.

"Now why did you have to go and tell the weapons master that?" Dragzel whined once they had left this room and entered a long hallway lit with sconces. "Are you going to give away my secret to everyone?"

Weapons master, Rivic thought. "I thought he tortured prisoners."

"Ha, prisoners!" Dragzel scoffed. "Nay, he takes wannabe Necroathelings and kicks their butts. Part of the training."

"At least now, in his mind, he'll always wonder if I have a bit of information he doesn't. 'Tis an advantage."

"'Tis that your theory? You plan on going around telling everyone in the castle that I can speak so you have some sort of mental dominance over them?"

"I'm still developing my plan."

Dragzel laughed, spitting little puffs of smoke as he did so. "I like you, Rivic. You're so transparent. Cirvel is going to twist your head right off your neck with his own hands."

Rivic knew that was a very real possibility. He remembered how he'd torn apart the first gargax. "Thanks. That builds up my confidence."

They left the first building and the warmth of the room departed as the cold mountain air hit his face. Cut stone walled them into the cobblestone street. Rivic wasn't certain he'd make it through the maze if not for Dragzel.

"Do you get brought back often? Does everyone know to return you when you get lost?" Rivic asked.

"I usually get chased back to my mistress," Dragzel said, his teeth showing in a smile. "But, aye, most people try to return me in order to gain favor with my mistress' master."

A short way down the street, they entered a second structure. Inside, the area opened up immediately into a large open room. Rivic was reminded of Sontre's cottage with its simple two room layout. He couldn't fathom what this building was used for, except maybe for grand gatherings. He kept looking for signs that would give him clues. Above him, wooden rafters held up the stone roof.

"Come on," Dragzel hissed.

From here, Dragzel led him back outside. A miniature city opened up before him. The cobblestone roads were lively with traffic. People walked out of one building and into another. Most of the businesses on the street levels had living spaces above them.

"Dragzel!" came a shout from down the street. Rivic saw the red-faced man grab a broom and start charging down the street after them.

"Run!" Dragzel said.

The cahaster dashed away, leaving Rivic to dull-wittedly follow. Dragzel skid around one corner and took a staircase.

"Hurry up, would you?" Dragzel said. "You're killing me!"

Rivic tried to run faster. He heard the man's footfalls thundering behind him.

Dragzel jumped over a gap between the buildings. Rivic stopped at the edge, teetering precariously. He looked down at the long drop to a cobblestone street below. "I can't make that," Rivic protested.

"Then you better learn how to fly." Dragzel turned as if he were going to leave Rivic behind.

"Talcor dun," Rivic said, teleporting to the other side.

The cahaster gave him an amused look. "The simple, dimwitted village boy is smarter than he looks," Dragzel said with a small amount of pride. "You might just survive this yet."

"At least long enough to meet Lord Cirvel," Rivic answered, seeing the man reaching the top of the steps huffing and puffing.

"Let's go," Dragzel said.

They turned a corner. "Go through the door," Dragzel said as he scrambled up the wall and entered through a window.

Rivic pulled on the door latch. He looked back before he

entered the building and saw the man, who had probably teleported across too, still running after them. Inside, Rivic slammed the door. "Cathida, venitis Plenelia." He turned to find Dragzel sitting up on his haunches, a stunned look on the cahaster's face.

Dragzel glanced between Rivic and the doorway and stretched out one of his forelegs to point at the latch. "Did you just lock that door with the password being that land without magic?"

"I did."

"'Tis almost brutal what you did there," the cahaster laughed. "Funny, but cruel. Do you think there is a maege in the land that could possibly say that place without cringing?" Dragzel turned and continued on. "Note to self: Rivic is devious. Keep an eye on him."

Rivic smiled as he knew that was probably the highest praise he'd ever get from the cahaster.

They went down a straight interior staircase, then entered a hallway with a spiral staircase going up near the center of the room. At the top, they went down another long hallway filled with entryways. This maze seemed to go on and on until they reached another set of double doors.

"Pick me up, then knock. Remember, you are returning me and that is your goal no matter what happens. Got it?"

Rivic lifted Dragzel back into his arms. "Got it." He tapped on the wood.

The doors opened and two Necroathelings stood in their dark purple robes on each side of the access. For a moment, Rivic thought he was looking at the two Necroathelings that had taken Nyree, but he quickly noticed that these dark maeges had silver and black braided cords hanging from their shoulders.

"I'm bringing the cahaster back," Rivic said, trying to

sound confident while standing in the presence the ancient enchantments swirling around these men.

"You could lose him forever you know," the Necroatheling on the left replied.

"Drop him off a cliff or something," said the other.

"That's the second time I've heard that," Rivic chuckled. "I'm beginning to see a theme regarding this beast."

Dragzel started to struggle in Rivic's arms. Not sure if the cahaster wanted down, Rivic loosened his grip. Dragzel came up snarling.

The Necroathelings stepped back, each raising a hand as if to cast a spell.

Rivic grabbed onto Dragzel and held him out toward the Necroathelings pretending to struggle with holding onto him. Dragzel began spitting fire as he growled.

"Go!" one of them commanded. "Get him back to his mistress."

As Rivic entered a different section of the castle, he heard one of the Necroathelings shout, "Next time, drop him off the cliff!"

"Doesn't anyone like you?" Rivic asked as soon as they were away from the Necroathelings.

"Not much. But then again, cahasters haven't been given the chance for most people to like us." Dragzel jumped down from Rivic's arms and strolled down the hallway with his ears slightly back.

"Why not?"

"We're going to outlive all of you," Dragzel said. "What's the point of making friends with a dead thing? Or, if we choose to become a vessel for a Necroatheling's soul, then we're bonded to that Necroatheling and you've seen what jerks they are, so who would want that? You'll never see me bonding with a Necroatheling."

Dragzel came to a halt right in the middle of a doorway.

"Root rot," he whispered, smacking a paw against the ground and shaking his head.

"What?"

Dragzel walked somberly into the room they were entering. In the center was a glass enclosure. A woman sat on a red pillow, imprisoned in the middle of the compound. She had yet to notice them, her attention tight on some needlework. Brown hair curled tightly around her face.

Calm permeated the room. "Who is she?" Rivic asked as Dragzel approached the glass and put a paw on it. For the first time since entering Gohaldinest, Rivic felt a sense of peace surround him.

The woman looked up and smiled as she saw Dragzel. Then she lifted her gaze to see Rivic and her face brightened further.

"'Tis my lady Lihn."

Rivic glanced at the woman behind the glass again. Ellonia had never mentioned the name of her sibling, only that the cahaster brought word from her sister. Could that be Lihn? He'd wait to learn more.

Rivic didn't see any doors in the glass. "Why is she in there?"

"'Twould seem she's displeased Lord Cirvel again."

"How would she do that?"

"Your guess is as good as mine," Dragzel said as the woman slid over near the glass to put her hand by Dragzel's paw. "She may have said the wrong thing to him, or wore the wrong dress today, or parted her hair on the wrong side."

Rivic couldn't stop staring at Lihn's soft, round face as she smiled at Dragzel. She certainly didn't seem injured or upset at her incarceration. "Is Lord Cirvel really that harsh? How long will he keep her in there?"

"I've seen him leave her in there for days, until the air was nearly gone." It seemed to be a painful memory for the cahaster. "I had to beg my mother to speak to him."

"Your mother has that kind of sway with Lord Cirvel?"

The cahaster looked up at Rivic as the creature took his tiny paw away from the glass and started to leave the room. "My mother," Dragzel said, "is the Guardian of Gohaldinest. Aye, she has sway with Lord Cirvel. Come along. I need to see about getting my mistress freed. Again."

CHAPTER 12

*L*eaving the woman in the glass prison, Dragzel headed up another staircase. Rivic took one last look back at Lihn as a strange and still melancholy possessed him. She sat, watching her stitching calmly, but he couldn't help feeling that she would rather be leaving with them. At length, and Dragzel's hiss, Rivic followed the cahaster to the top of the stairs. There, everything changed.

Rivic opened the closed doorway before them and entered a hallway with windows of diamond-shaped quarries that made brilliant latticework shadows on the white and black tile floor. A stone bench sat against the rock wall opposite the windows. A long lantern with three layers of unlit candles hung from the ceiling. He imaged that at night it would be quite the beautiful sight.

"Quit gawking," Dragzel said. "Every moment you delay, the more time Lord Cirvel has with your sister. You've seen how he treats people he supposedly loves. Now imagine how he treats someone he detests."

"He would hate her because she doesn't have magic?"

"Chances are, he despises her because he envies her lack of magic?"

"Envies?"

"Lord Cirvel's life has not been easy. His own magic has caused him a great deal of pain."

Footsteps headed toward them. Dragzel pulled back against a wall, but it was too late for Rivic to hide as the guard spotted him.

"Who goes there?" the man in red armor shouted.

Rivic looked to Dragzel, but he couldn't see where the cahaster had gone. Rivic bowed. "I am Rivic. Lord Cirvel has requested my presence."

The guard glanced him over. "Oh, I bet he has. Put your hands on your head!"

The sooner he got to Lord Cirvel, the better he'd be, Rivic decided. He fulfilled the guard's command.

As the guard approached, Dragzel came blazing out of the shadows, growling and snapping at the man. Dragzel latched onto his red cape with teeth and claws. Seizing the material in two hands, the man simultaneously held it away from him as he jerked it around attempting to shake the cahaster off. Dragzel snarled while dangling, refusing to release his hold. Clearly afraid to grasp Dragzel lest it give the beast opportunity to bite into flesh, the guard turned his attention away from Rivic.

Taking advantage of the distraction, Rivic ran for the door the guard had come through at the other end of the hallway. Beyond was a large chamber with a staircase running along the four walls with landings at every corner. Tall, white marble sconces scaled the walls. Here, the candles were lit; otherwise it would have been dark. The flames lit every section of the white marble walls and reflected in the golden railings along the stairs.

Without any other ways out of the room, Rivic progressed up the stairs.

At the top floor, he opened a door into a long room with arching windows at the opposite end. Even though there was a good deal of light coming through the windows, two chandeliers, each holding twenty burning candles, hung from the ceiling and illuminated the room.

Rivic stepped inside, his gaze taking the in whole area. A long table covered with a black and silver runner sat in the middle of the room with a candelabrum holding five additional burning candles. Tucked against the table were several wooden chairs. The space felt empty and strange with no one else present. He fought rubbing his arms against the chills running up them, especially as he took in an odd sight.

On every wall, there sat two tall, round wooden tables on each side of the doors with what looked like golden teapots. He felt magic and itched to examine them closer.

With one glance behind him, he wondered if he should continue on into another room. But which door should he take? How would the cahaster know which way he'd gone? Would Dragzel be capable of following?

As these questions entered Rivic's mind, a man with long, loose black hair entered the room holding an open tome in his hands. He stopped just beyond the entryway, standing perpendicular to Rivic. His gaze lifted from the book to the room straight ahead of him.

Rivic, holding his breath, could see the man's eyes flicking as if searching for something. Then, the man turned.

A prickling ran across Rivic as the man's dark regard eventually landed on him.

After a moment of stark assessment, the man said, "Greetings."

Rivic found himself swallowing hard to clear his throat. "Blessings," Rivic said with a bow of his head.

The man closed his book and turned fully toward Rivic, folding his hands on the text in front of him. "Is there something I can do to help you?"

"I am looking for Lord Cirvel."

The man looked to his left through the door in which he'd entered. He raised a hand as if halting someone about to come through and gave a curt nod. "Why do you come seeking the master of this realm?"

"Some of his men have taken someone important to me."

"Indeed." The man walked to the table and set the book down on it. He drummed his fingers in contemplation. "Do you care to describe these men to me?"

"They were Necroathelings. I didn't get a good look at their faces, but one of them was called Kalt. That they spoke Lord Cirvel's name is enough for me to know they worked for him."

Invisible fingers crawled along Rivic. The man was feeling out Rivic's magic, seeing how strong it was. It took all of Rivic's strength not to step back.

"The Necroathelings always collect things that might interest their lord. You will have to be more specific in who you are looking for."

"She is my sister," Rivic said, letting there be a little pause. "My twin."

The man remained unimpressed.

"Since you can feel my magic," Rivic said, spelling it out for the man, "you know that my twin would not have power. Why this Lord Cirvel would want her, I do not know. Except that it would draw me in. I am here to secure my sister's freedom."

The man looked around again. "Mind telling me how you got in here?" The door behind him slowly started to close.

Dragzel burst into the room, darting between Rivic's legs. He jumped up on a chair, then to the table. His claws clicked over the polished wood. "I brought him. He's my bounty."

"Bounty?" Rivic whispered.

"Really?" the man said. The arching of a thin, dark eyebrow indicated his intrigue.

"Aye." Dragzel sat up, rising back on his haunches. He put his paws together. "Your Necroathelings had failed. I convinced him to come for his sister, and of his own free will." Dragzel said the last two words, free will, as if they carried special meaning.

"And you got him around my Domini as well?"

The cahaster showed teeth, something akin to a smile Rivic presumed.

"Indeed." The man thumped on the book again as he blinked slowly, calculatingly, at the cahaster. He seemed completely without care that Rivic was in the room. "I suspect I know what you'll request for a reward," he said.

Dragzel crossed his forelegs over his chest as his tail gave a little flick.

An icy chill swept through Rivic. He'd found himself face to face unknowingly and unannounced in from of the Lord of Gohaldinest. He waited to see what would play out between Lord Cirvel and the cahaster.

"You have indeed brought him here," Cirvel said. "Go be with your mistress."

Dragzel seemed to realize he was in trouble the instant Cirvel raised his hand. The cahaster started to protest, but Cirvel snapped his fingers and Dragzel disappeared. "If you are so good at convincing people to your will," Cirvel commanded to the air, his head lifted slightly to the right, "make your mistress conform to my bidding." Then, a little calmer, he added, "If the lad turns out to be all my Necroathelings said he is, I will consider letting you both free. If not, well, you know what will happen."

Rivic suddenly realized that, along with his sister, Dragzel and his mistress' life now depended on what Cirvel thought of him.

Cirvel turned his dark eyes toward Rivic. "This is certainly not how I would have dressed had I known we were going to meet," Cirvel said.

Rivic dropped to one knee and bowed his head. "Forgive me, Lord Cirvel. The intrusion is all my– "

"The fault of an ambitious cahaster," Cirvel cut across him. "Although, 'twould seem that he did indeed succeed where my Necroathelings failed." Placing the book on the table, Cirvel slid into a high-backed chair at the head of the table.

Rivic remained kneeling for a long moment before Cirvel requested that he stand. He wondered if he should sit but didn't dare move. He wasn't quite sure that he could budge. His legs seemed locked in place and his feet firmly rooted to the floor. If he could be as still as one of the tables with the strange teapots on them, he would have gladly done so. He didn't even want to breathe lest he offend the Lord of Gohaldinest.

The book flipped open without Cirvel touching it. Rivic smelled the magic coming off the pages, but he refused to be impressed, though he was curious about what on the pages held the lord's attention.

"I know you are not from the tribe you were with," Cirvel said as his fingers skimmed the words written on the page and his gaze never left the book. "Where are you from originally?"

Fear jumped into Rivic's stomach. How could he answer that he didn't know? He decided for the something as close to the truth as he could come. "My sister and I have been on our own for a while. I felt it was time for us to find someone to start a family with."

Now Cirvel's black eyes raised to him, an edge of humor playing wryly on his lips. "Did you find that special someone?"

Rivic thought of Ellonia and felt the blood rush into his face. "Aye."

"But your blood family is more important than the ties you wish to make with the one you found?"

"If you are asking that I would choose my sister over the woman in the village, aye, I would. My sister and I have only had each other for many cycles now. I cannot imagine life without her."

Cirvel gave a slow, thoughtful nod as his hands closed the book and his fingers lingered on the cover. "Your magic is very powerful, but untrained. Is it possible that you have taken the magic of another?"

"I do not get your meaning."

"My Necroathelings have informed me of your power. You defended against them well enough, but as you stand before me, I sense the strength but not the knowledge behind your abilities." Cirvel waved his hand and the book vanished from the table and appeared on the stack of books nearby. "Your magic is a confused jumble. Is it possible that one of your parents was not human?"

"I don't remember my parents. When I was very young, I destroyed the village where we lived." Again, he could tell some of the truth, but not everything. "We were taken in by our aunt and uncle's tribe."

"You performed magic as a toddler?" Cirvel looked Rivic over as if fascinated, but still hedging with disbelief.

Rivic nodded. "Aye."

"Then you may have inadvertently taken advantage of another's magic, then killed them when you destroyed the village. With no body for the magic to return to, you are stuck with it." Cirvel's eyes widened with sheer excitement. "You must stay and let me study you."

"Nay." Rivic's gaze drifted toward the little tables standing guard before the doors. Candlelight flickered off the curves of the golden metal pots. Power emanated in concentric circles, each rise like another omen warning Rivic to leave. He knew accepting Cirvel's offer was exactly what his dragon mother wanted him to do, but faced with Cirvel and his perfected abilities, as well as the strange magicks floating in the room, Rivic saw no way of defeating him. He didn't know enough about his own powers, as Cirvel had said. He needed more time, as his own sister had tried to forewarn him, to grow his own skills. "I would prefer to take my sister and return to our tribe."

Cirvel issued an amused scoff as he rose and came around the table. He waved his hand toward the strange pots. "Do you know what these are?"

"Nay," Rivic said with a shake of his head. With Cirvel drawing Rivic's attention closer to the curving teapots, he found himself drawn to them and could barely pull his gaze away from them. "What are they?"

"Magical lamps."

Rivic tried not to look down, though he certainly wanted to. "I'm sorry. I don't know what a magic lamp is."

"Have you heard of genie lamps?"

"Nay."

"A magical lamp is just that, a lamp with magic. There is nothing else inside." Cirvel picked one up by the ring at the end of it and let it dangle for a moment while he turned it for Rivic's inspection. Then he lifted off the lid and let Rivic peer inside. As the lord had stated, nothing was inside except for a bit of dust around the indented molding line where the base attached and a stale, metallic odor.

Replacing the lid, Cirvel carefully put his hand beneath

the spout and set it down on the long table in the middle of the room.

Then he turned and reached out his hand. One of the strange golden teapots from the opposite wall floated over to him. "This is a genie lamp. If I were to rub it, a genie would come out."

"What is a genie? Is that like a person?"

Cirvel appeared amused by Rivic's question. He stood up and started to pace the room. "Genies have form like a human, but they are not human. They are abominations."

"What purpose do they serve?"

Cirvel laughed as he picked the genie lamp up from the table. "That is the question indeed! What purpose do they serve, these abominations? They have powerful magic and are said to grant wishes. But every wish that gets granted has dire consequences."

"Why would you want these genie lamps then?"

"Because I'm a kind of collector."

Rivic felt totally confused. "Why would you collect these? They sound like more trouble than they are worth."

Cirvel set the genie lamp down on the table. "Because I collect all things magical."

The way Cirvel was looking at him now made Rivic feel uncomfortable, and in this he realized he was being set up. "My sister has no magic. What purpose does she serve you?"

"I haven't yet met your sister, but my men tell me she's been quite… accommodating." He paused to have slow articulation on the last word, making sure to leave Rivic wondering what exactly Cirvel meant by it.

"If she's been hurt—"

"Calm yourself. There are no trials for her to endure here." Cirvel slid back down into his chair with an easy grace. "She is fine. In fact, I am told she is enjoying herself and is quite relaxed here, though confident her brother is coming for her. We both have been patiently waiting for you."

Rivic wasn't certain why Cirvel would want to see him, but he was certain it wasn't a good thing. "Is that why you have brought me here, to collect me?"

"Would you like to be collected?"

A shiver ran through Rivic as Cirvel's magic danced around him as though happy to have found a playmate. "If all things were equal, Lord Cirvel, I would like to get my sister and leave."

"Do you not seek to further your magical training?" There was a slyness to his smile which reached into his black eyes. "My Necroathelings said you were minimally trained but had such potential."

"I have magic, but I don't seek power or glory. I don't have any magical ambitions." The words were hard for Rivic to say as every fiber inside him screamed for him to accept Lord Cirvel's offer, yet he knew he should be terrified of this man too. "You have nothing to fear from me."

"Why would I fear you?"

Even though Cirvel seemed amused in asking his question, his energy snapped around Rivic. Realizing he'd crossed a dangerous line, Rivic lowered his head. "I meant nothing by it. Your power is known throughout the land and I would never want you to think that I presumed mine better than yours."

Now Cirvel's eyes narrowed on him. The magic withdrew as if sinking back into a coil before striking out. "I do not think you know my power as well as you claim. Or your own. Why have you really come here?"

"I told you: for my sister."

"What would you do if I let you and your sister walk right out of here?"

Honestly, Rivic hadn't thought that far ahead. The dragon

had said that Rivic needed to defeat the power in Gohaldinest and that was obviously Cirvel. But now that Rivic had met the man and felt his power, Rivic wasn't certain he was up to the challenge. His own magic called him to learn from Cirvel. "Go back to the village."

Cirvel leaned forward and placed his fingers on the table's dark, polished wood. "Do you know what kind of life could exist for you inside of Gohaldinest? What I could offer you?"

"Nay, my lord. I do not."

Cirvel smiled as he pushed himself back in his chair. "Did you fall out of the sky?" Cirvel looked genuinely confused.

"Nay, my lord, but I have been very sheltered."

"Are you nobility?"

"Nay," he said, though every fiber of himself wanted to scream that he was.

"Then you know how hard life in the tribe is." Cirvel looked smug. "Let me tell you what awaits you outside of Gohaldinest. A life of labor, hunting, gathering, and living in small, huddled groups waiting for the gargaxes or gaxlors to come rip you apart unless you remain constantly nomadic and on the move. Do you want to scurry around like a rat all the time?"

"Nay, my lord."

"Would you condemn your sister to that life, to toiling by your side?"

"I would prefer if she had a husband who would care for her and provide her with the life I never could."

"I could ensure that she has that here."

Rivic's gaze darted toward the door. How fast could he run from here? He should never have come.

Cirvel raised a flat palm toward Rivic as if to shush him. "I get ahead of myself. Let us take this more slowly."

Rivic forced his attention back to Cirvel.

"You won't make it down out of the mountains in time. The snow has begun to fall. Besides that, does your tribe really need two extra mouths to feed?" Cirvel paused. He tried very desperately to hide a conspiring smile, but failed. "There is nothing that you can do to help your tribe at this point, even if you could make it back to them before the weather gets really bad. Stay with us here until growing season. By that time, your fellow tribesmen will need you. They will want the extra hands to begin preparing for next snow season. Stay here until the thaw and I will let you leave with my full blessings. I will even mark your tribe as sanctioned and let you all live in peace free from the gargax attacks."

The proposal sounded too good. The safety of Ellonia's tribe in exchange for staying one mere season in Gohaldinest.

"But our staying here will tax your storages just the same," Rivic said, knowing that something was never given for nothing, "What would I have to do in exchange? What do I give you in return? What do you expect as payment?" His legs craved to move him forward closer to Cirvel, but he resisted and kept his feet planted. "I doubt I could offer anything you would possibly need in return."

Cirvel seemed to think about it for a moment, but Rivic sensed it was an act feigned his for his benefit. Cirvel let his head move back and forth a little as his eyes looked up toward the ceiling. Then they snaked their way back down and Cirvel pinned him hard with that dark gaze. His lips twitched with the faintest of smiles. "A drop of blood from you and your sister."

"One drop?"

"'Tis all I need. But should you like to give me two or three," Cirvel said with a hint of shock, "that would be glorious as well. A bona fide gift."

"Would I be free to move around the castle and city as I pleased? My sister as well?" Rivic asked, determined to find the boundaries of this bargain.

"Of course."

It all seemed unreal. "I don't understand why you are doing this for us."

"You underestimate your potential, lad. Your abilities are merely untapped and untrained."

"I have fought to control my magic. Sometimes it seems to much. Destructive." Rivic wasn't certain why he was admitting the flaws in his abilities, maybe because he hoped it would give Cirvel cause to send him on his way. Yet, it also felt good to admit it.

Cirvel's dark eyes seemed to brighten as he smiled. "We can help you with that."

Rivic's magic was singing. Cirvel would allow him to stay and train. The agreement seemed too astonishing. "Will you really remain true to your word?"

Cirvel chuckled. "Of course my word is good. I make this arrangement all the time, except most come willingly to beg for such a chance."

"Why?"

His amusement continued. "For just the very reasons I have mentioned to you. Their tribe needs to feed fewer mouths over the snowing season. They come here to ease those pressures from their people. When they leave here, I have a man inside their tribe who I trained, who I can trust. I can depend upon you, can't I?"

The tides had turned. Cirvel was now asking Rivic if he was a man of honor. As apprehensive as he felt, Rivic nodded. If Cirvel kept his word and let them go as soon as the snow was melted, then Rivic would stand by his promise and be loyal to Cirvel. Especially, if it provided safety for Ellonia's tribe. He could maintain residence here for short time knowing that it would protect her for much longer. "Very well then. We accept your generosity, Lord Cirvel. We shall stay during the snow season and leave in the rain season. Your oath for mine. 'Tis a bond."

Cirvel tipped his head. "I'm glad we came to such a bargain so easily." He stood and pulled on a cord hanging along the wall. Somewhere beyond the doorway, Rivic heard a bell ding. A moment later, a beautiful, young woman in white robes appeared. Magic churned in the air. The candle-light sparkled in golden flashes off her wavy red hair.

"Your bidding, my lord?" the girl asked. Her voice had the smoothness of an ethereal being and made Rivic's heart quicken.

"Alityka, this is Rivic. He is our newest acolyte. Please make sure he is well attended."

Her blue eyes assessed Rivic. "Very well, my lord." She came around the table towards him, reaching out her hand.

"Once he is settled, show him to Nyree's quarters," Cirvel added. "Rivic is her twin."

For a second, a shocked expression came over Alityka's face, but she quickly hid it. "Aye, my lord."

Rivic took her hand and allowed himself to be escorted from the room. Before she opened the door, Rivic turned. "Lord Cirvel, I hope you are pleased enough with our meeting that you will release Dragzel and his mistress."

Looking back down at his book, Cirvel smirked.

CHAPTER 13

"You will need to put these on," Alityka said, pulling a pair of light gray pants and a matching tunic from the shelves of a closet once they had reached another building. She pointed to a trifold panel. "You may change over there."

Rivic stepped behind the changing screen, began to remove his garb, and donned the ones she had given to him. He'd never felt such soft fabric in his life. He pulled the ties on the pants and tucked them into the band. "How long have you been here?" he asked.

She replied from the other side, but it sounded like she also faced the wall. "Nearly two cycles now."

"Where are you from?"

"Like most of the acolytes, I'm from a tribe beyond the Palin Mountains."

That didn't seem like a specific answer. He pulled the tunic over his head, then gathered his discarded wardrobe and tucked them under his arm before coming out from behind the partition.

"When you need a change of clothes, you may come here

and get them. Take two more sets. You will be able to store them away for now." She paused while she waited for him to follow her instructions. Then she pointed to a square hole in the wall that looked like it had a tunnel leading downward. "When your acolyte outfit is soiled, place it here to be taken down to the laundry and washed. You may put your travel clothes there now. They will be cleaned and held in the laundry room until you can get them."

Holding onto the blue traveling cloak that Ellonia had made for him, Rivic put the rest of his clothes on the ramp and sent them down. He listened to see if he could tell how far down the chute was, but he didn't hear a sound when they had landed.

Alityka pointed to the cloak. "That too."

"I'd rather not."

Alityka shrugged, then moved on. "We are on a chore rotation. You will find yourself in the laundry room during some fortnight period."

Men and women in red and gold armor watched many of the hallways where they progressed through.

"Who are they?" Rivic asked.

"They are the Domini, Cirvel's elite guardsmen." Alityka fell silent and kept her head down as she passed by another of the sentinels. Once around the corner, she began speaking lowly again. "Acolytes wishing to progress become Domini. Those that survive go on to being promoted to Necroathelings. 'Tis best that you don't encounter either Domini or Necroatheling, but if you really need aid, then find a Dominus. They have not become as cruel yet."

She once again reached out for him, then led him toward a staircase. He followed her up, still letting her have his hand though he felt as if he should draw away.

They came out in a shadowy room with a huge sloping gable. Wood planks with large rafter supports and exposed beams ran across the roof. Six windows, three on each opposite wall, allowed light into the area. The dark, ragged wood of the uncovered walls made it seem murky in here, as if it couldn't get enough sunlight.

Three beds lined up on each of the outer walls, each separated by a window, while in the center were two sets of six, three against three, with a small walk space between them. Simply constructed, the small wooden frames raised about two feet off the ground and the mats were covered with white blankets. A small trunk rested at the foot of each bed.

Alityka stopped beside one of the beds against the wall. "This will be yours. The boy who was sleeping here recently had an accident." She broke her hand away from his to gesture toward the space.

"An accident?" A draft ran across the back of Rivic's neck.

"He lost control of his magic." Her eyes looked sad, too sad for someone her age. He wanted to make her smile, for someone as lovely as she was should never be sorrowful. "There is a lot of residue in this castle. When it comes whispering to you at night, I suggest you shield your heart from its lies."

"What happened to the boy?"

"The gargaxes devoured him." She turned her head away as if she could defend herself from the memory. Then she straightened her posture. "'Tis hard, but every now and again we lose acolytes who are not prepared to be here. Boys and girls of varying ages stay in this dormitory until we are promoted, so we get to know each other. 'Tis devastating to lose someone you know well."

"You stay here, sleep here too?" Rivic set his extra clothes on top of the blankets and stepped over to the nearest window. Each one had a padded ledge for sitting on while staring outside. He looked out on a space between the buildings and the alleyway beneath. Examining the sills, he noted that the walls of the room were at least two feet thick.

Alityka looked around as if it depressed her. "Aye." She drifted across the room to head to the far back corner diagonal from him. "'Tis my bed here. I'm the oldest in this room, so 'tis my job to watch out for the others."

Rivic took a quick count. "So, there are eighteen acolytes if all the beds are filled?"

"Aye, in this dormitory. Lord Cirvel tries to keep it balanced with nine girls and nine boys, but it doesn't always work out that way. Right now, with you included, there are twelve girls and seven boys."

"That's nineteen."

Alityka smiled and it made his heart sing at the revival of her beauty. "Very good. You have basic math skills," she said proudly. "Most who come here do not know how to read, write, or do math. Do you read and write as well?"

"Sontre' taught me."

"Sontre'?"

"'Tis what we called the woman who raised me and my sister." Though it was the truth, it felt strange talking about something that hadn't been real, but rather more like an intense dream. "She was my Sontre'."

"Sontre'... Sontre'..." The girl seemed about to laugh, but then her blue eyes started to flicker back and forth as if she were reading something over her head. The smile faded from her lips. "A teacher of the Onesong." She grabbed his wrists. "Does Lord Cirvel know that you are connected to the Onesong?"

"I don't... I don't think so."

"How could he not!" Alityka stepped away from Rivic. "'Tis why he wanted you here. You must not tell anyone. 'Tis dangerous, you hear? If Lord Cirvel found out..."

"He won't."

She released him and glanced around the quiet room. "We should carry on, pretend this conversation never happened."

"Aye." He felt relieved at being liberated from this discussion. "I am anxious to see my sister."

They left this building and proceeded into the next. Alityka pointed out classrooms and training areas, but her attitude was different now, shorter, sharper, as if she were in a hurry and didn't want to be around him any longer.

Going through another entrance, the quarries in the windows and the tiles reminded Rivic of the hallway he'd entered before coming to Lord Cirvel's room. He glanced around to see if any other features would give him his bearings. "Are we back in the castle?" Rivic asked.

"Another wing of it," Alityka replied.

As they approached a staircase, Rivic realized he'd been up and down so much today that his legs were beginning to hurt. How much more would he have to endure?

"You're almost there," Alityka said as if she could read his thoughts.

It gave him the fortitude to continue on. In a long passage with doors lining both sides, Alityka knocked on the fourth doorway down to the left.

"Come in," Nyree's voice called from inside.

Alityka opened the door. "I've brought someone to see you." She stepped inside and moved out of the way for Rivic to enter.

Unlike the dormitory where he was going to be staying with the acolytes, Nyree's room was bright and lavish. It seemed to fit the castle better than the drafty attic accommodations. The bed had four long poles, each as thick as the posts which made the frames of the lodgings in Krithstand's village, rising from each corner. The curtains on the windows were pulled back to allow the daylight into the room, but after dark a chandelier with four candles would illuminate the room. Nyree sat near the window. She put her book down on the round marble table beside her and jumped to her feet. A short way off was a small writing desk and another chair.

"Rivic! You're finally here." Nyree ran over to him and threw her arms around his neck in a tight hug. He lifted her close to him for a moment then dropped her back down to her feet. "Come." She grabbed his hand and led him toward the fireplace where there was a small sofa.

Nyree sat down and motioned for Rivic to do the same.

Alityka, who had remained by the open door, spoke up, "I'll leave you two to visit. Nyree can take you down to dinner in a bit. I will catch up to you later to lead you back to the acolytes' quarters."

"Thank you," Rivic said.

As the door shut behind Alityka, Rivic faced his sister. "Are you all right? No one's hurt you?"

"I promise you, I've been fine. I'm not sure that what they say about Lord Cirvel is true. Everyone here is wonderful and seems so happy." She rubbed her hands over her knees as she smiled at him.

He couldn't find the words to speak.

"When do we go home?" she asked.

"We're not. Not until next season." He paused. "I've agreed to continue my training while we are here."

"'Tis great." She sounded genuinely pleased.

"But we have to do something for Lord Cirvel to repay his kindness. I have agreed to his terms."

She looked at him suspiciously. "Terms?"

"His request, what he wants in payment."

"Which is?"

"A few drops of our blood, nothing more."

Nyree nodded, smiling. "'Tis nothing much for what we are getting in return. The wound will heal." She reached over and took his hands in hers, her eyes alight with excitement. "You should see the library here. Books from floor to ceiling. I have been allowed to read at my leisure and there are so many wonderful things."

Recalling Ellonia's words about appreciating the things he'd been given, Rivic closed his eyes and thanked the Onesong for keeping Nyree safe. Lord Cirvel had been truthful in saying that Nyree was unharmed. Maybe, just maybe, Cirvel wasn't as bad as the stories of his reputation. However, Rivic had also seen what it was like to be on the receiving end of his temper. Nyree hadn't yet met him. Time would reveal the truth.

CHAPTER 14

*R*ivic sat on his bed in the tower dormitory, his back against the wall. A cool breeze blew through the aged planks and stirred against his tunic. He thought about putting a blanket behind him to keep the draft away, but if he were to be here for a while, he'd better get used to it.

The acolytes began to return and as the room collected with people, the chill left the air and the noise level grew. The girls all wore white dresses while the boys all had light gray pants and tunics. Ages seemed to range from eight to nearly fifteen cycles. Some of the kids were sitting in the window seats reading. Others were practicing the day's lessons.

Magic stirred around the room, reaching out from the wood, especially around the acolytes practicing their current studies.

Rivic reached out his hands, touching the little wisps of magic that circled near him. It played around his fingers, twisting through as he moved them, watching the sparkling line slither ever so close to him. Gradients of red, blue, yellow, and purple all ran through the string, shifting within it like fluid. He looped it around, capturing the sublime tangle. As it tugged away from him, he watched it curl its way along the edge of his mattress and sink into a gap between the wood of the floor. When he looked back up, he noticed a girl had moved to the foot of his bed and realized it was Alityka. "I understand what you mean now about residue."

Alityka moved a little closer, curiosity in her eyes. "What happened to you? How did you find a Sontre'?"

Rivic shifted uncomfortably. What would she think about him if she knew? "I was magic spun when I was about five cycles old. I accidentally destroyed the village where my parents lived. My sister and I got sent to live with my aunt and uncle after that. The same thing happened. Nyree and I were the only ones to survive."

"You decimated two villages?" she asked.

"I did." Rivic's chest tightened at the admission. He continued before he could no longer get the air out, "Nyree and I wandered through the forest for days before Sontre' came upon us. She took us in." That was close enough to the truth.

Her eyes narrowed briefly on him. "I heard that Necroathelings found you and your sister. Why didn't Sontre' stop them?"

"She died recently. We've been on our own for a while. We went to live with a tribe."

Alityka nodded, but said nothing further.

"You said there are currently nineteen acolytes," Rivic said when Alityka didn't speak again. "Who is this extra person? Where does he stay?"

"She." Alityka sat down on the corner of the bed, turning and folding one leg in front of her. "The extra would be Lady Lihn Harvestendale." When Rivic shook his head because he didn't understand, she continued, "The cahaster's mistress."

"Dragzel's mistress? The woman in the glass prison?"

"Aye." She gave a faint smile. "And thanks to you she is free again tonight. Now if she can only keep Lord Cirvel happy for the time being."

"What does she do to displease him?"

"She keeps from him the secrets of the Onesong which he wishes to know."

Rivic paused, taking in this information and trying to process it. Why would Lihn do that? Was she the other champion the dragon had referred to? Or was she another teacher of the Onesong? He couldn't help the flicker of hope which flared in his chest. "She is a Sontre'?"

"Nay, but she does have incredible knowledge about the Onesong."

Rivic refused to show his disappointment as his wish of finding another Sontre' broke. "Why would she keep it from him?"

"She was sent as an emissary from her people. She was to cultivate peace with Lord Cirvel. That was the first time she displeased him. Since then he has kept her as a prisoner. He has assigned her to the worst tasks and makes her sleep alone in the high tower. If not for Dragzel taking a shine to her, I don't know what would have happened to her by now."

Rivic felt his heart begin to race. Lihn had to be Ellonia's sister. Was it really possible that she was the other champion too? "But even with her knowledge of the Onesong, she's an acolyte too?"

"'Tis too strange for me to understand as well," Alityka said with a smile. "But if I were you, I'd keep what you know about the Onesong to yourself. So far, those who know about it and reveal it are liable to be in great danger from Cirvel."

"Why?"

A strange look twisted on her face, almost as if she were

trying not to show irritation at his question. "I do not know specifics, but he seeks dark and terrible secrets."

That made sense to Rivic. Cirvel had told him how he collected all things magical. That wouldn't just mean light and fluffy stuff, but the horrible as well. It worried Rivic that he longed to seek out the same dangers. "How is it that you know of the Onesong?"

Alityka smiled and turned her face as if to hide her mysteries from him. She didn't look at him as she spoke. "Let's just say that I've done my own quest." She patted him on the knee, then stood up. "All right everyone. Time for lights out. Classes begin early tomorrow."

A collective sigh rose from the room as everyone grumbled their way to bed. As the lights went out, Rivic watched the white sway of Alityka's dress as she moved down to her bed and pulled back the blankets. He stayed on top of his cover until everyone was tucked in bed and he began to hear some people starting to snore softly.

"Lights out," Alityka hissed through the darkness. Rivic saw a dim glow from under a blanket of a bed not far from her. Someone was trying to read under the blanket. It quickly went out. He saw her roll over in the dark, her face pale in the moonlight. "You too," she mouthed at him.

He nodded and kicked the blanket back before slinking down on the bed. His mind was too active. He didn't know how he would sleep. He closed his eyes, certain that it wouldn't help.

Next thing he knew, it was morning.

"Come on, sleepyhead," Alityka said as she raked her fingers through her hair to comb it. "You best get up if you want breakfast."

Already the younger kids were screaming from the dormitory and running down the stairs. Rivic tossed back the thin blanket and put his feet on the floor. "When will I get to see my sister today?" he asked.

"Probably not until near evening. Yesterday was a catch-up day, where we can get through our extra chores, home-work, or just play. This day will have much more structure to it and you'll be quite busy."

At breakfast, he sat at the table with the other acolytes, but found that Alityka was seated at the other end. She smiled down the length when she caught him looking at her.

"So, Rivic," said a young boy named Melodin, "I've heard that your twin is here in Gohaldinest, that you both came so that you could train."

"Aye," Rivic answered, knowing that the story was close enough.

A pot passed from person to person. Each took one ladleful of the oatmeal and slid it down. Melodin passed the pot to Rivic.

"Your twin, a brother or a sister?" Melodin asked. When Rivic answered, he continued, "How is she faring with her days? She must be bored, stuck here, not able to work with magic. Why did you bring your sister? Afraid of the dark without her?"

"We're the only family the other has."

"So you come here to loaf off of the Lord of Gohaldinest?" asked another boy just down the table. "Think he'll take care of you and your sister for free if you become an acolyte, do you? That's pathetic."

"Oren," Alityka growled, "that's quite enough from you. I won't stand by and let unfounded accusations fly. You don't understand his circumstances."

"Why else do orphans end up here?" Oren retorted. "We're supposed to be elite. The best of the best. We're training to be Necroathelings and serve Lord Cirvel. But now we're taking on rift-raft."

His voice raised as he spoke and two Necroathelings moved toward him from the doorway. "Shh," Alityka warned, noticing them. Oren sat up a bit straighter. They tapped him on the shoulder and motioned for him to come with them.

"'Tis about time I get noticed," Oren said as he lifted his leg over the bench to get up. "Losers!" Oren rolled back his shoulders and proudly followed the Necroathelings from the room.

They were still down to seventeen in number when they arrived at their first class; Oren didn't show. As they were seated, Lady Lihn entered the room and sat down just slightly off to the side. Rivic couldn't look away from her as she met his gaze and smiled. He noticed Dragzel curled up in her lap.

The lesson seemed to roll into time without end. Rivic found himself drifting off to sleep. He understood only some of what they were talking about and Sontre' had always made his lessons into action tasks, not lectures. Sitting still this long made him ache.

During break, Rivic moved toward Lihn, who was standing off in a corner of the room by herself.

"Blessings, Dragzel," he said, not quite sure how to start a conversation directly with Lihn. "I'm glad to see you're out."

The cahaster raised his head and hissed at Rivic.

Lihn turned to face the wall. "I'm sorry," she whispered. "We can't be seen talking."

That seemed like the silliest thing he'd ever heard. "Why not?"

"Because we can't. Cirvel won't like it."

"He's not here to know."

"Anyone seeking Cirvel's favor would be more than willing to tell him." Lihn's scared gaze circled the room. "Please, go away. I have no wish to get you into trouble."

Rivic sighed. "Sorry. I guess I don't understand anything

here." He turned to leave.

"Thank you for reminding Cirvel about his promise to Dragzel," she whispered as he stepped away.

Rivic said nothing as he went back to his seat for the rest of the class. After what felt like forever again, they went into another room that had tables with benches on both sides. Here, they actually worked hands on. Today was an herb mixing class, and that was something that Rivic felt his participation was worthwhile. If nothing else, he might learn some techniques he could share with Ellonia. Maybe he'd learn enough to understand what she was doing.

"You hated today, didn't you?" Alityka asked as they made their way back to the dormitory before dinner. "I saw you nearly fall asleep three times."

"Only three?" Rivic said. "I don't understand half of it because 'tis practical theory and the other half is something I'm way beyond. I really don't know what I'm doing here."

Worse, his chore assignment had been to help cook meals for the acolytes. Nyree and Sontre' had always cooked. And, he had to do it without the use of magic. Apparently, Lord Cirvel was very big on actual manual labor. Rivic didn't have to clean up the kitchen afterwards, not this fortnight at least. That chore rotation would come.

Oren didn't return to the dormitory that night. Nor was he at breakfast, or class the next morning, or the following. Rivic's days started to blur together with the sameness of it all, leaving him wondering why he'd chosen to remain here. He found much of his training too hard; Sontre's teaching had been pragmatic and hands-on, not the theorems and concepts of why magic was what it was. It fascinated Rivic and bored him at the same time. Maybe if he'd had these foundations from day one, he'd understand more.

Rumors of the Necroathelings killing Oren began to circulate. Part of Rivic envied him for getting out of this dreadful life. Not only did Rivic resent his decision to stay, but he hadn't been able to see Nyree either.

With only his evenings free and being so far behind on his theoretical studies, he had been using the time to catch up. But not tonight, he promised himself as he left the meal hall and headed over to the wing of the castle where Nyree was quartered.

He entered a hallway where the windows set high in the walls caught the orange cast of evening light. Empty sofas and an odd assortment of tables lined the gray stone walls, the wood seemingly bright compared to the rock of the castle as it reflected the sunset. He felt himself being watched. Dark shadows spread along the crevices. Rivic walked through, unable to shake the sense of wariness.

Glowing blue eyes in the deep, jagged shadow of the staircase caught Rivic's attention. "Dragzel," he called out, with a breath of relief, "Why did you get away from your mistress this time? Is she in trouble again?"

As he bent down to see Dragzel, the cahaster zoomed out from his hiding spot and zipped up Rivic's arm. The cahaster stretched out behind Rivic's neck and nuzzled under his long dark hair. "My mistress requests a meeting with you now."

"I'm on my way to see Nyree," Rivic answered. "Tell me where she wants to meet, then inform her I'll be there later."

"There is no time for delay. She only has a few moments."

Rivic tried to hide his disappointment. He supposed one quick visit, if Lihn had only a short time, wouldn't hurt. Then he could spend a tranquil evening with Nyree. "Lead the way."

"Leave here the way you came in."

Rivic had been hoping the cahaster wouldn't remain curled up around the back of his neck, but he was sure that Dragzel had his reason for staying there. Departing the building, Rivic walked straight between two structures. The night sky had darkened, but the moons hadn't risen yet, letting early stars begin to shine.

"Turn left and go through the courtyard," Dragzel commanded. "We want to go to the tower just beyond."

Coming out from between buildings, the brick pattern work of the road divided around a rectangular section of grass. Tall vases cultivating vines that grew the largest blossoms Rivic had ever seen sat atop marble pillars marking the corners of the courtyard. The flowers, yellow near the stamen and gradated to blue further down the pedal, were open to the night sky.

"Get down," Dragzel hissed in his ear.

Rivic ducked behind the marble pedestal. A moment later he saw why Dragzel had told him to hide. Two Necroathelings strolled through an archway and headed down the road opposite them in the courtyard, followed by Lord Cirvel in robes of black with silver hems. Even though there was no moonlight yet, the shiny cloth seemed to glow as if reflecting all the starlight.

Beside him walked Lihn Harvestendale, looking so much like a grand princess that Rivic hardly recognized her. She wasn't wearing the white dress of an acolyte, but rather a long satiny silver dress with white lace around her neck and down the forearms. Her skirt had a light billow to it, which forced some distance between her and Lord Cirvel. Her brown hair had been piled up on top of her head with curling wisps left to fall around her neck and face.

She laughed at something Cirvel had said, turning slightly toward him as she did so, and stretching to lay a gentle hand on his arm. Rivic felt the magic between them even from this distance. Hers danced and swirled in a teasing way, while Cirvel's responded with playful, predatory stalking. It twisted sharply, as if always keeping her bewitchment in full view at all times.

A Necroatheling in the lead stopped and raised his right hand. Both Necroathelings looked around.

"Uh-oh," Dragzel said.

Rivic realized that the Necroathelings had sensed his magic. He crawled to the other side of the pillar and saw two more Necroathelings which had been following Lord Cirvel. Even Cirvel's power assumed an attack position.

Rivic pulled back his magic, imagining himself as small as the cahaster.

"Carry on," Lord Cirvel ordered at last. They continued through the courtyard and Rivic finally allowed himself to breathe. Remaining silent, Rivic peeked around the pillar to watch Lihn and Cirvel enter what could only be the tower Dragzel had mentioned earlier. The circular section of the castle rose taller than the surrounding walls.

As the door closed, Rivic noticed it was glass. Only once Cirvel and the Necroathelings were inside the tower did Rivic speak. "That was close," Rivic said. "Do you think he knows 'twas me out here?"

"Oh, he knows," Dragzel confirmed. "'Tis just that he doesn't see you as a threat. But don't be surprised when he calls you in to question you tomorrow."

"I'll just tell him I was out looking at the stars and when I saw them coming, I didn't want to ruin their mood, so I hid."

"Good idea. I'm not sure he'll buy it, but you can try."

"How can he dispute it?"

"He doesn't need to debate it. All he has to do is not believe you and then decide to suck out your life force. Not a single person can stop that from happening." Dragzel looked around. "Head down the street a little. In one of the alleyways, there's a trellis you can climb to the balcony. We'll wait up there for Cirvel to leave."

Staying low and crouched, Rivic ran for the street. They came into the alley and Rivic found the lattice Dragzel was talking about. "'Tis too thin," Rivic said. "'Twon't support my weight. I can't climb it."

Dragzel hissed, then ran onto the framework. "Fine. You stay down and I'll keep a look out."

The cahaster climbed up the trellis and sat on the edge of the balcony as if he'd done this hundreds of times before. Rivic stayed back, tucked in the shadows, and watched Dragzel being vigilant for Cirvel. "You do this often?" Rivic asked.

"Every night when she goes out with him." Dragzel said the last word as though the thought of Cirvel was poison on his tongue.

"I realize he's not the nicest guy in the world, but why do you have such animosity against him?"

"I hate the way he's treated my mother," Dragzel said. "He made her Guardian of Gohaldinest and then keeps her trapped when she should be flying free."

"I'm sorry. I'm sure that is hard on you."

At the sound of Dragzel's hiss, Rivic saw Cirvel leaving the tower and ambling across the courtyard. The Necroathelings spread out across the grass and walked toward where Rivic had been hiding. Rivic pulled back deeper into the shadows of the alley, not wanting them to see his head should they look back.

After the Necroathelings and Lord Cirvel had gone inside the main castle, Dragzel came down the lattice and jumped onto Rivic's shoulder. "Let's go." Rivic dashed down the street with Dragzel once again curled up behind his neck. They slipped into the tower. The interior seemed surprisingly smaller than the outside. Practically just beyond the door was the first step of a spiral staircase. Rivic tried to look up to see where it went, but saw nothing except darkness. For what it lacked in width, it made up for with height.

"Why does Lady Lihn wish to see me?" Rivic asked. "She

has said nothing to me in class other than to warn me to stay away."

"She has to tell everyone that. He doesn't like the thought of her consorting with anyone other than him."

Rivic knew that Dragzel meant Cirvel.

"Why? What harm would it bring?"

"You do not know what a selfish man he is."

Rivic thought about his own deal with Lord Cirvel; Rivic and his sister staying in Gohaldinest for a season in exchange for a few drops of blood, which Cirvel hadn't even come to collect yet. It didn't seem selfish to feed two extra mouths and provide magical training essentially for free. In fact, the offer seemed too generous. But Rivic had always felt in his gut that the situation was too good to be true. There was more that he had yet to see.

Rivic started to climb the staircase. Silver lights lit up words across the top of the next step before him. *Those who know shall show their reverence*, it read.

"Kneel," Dragzel said in Rivic's ear.

"What?"

"Kneel!"

Rivic dropped to his knee hard enough on the step that he knew he'd end up with a bruise. A transparent image of Lord Cirvel appeared on the steps. Magic singed the air. "Pada'su raysa kada'zil," the image spoke. Rivic felt a rush of magic over his head.

Rivic froze as the image of Cirvel faded from view.

"Anyone without magic who tried to enter here and go up the stairs would be killed," Dragzel said. "'Tis the first precaution."

"There are more?"

"Two more. Do as I say and you'll be fine."

Though he didn't want to move, Rivic stood and continued up the stairs. He stopped as soon as he saw silver writing appear several steps later. *Too many to speak, too many to name, but all with equal opportunities and infinite possibilities.*

"What?" Rivic asked as he realized this was a riddle.

"Dimensions that the Necroathelings can travel in."

Rivic felt magic gathering in the air.

"Hurry!" Dragzel ordered.

"Dimensions that the Necroathelings can travel in," Rivic repeated. The words faded from the step. "I really don't like this game."

He walked through a rush of steam that surged from the ceiling.

"Ah, root rot! Run!" Dragzel said as he jumped off Rivic's shoulder and dashed up the railing.

Rivic rushed up the next few steps. A stone in the wall exploded next to him. The blast knocked him against the railing and flipped him over it. His hands caught the upright supports.

"Talcor dun," he said, wanting to be back up on the staircase, preferably at the top. Nothing happened.

"The steam drained your magic," Dragzel shouted. "Didn't you feel it?"

Rivic lifted himself up, feeling the strain through his elbows. He reached for the railing and grabbed hold. His fingers felt cold and clammy on the metal. At last, he was in a position where he could swing a leg up and haul himself over the railing. He lay on the steps panting for a moment.

The staircase transformed to a ramp and Rivic started to slide down it. His fingers smacked the first couple of the handrail's support struts as he tried to grab them, then the attempt succeeded and he stopped from sliding. The steam shot down on him again. He closed his eyes and turned his face away from the blast.

"'Tis not worth going to visit your mistress," Rivic shouted. "Next time, she comes to see me."

CHAPTER 15

The blackness of the tower made it difficult as Rivic climbed toward the top using the railing's struts as if it were a ladder. The seams of the stairs where they had flattened together to make the ramp chafed against his arm, hip, and thigh. He kept telling himself that if he made it to the top, he'd be done.

At the landing and after getting upright to his feet, he bent over and put his hands on his knees to breathe for a moment. Then, following the short rest, he realized that he was in an empty room at the very top of the tower. "Where is she, Dragzel? This better not be some sort of trick."

"You have to call forth the column."

"What?"

Dragzel sat back on his haunches and pointed toward the ceiling. "There's a column that comes down when you speak the magical words for it."

"Great, Dragzel. I don't know the words. Do you?"

"Hello, cahaster here! Do you think my mouth works like a human's? Even if I spoke the words, you wouldn't understand them because it would be garbled."

Rivic threw his hands in the air. "You speak well enough. You can manage that, but when it comes to spells, all of a sudden you're impotent?"

"Woah, now that's uncalled for!"

"Well?" Rivic tapped his foot as he waited for the cahaster to come up with the answer.

"My lady Lihn said that if you were the one, you would know how to do it."

"Great!" Rivic turned, feeling angry that he'd wasted the whole evening trying to see this woman instead of his sister and now he couldn't even manage to find out what Lihn wanted. But even as the emotion hit him, he realized it was wasted energy. With a deep breath, he pushed the hot anger down through his feet and out of him. In that clearing, he felt his magic returning and recovering from the steamy blast he had taken.

The answer whispered with curls of ancient magic through his mind.

The words rolled off his tongue. "Vocha chia cada'dada."

He didn't realize that he'd closed his eyes until he heard the cahaster issue a noise that sounded like a victory cry. A silver column had come down in front of him. "Vochey," he said as the next thing that felt right to say.

Within the silver column, an assortment of images unrolled before him.

"She's in the second row down, third column over."

As Rivic found the picture, he saw Lihn moving around in a room beyond this one as if he were merely watching from the doorway. Then she stepped from view never knowing he was spying on her.

Dragzel jumped from the railing over to Rivic's shoulder. "Touch the image."

Rivic reached out for it. As his fingers entered the silver column, the magic tingled along his skin. At contacting the picture, a rush surged through him and automatically he closed his eyes. Opening them again, he found himself in the room with Lihn.

She sat before a vanity, brushing out her long brown hair. Her reflection in the mirror smiled at him. "Blessings. I'm glad you made it." A large window by the vanity looked out over a town far below. Lights were still on at many of the homes below. A thin dusting of snow covered the rooftops, but the sky above was clear.

Lihn's room seemed nearly as drab as the acolytes' dormitory where he slept, save that the light held more of a brown cast here rather than a gray. All of her belongs were neatly set in their place among the furnishings of a bed, vanity, desk, dresser, several bookshelves, and round table with two chairs. Rivic couldn't spot a single place where she would store a gown like the one he'd seen her in only a few moments ago. Her nightclothes, made of a thick material that looked soft but he couldn't identify, lay across her bed ready to change into. She currently wore the acolyte's outfit.

Dragzel jumped from Rivic's shoulder and ran toward Lihn. He took a spot on the vanity so she could adore him for a moment and pressed his long head against her palm as she indulged him. The cahaster's eyes shined blue-green in the murky light.

Rivic remembered the stone he carried from Ellonia to give to her sister.

Setting the brush down on the vanity, she rose and moved toward him. The white skirt of her acolyte dress twirled about her legs.

The dark wood of the room, though polished and shiny, was no less old than that of the dormitory, just better taken care of. Stone accented the wood. Lihn walked by one of the many bookshelves by the desk and an extra pile of books rising from the floor. The whole room swirled with magic.

"'Tis some protection which Lord Cirvel has on you," Rivic commented, his gaze once again going toward the window and out beyond the undrawn curtain. The courtyard he'd been in this evening had seen no sign of snow and he wondered if the grassy area outside was magically protected. Perhaps they were not in Gohaldinest any longer, but rather some place where the winter was settled firmly in now.

She smiled and it held such a calm that the tension of the last few moments drained right out of Rivic. "The lord does like his collectables."

"So I've heard." Rivic looked around her room hoping it would give him some sort of clue as to why he was there. Yet it was the window that kept drawing him back. "Is that Gohaldinest?" he asked.

"Nay, we are far away from Gohaldinest. Another dimension entirely."

Rivic nearly choked. "Another dimension?"

"Aye. Cirvel thinks that keeping me locked away will keep me safe no matter what happens in Gohaldinest, but I enjoy it because it keeps me mostly out of his vision."

"Does that mean that you can do whatever you want while you are here?" He wanted to be perfectly clear about this.

She smiled again, but shrugged. "For the most part."

"So, he doesn't know I'm here either?"

"I knew I was taking a risk of being found out when I had Dragzel bring you here. But if Cirvel did know," she said, placing her hand upon his arm, "he'd be here already."

Feeling as though they were safe for the moment, Rivic reached into his pouch and pulled out the wrapped stone. He unfolded the brown cloth to reveal the blue teardrop gem within. "Your sister said this was yours and that I should give it to you."

Lihn leaned forward to look at it. "'Tis not mine.

However, I have heard a story from Alityka that she was born with a blue gemstone in her mouth." She laughed as if the preposterous idea brought her great humor. "'Tis silly, is it not? A baby born with a rock in her mouth?"

"So Ellonia is not your sister?" Rivic asked, wondering how he could have been so wrong. "Dragzel went to her to warn her that the Necroathelings were going to attack her tribe. She said the message came from her sister."

"Dragzel did indeed carry the message from Alityka for the tribe," Lihn said. "But he was also on a mission for me."

He folded the stone back up and returned it to his pouch. So he would have to give it to Alityka. His mind tried to mentally find the resemblance between Ellonia and Alityka and couldn't see it. Lihn bore more of a similarity. It brought a strange emptiness to him. Nearly the same kind of hollowness that this room held. "To bring me to Gohaldinest?" His words also reflected the strange void pressing through him.

"Aye."

"So why am I here?" He was ready to be down to business.

"I am told that you have knowledge of the Onesong." She went to sit down on the edge of her bed and offered him the chair beside her writing desk. Dragzel left his seat on the vanity and curled up next to Lihn on the bed.

He wondered who she had been talking to. Had Dragzel told her, or Alityka, or the Onesong itself?

When he didn't say anything, she asked, "Can you commune with it?"

Rivic laughed dryly. "Everyone is connected with it. 'Tis all in how well you listen back when it speaks." That had been one of Sontre's favorite sayings. His answer seemed to please Lihn. How could he admit that his communication with the Onesong had been hampered, or at least that's what he'd been told?

Then her demeanor darkened again like a cloud covering

the sun. "Cirvel wants me to give him the secrets of the Onesong, but they must never fall into his hands."

"You're stating the obvious."

"The Onesong tells me that I can trust you, that I should trust you. The Onesong wants me to give you the secrets so that you can help me."

Rivic leaned forward in the chair and put his elbows on his knees. "Why are you so certain that I wouldn't give the secrets to Cirvel myself? Or that I have any desire to help you in whatever you are plotting?"

"I don't. But Alityka and I know that we need someone else to help us. We cannot succeed alone."

"What is it you are doing?"

"We must overthrow the false king."

"False king?"

"Lord Cirvel is not a rightful ruler. He came to this land and took Gohaldinest by force of his magic. He has scattered the people on this continent all over and keeps them scared. He hunts across the dimensions without caring for the ramifications to the Onesong. His Necroathelings are stealing magic from other realms and cutting them off from the Wells. Worlds will die. He must be stopped."

"You believe I'm the one to help you in taking down the Lord of Gohaldinest?" He didn't wait for her to answer. Instead, he continued on. "I just want to go home. I was far away from Gohaldinest and safe."

"Safe?" she asked. "You were watched by Cirvel and the gargaxes, where if a tribe's magic becomes to significant it is culled. You call that 'safe'? Even if you were to go home in the growing season and rebuild your life, you know too much. You will always be looking over your shoulder. You will never feel secure again, especially with the Necroathelings knowing of your existence. As far as Cirvel is concerned, he is fattening you up with magic to feed his Necroathelings on later. You are a pig going to the slaughter."

Her words sent a terrible chill through him. He'd always known there was more to his bargain with Cirvel, but he'd never thought about how his own education and growth in magic could be beneficial to Cirvel. Now that the words were out, he admitted that she made perfect sense.

"I can give you the secrets of the Onesong, all of them, quickly and easily," she said in a tone so softly he wasn't even sure he heard her or if he believed it. Nothing was simple like that.

"How?" he asked. Was it possible? Would it even work considering his connection to the Humline had been broken by the Necroathelings?

"That is something you will have to experience. But you should be warned that the knowledge will make you powerful. Alityka says you are timid with your magic, afraid to experience it. If you accept the secrets of the Onesong, you must realize that you will no longer fear your life. You will be noticed and stand out. Even Cirvel will be inexplicably drawn to you, but you will be able to hold your own against all challengers, even the Necroathelings."

For a moment, Rivic couldn't even find the words to speak. He hated bargains where he couldn't identify the cost and here was another one being set before him. Cirvel's proposal to stay and train had been the first. "Have you offered this to Alityka?"

"There is no need. She came to the Onesong by her own route."

Rivic felt his lips tighten. If he could have only asked Alityka about her experience. If he could speak to his sister and see what her strange vision would tell him. "Can I think on this?"

"While I have the time to give you, I'm not certain you have the time."

"What does that mean?"

Lihn folded her hands in her lap and glanced down at them. She had such a beautiful round face that Rivic wanted to put his hands around it. She smiled, her eyes filled with a strange knowing and it reminded Rivic of way his sister looked at him with her new, abnormal eyes. "I fear coming events may push things too fast and we will be separated rather than having another chance to come together like this again."

"You can see the future?"

"Immediate events are always clearer than those which are distant, but anyone who observes people can surmise pretty much the same thing."

"So, what will I choose to do?" he asked.

"Same as you always have: to do what is best for your sister."

"Keen observation," he remarked dryly.

"Spells aren't the only way to predict the magic of the universe."

For but a moment, Rivic saw a flash of something in her face. He wasn't sure what it was but it seemed like she saw a bigger picture than most people saw. "Who are you?"

She raised her head and tilted it slightly. "A child of destiny."

Chills swept down his arms. Her certainty in knowing who and what she was blew past every conceived notion he'd ever held of himself.

"That's right," she said. "You are one too."

Rivic slapped his knees as he stood up. "I don't want to be. I just want to have a nice, quiet life." He held his hands out in front of him as though he could catch the air and strangle it. He had no need to save the world or even to change it? It was perfect just the way it was and only got messed up when someone got grandiose ideas. The dragon had been wrong about him; no champion resided within him.

But a little part called out, wondering if he were to do nothing, would his inaction be as destructive as his magic?

Rivic swallowed the question, burying it so deeply inside him that he hoped it never came up again.

Fighting to control his breathing, he walked back the way he'd entered the room. He had no door to go through and a panic swept over him. "I need to think. How do I leave?"

"Vochey," she said.

The column opened up on the wall.

"Some doorways close and lock behind you," she said. "Don't block off all your routes."

In the silver mist, Rivic found his destination: the tower in Gohaldinest. He hesitated, and then touched it. The next moment he was back home.

CHAPTER 16

*R*ivic got up and dressed the next morning before any of the acolytes woke. He ran out of the dormitory and hurried to the kitchens to cook breakfast, finding himself there before any of the other acolytes on this rotation, but still later than some of the castle's regular cooks. Since helping out with the cooking rotation meant he got to eat in the kitchen, he didn't have to face Alityka. All night he'd been wondering what she'd told Lihn about him. He regretted telling her so readily about his past.

Once he saw Alityka finish breakfast and leave the hall, he went in the opposite direction than the way he knew she'd be going. He hurried toward Nyree's wing of the castle and knocked on her door hoping it wasn't too early to see her.

A man in a dark purple robe answered the door. "Aye?" the Necroatheling asked.

"Nyree?" Her name choked in his throat.

"In here, Rivic," he heard Nyree call from within.

Rivic squeezed by the Necroatheling into the room. Nyree was sitting in her nightclothes on the couch by the fireplace. A silver plate piled with fruit, cheese, and bread was in her hands.

"'Tis good to see you." She waved Rivic over. Then, to the Necroatheling, she continued, "I will see you tomorrow, Kalt. My brother hasn't been by in several days and I'm excited to speak with him."

Rivic watched the Necroatheling to see if he'd notice the switch in Nyree's voice, or had Rivic been the only one to notice it. She was testing the Necroatheling, but why? What did Nyree know? He couldn't help but feel some resentment at knowing if he still had his connection to the Onesong he'd be fully aware of what his sister already perceived.

The Necroatheling bowed. "Very well."

As the Necroatheling closed the door behind him, Rivic turned to his sister. "What are you doing talking to a Necroatheling in your nightclothes? And when did a Necroatheling give you his name? They don't have names!"

Nyree laughed. "Of course they do. His name is Kalt. He brings me breakfast every morning."

"He's a Necroatheling! If nothing else, you should be addressing him as Kalt-na and not in the familiar."

Nyree shook her head and laughed again. "You're acting like he's not human."

"He's not, Nyree. He's traded his soul for magic and power."

"I know. You won't understand my reasonings for needing to befriend Kalt, so 'tis best we don't even speak of it." Nyree held out her plate to offer him something from it.

The thought of befriending a Necroatheling made his stomach churn and he held up a hand to refuse. Instead, he reached out, took the dish from her, and slid it across the table.

"What's gotten into you?" she asked, staring between him and the plate.

Rivic rubbed his face. "I'm tired. I haven't slept well in days and I don't like being here. I feel… caged." He sat down in a wooden chair with paddings on the seat and back, yet still looked uncomfortable enough to not let him enjoy any of the luxuries of the room.

"'Tis a beautiful city. You should enjoy it."

"I can't. I'm too busy training."

"But you're here today." She got up from the sofa and moved toward a standing wardrobe over near the bed. "I'll get dressed and we'll go walk around the city. I'll show you all the wonders I've found here."

"I don't like the idea of you going out unescorted."

"I haven't been." As soon as she said the words, she popped her hands over her mouth.

"Kalt-na was with you," Rivic said, his tone weary.

"Rivic, please," she said dashing across the room to him. She dropped to the floor before him in the chair and placed her hands on his closest knee. "He's a nice man. You should get to know him."

"We're not here to make friends. You will have to leave all of them behind when we finally depart here."

Nyree issued a disgruntled breath as she got up and walked to the wardrobe. Throwing the double doors open, she disappeared behind them. "What if I don't want to leave? I like it here. I like the city. I don't want to go back to the forest."

He heard it in her words: she thought the streets of Gohaldinest were paved with gold. This was her adventure. Of course she didn't want to return to the tribe. Here, she lived in luxury. Rivic fought against telling her that all the extravagances surrounding her were actually Cirvel's and he could remove them in an instant, but Rivic couldn't trouble her with that knowledge. Let her enjoy what she had for the moment.

"Get dressed," he said. "Then you can show me what you love so much about the city." Maybe it would give him some small measure of reassurance that he'd made the right decision in agreeing to stay.

They spent the morning in Gohaldinest, which was a much bigger city than he'd seen when he'd been making his way through the narrow back streets with Dragzel. He realized that the cramped quarters from the gate were to keep invaders from making it this deep into Gohaldinest. Anyone thinking to make battle within the city's center would have to leave horses and equipment behind. Then they would be lost to the maze of buildings, allowing Gohaldinest's forces to take invaders down one by one. Even teleporting into the city would be dangerous in the tight outer walls, not to mention the enchantments which prevented most outside magicks from getting in. A war to overthrow Gohaldinest would have to come from inside.

Nyree smiled at Rivic and he wondered how much of that was from her sensing his realization about the defensive structure of Gohaldinest. Or was it because she was merely glad to be with him?

The day had a slight chill to the air, but not enough that Rivic ever felt cold. Though the high towers of the castle were visible, tall walls lined the streets and he had to look nearly straight up to see the blue sky.

Without really paying attention to where they were going, he found himself in front of a shop with a large glass window.

Nyree pulled on his arm. "Look, Rivic, a tea shop. Let's stop and have something to eat."

The words *Orcee's Supreme* arched over the final word *Tea*. It seemed that Madame Orcee's ego might very well rival Lord Cirvel's. The surrounding businesses here had only small windows and some even covered with bars as if afraid that the gargaxes would riot and toss rocks through the glass.

"I don't have any money," he confessed to Nyree.

Her eyes lit up. "I do. Kalt gave me some tokens so I could buy something for myself."

"The Necroatheling?" he asked, coming to a complete stop in the street as she continued to tug on his arm as she directed him to the shop. "Why would he give you money?"

"'Tis more to the Necroathelings than just the stories told about them," she grinned. "Kalt is a nice guy, very smart too. You'd like him if you got to know him."

A ripple went through Rivic, a thread of apprehension over Nyree's words. He doubted very much that he'd ever be friends with Kalt-na.

"Come on," she said, dragging on his arm once more. "Having lunch with you will make me happy, which is what both you and Kalt want. So, let's do it."

Rivic allowed Nyree to haul him into the tea shop. It smelled of earthy leaves and spices, along with the scent of a tallow candle burning. The odd sensation he'd had only a moment ago over Kalt-na now circled his chest with strangling tightness. He shouldn't be here.

That wasn't quite right: Nyree shouldn't be here.

For a second time, he stopped and the abruptness yanked Nyree backwards. "Let's go," he whispered to her.

"But we –"

Nyree's protests were cut short as an elderly woman with gray hair pulled back into a bun came from behind a curtain and called out to them in welcome.

"Blessings, acolyte," she said as her eyes roamed over his clothes. "Strayed a bit far today, haven't you?"

Rivic felt his mouth go dry. "My sister and I came out for lunch in the city."

"I see. A bit early for lunch, but that can be accommodated. Please sit."

Nyree dropped down into a chair at one of the small tables while Rivic stood behind her watching the woman as she went back behind her counter.

"I take it that you'll both be having tea?" she asked.

"We will," Nyree answered quickly. "Are you Madame Orcee?" She glanced up at Rivic, then shot her gaze to the chair, silently indicating that she wanted him to sit down.

Rivic slid into the seat and leaned over the table. "You knew about this place? You wanted to come here, didn't you?"

Nyree shrugged, along with a half-smile. She reached across and put her hands on Rivic's. "Please?"

Rivic withdrew his hands from her warm touch, leaned back in his chair, and folded his arms across his chest.

The woman came over to the table with a small silver tray, along with two cups and a pot that looked similar to the genie lamps in Cirvel's reading room. "I am Madame Orcee."

Nyree appeared even more pleased.

"But I don't suspect you needed to come see me, now did you, child?" Orcee asked with a light touch on Nyree's shoulder after setting the tray down on the table. "Nor does your brother need my gift, not right now at least with your own sight."

Rivic knew they had come for a reason: Nyree had brought them here.

"Show me," Orcee requested.

Nyree didn't even blink and her eyes changed. One moment they were blue, the next they were black with the yellow torch.

"Beautiful." Orcee slid a chair over and sat down at the table, never looking away from Nyree and completely heedless of Rivic. "I can see why they are enchanted. Tell me what you see."

Nyree's immediate expression of delight gave way to fear. She glanced around the shop. "I see it all burned. I see it dark. Wait, there is a light. She comes."

"Who?"

"I can't see her face, but her magic... I can feel her magic." Nyree looked to Rivic. "She's a temptest. For cycles she has been here. She's been waiting for her dark lord to rise again."

"Interesting," Orcee said. "What else?"

Rivic reached across the table to Nyree as he felt an odd, rippled, buzz go through him. It lasted in his foot the longest, a vibration that felt wrong. "Nyree, stop."

Orcee lightly smacked his hand twice in rapid succession. "Leave her alone. Let the vision be. You should know by now not to interrupt."

A sensation rose near the surface of his emotions and moved dangerously through him. Rivic wanted to stand up and slash her with his claws. His gaze held on her fingers as they slid off his skin after her second tap. Hearing Orcee's heartbeat quicken, Rivic glanced up. She watched him with a look mixed of pure delight and distress. Not only was Orcee's discomfort a success for Nyree, but for him as well. What did she want to discover about him?

Nyree leaned forward to gain Rivic's attention. "The Lord of Gohaldinest has asked her to find out why he finds you so intriguing. She has told him that it is because he is afraid to see a reflection of himself in you."

Nyree's words seemed to startle Orcee, who moved towards Rivic very slightly.

"And now she is afraid that I am a reflection of her," Nyree said with a smile.

"I think your brother is right," Orcee said. "That is quite enough."

Nyree blinked, her normal eyes returning. "Enough of the demonstration for you?"

Rivic found himself shocked by Nyree's sharpness. He wasn't accustomed to her being rude. What had happened to her since they had reached Gohaldinest? In every visit, she had seemed just a little more different. He barely recognized her. He wondered if this was an effect of her coming out of her visions. Rivic leaned close to Nyree and whispered, "Can we be going now?"

Nyree stared at Orcee. "Not until we've had our lunch. Wouldn't you like something to drink? I do believe you should try her tea."

Orcee smiled. "Aye, by all means, you should have a drink." She picked up a spoon and stirred the tea. Then she handed the cup to him. "Drink."

He accepted the warm teacup in his hands, enjoying the feel of the heat on his fingers. The orange scent tingled at his nose as he brought it closer to his face. He took a sip, finding the liquid pleasantly sweet.

"Hold the cup there," she said as she reached up.

"Why?" he asked, lowering the cup away from his lips.

She looked disappointed. "I said to hold it. You have to be drinking the tea while I do this." Even though she snapped her answer, it seemed as if she'd repeated these words a few hundred times or two.

"All right," he said, beginning to drink once more.

She touched the bottom of the glass and he felt a slight pressure. "Orcee ockree." Whipping around, she flung her arm toward the wall as if flicking something off her fingers. What appeared like enlarged black tea leaves splattered like rain on the white wall. They shifted, as if they were sliding down the polished surface, except that some flowed in an upward direction.

Rivic lowered his cup and looked down into it. The

browned water wasn't completely clear, but he could tell there were no tea leaves remaining within his cup. "What is this? Some sort of elaborate tea leaf reading?"

At seeing Orcee paying close attention to the markings, Rivic glanced to Nyree, who seemed to be watching as well. When she noticed Rivic looking at her, she gave him a smile back.

"Clever, clever, that your true power be hidden. How did you accomplish that, boy?" Orcee continued to watch the smear as she rose from her chair and moved toward the wall. A spell came off her fingers and the image of the leaves quaked a little and scurried apart. "Shadows creep around you," she said.

Already he was not impressed with her abilities. He was certain that shadows crept around most people coming in here hoping for answers.

"Come on, Nyree. Let's get going. There's nothing for us here," he said to his sister, who continued to watch Orcee as the shopkeeper moved around behind the counter to take a closer look at the wall. He felt so removed, as if he were viewing a contest between these two women as one might read an imaginary tale. Didn't Nyree understand that there was nothing to be gained here? Whatever power Nyree had to see the future, Orcee's abilities paled in comparison, especially considering that the shopkeeper had to use magic to alter or interpret them.

"Aye, shadows move around you." Orcee leaned forward on the counter over her elbows. "'Tis whatever you want to make it out to be. If 'tis fiction you want, then that 'tis all you will see. But, if you seek meaning in the greater truth, the leaves can point that out to you as well." She jerked her thumb in the direction of the splatter on the wall. "You choose, acolyte."

"Give it a chance, will you?" Nyree whispered.

"Fine," he said, sitting back in the chair. "What do you see?"

"I see why our Lord is enchanted with you. So much is going on around you, as if you are a maelstrom on the verge of coming into being. All you need is one slight push and everything changes like a series of locks being turned to open the door. Why do you refuse to let it in?"

"I'm not resisting," Rivic said, but he looked to Nyree to see if his sister also caught the lie. He knew he restrained himself, not wanting to touch completely upon the power inside him. He'd destroyed enough lives already. If he didn't keep that power so firmly in check and secured behind the locked door Orcee referenced, who knew what would happen. Was he capable of bringing down all of Gohaldinest?

Orcee began working behind the counter, but she paused to let herself point momentarily at the wall. "The leaves do not lie to me. What it tells me about you is that you are bound to a moment in your past, one you must overcome. How terrible of a nudge must you receive to learn that the abilities you have been given are not ones that can be fortified behind willpower alone?"

"What are you saying?" Nyree asked, her voice low and fearful.

"I'm saying that even you do not see the true nature of your brother." Orcee paused for a moment, then she came out from behind the counter carrying two plates loaded with meats, cheese, fruit, and a slice of bread. She brought them to the table and set them down. "He has been obscured by a powerful force, like a shell that cannot be cracked. Only he can emerge from within that egg."

Orcee raised her hand as if she were wiping away the smear on the wall and it vanished even though she was still by their table. "I'm not sure either one of us wants to be nearby when he does. The results might be blinding." She started to walk back toward the counter. "Whatever force it takes to crack that egg, will be painful indeed."

CHAPTER 17

*R*ivic and Nyree returned to the castle just after midday. Having missed his lunchtime shift, he hoped that no one had noticed his absence, but wasn't willing to take the risk a second time for evening meal.

Still feeling apprehensive about the meeting with Madame Orcee, Rivic couldn't bring himself to ask Nyree if she believed any of the tea reading. They were in Gohaldinest and he was receiving training for his magic, so there was nothing more to fear.

Right?

They arrived back at Nyree's chambers. Nyree took Rivic's hands in hers. "Thank you for spending the day with me. These memories mean so much to me. I will hang onto them for a long time."

That sensation of Nyree's words being more than what she spoke came to Rivic just as it had when she'd been speaking to Kalt earlier this morning. "What aren't you telling me?"

She reached in and hugged him. "Nothing," she lied. "I told you that Gohaldinest would change our lives, and that we needed to be here. Trust this path and keep walking, even when it gets dark."

"Nyree, what's going to happen?"

"I don't know. Certain aspects of this sight have been withheld from me. I only see that it involves you and Kalt, and that it was so important for me to get to know the Necroatheling. What comes to pass must happen to fortify you to defeat Cirvel. 'Tis nothing that you can't handle. I hope Kalt proves to be an ally." Nyree stepped back and released him. "You should go now."

He wanted to press her for more, but was afraid that she'd turn to deceit to escape his questions. If she trusted he could handle what was coming, then he believed her. He smiled once more before he hurried down to the hall to begin preparation of the evening meal.

After dinner, he headed back to the dormitory feeling like he might actually be able to sleep well tonight.

"You were missed in classes today," Alityka said from her bed as Rivic entered. Her words carried a soft threat. There was no one else in the dormitory.

Rivic sensed that she cleared the others out so she could have this confrontation in private. "I spent the day with my sister."

"You shouldn't have done that. Missing class isn't good," she said, swinging her feet off the bed. "Neither is missing your chores."

"'Tis only one day. 'Twill be fine."

"Doesn't work like that. You can't just skip out on class and expect to make it up."

Rivic shrugged. "That's what the free days are for, right? To catch up? I'll do the work then."

"You are being reckless," Alityka said.

"'Twas a day off," Rivic protested loudly while raising his hands. "'Tis not like I broke any major laws."

Yet in light of Nyree's words, he wondered if there was more to it. He really ought to ask Alityka what punishment would come, but Nyree had already told him he could handle it. Walking in the fresh air all day had relaxed him and he needed the sleep he felt approaching.

Alityka's eyes filled with sorrow until she forced herself to look away from him and shake her head. "'Twill see if that's how you feel about it tomorrow night." She exhaled an exasperated breath, and then changed the subject. "Lihn says she spoke to you."

"We did. I haven't come to a decision yet, if that's what you're wondering."

"Nay, you haven't. You're going to stall that too, run away from it like class today, and hope that nothing bad comes as a result."

"I'm tired. I'm going to bed." He pulled back the blanket and crawled beneath it.

"My lady Lihn was too nice to you."

Rivic yawned and nestled down against his flat pillow. "I'm sure she was."

"She doesn't know you like I do. You told me what you are."

"So? I don't know how any of that factors into my decision." He hated her questioning him and, thinking of the blue stone in his pouch, he suddenly didn't want Alityka to be Ellonia's sister. Bitterness rose through him. He'd done nothing wrong except spending the day with his twin. Maybe Alityka admonished him because she was jealous.

"Aye, you do know your choices matter. You only need to touch the Onesong to know the truth of it."

He scoffed. "Which is? What is the truth?"

"You are already a murderer," she said.

His chest tightened and he bolted upright in bed. How dare she use his past against him? "I don't want to be that person. I was too young to control the magic and there was not anyone around me who could help me. I didn't mean to do it," he blurted.

"Aye, you were young, in both instances, yet you have let them haunt you for cycles. Do you think you can hide away behind a nice, quiet life from this emotional demon that plagues you? 'Twill always remain until you accept what you have done, quiet life or not."

"It does plague me. 'Tis why I really don't want to be around anyone else. I don't want to lose myself to the magic again. 'Tis given me a great deal of pain. I worry that I won't always be able to control my magic. But the answer is with me, not the Onesong. I have to control the power. 'Tis my fate and I say I am better off doing it on my own and being alone."

"Really? You know better how to handle this than the universe? You have a gift," she said. "Your magic, in being a twin, is a special thing. It might have gone to your sister just as easily as it came to you, but you were chosen by the Onesong, not Nyree. If I were you, I'd want to know why the Onesong chose me."

Rivic dropped back against the mattress and pulled the blanket up around him. "Well, I don't want to know," he insisted. Much like he didn't want to know if Alityka was Ellonia's sister.

The sound of stomping footsteps on the stairs intensified as the dormitory door opened. "Can we come in now? We're tired," a girl asked.

"Aye, come on in. We're done here," Alityka responded.

The room filled with acolytes and chatter, noise which dwindled in slow time, giving way to the sound of sleep all around him before Rivic himself found peace behind his closed eyes.

A Necroatheling dumped Rivic out of bed. "Get up."

Rivic jumped at the sound and fought to shove off the soft mattress folding around him. He figured everyone in the dormitory had been awoken, but no one else moved. It felt like only moments since Rivic had fallen asleep, but the orange-pink light tinting the window revealed it was just before sunrise the next morning.

"Pick up the mat and get your bed made," the Necroatheling yelled.

Still, no one moved in their sleep as if the rest of the dormitory heard nothing.

"I said—"

"I heard you," Rivic said, grabbing the mattress and putting it back on the shallow wooden frame. After he had it done, the Necroatheling flipped it again. The mattress hit Rivic and knocked him backwards into an invisible wall. He realized that the Necroatheling had put them into a magically created bubble.

"Get it made!"

Rivic slammed the mattress down again and flipped the blanket over it. He quickly leaned in and said, "Palixa jotal." The bed transformed into a chair.

The Necroatheling smiled beneath the deep hood of his cloak. "You do learn quickly, acolyte. Bored with your classes yesterday? 'Tis that why you skipped class?"

"Sure," Rivic answered flippantly. "I'm only here for the season. What does it matter to you if I attend or not?"

"Because of you," the Necroatheling said as he lowered his hood, "I don't get to have breakfast with your sister today."

"Kalt-na?"

"Aye, and I was the last one to see your sorry butt, so I get to give it a workout. I really wish you hadn't skipped class." Kalt raised his hand toward the chair. "Cazidor."

The chair burst into flames and filled their bubble with smoke.

"Radin lukion," Rivic coughed.

The bubble and the fire stopped, but smoke remained in the air.

Kalt grabbed Rivic, the Necroatheling's hand around the back of his neck. "Talcor dun."

Rivic found himself outside on one the crenellated walls of a tower. He couldn't identify which one and he didn't exactly want to look down.

"You know what you missed yesterday," the Necroatheling asked, still bracing Rivic. "A lesson on how to fly."

Kalt shoved him. Rivic twisted as he toppled and began to fall. He tried to grab the Necroatheling's arm as he tumbled backwards, but he couldn't get a hold. His fingers held memory of skimming Kalt's soft, thick robe and the flesh beneath as he fell away.

"What? Don't you have any spells now, acolyte?"

He heard the taunt, but his own mind was too busy racing through all the spells he knew and not a single one to stop his plummet.

Wait.

"Talcor dun," he shouted. He reappeared in the dormitory. Let the Necroatheling find him now!

Rivic felt a tap on his shoulder. As he started to turn, Kalt picked him up. "Predictable," the Necroatheling said as he lifted Rivic over his head. "Try this on for size. Makal cho'-darenscia."

The Necroatheling threw Rivic at the dormitory wall. Rivic expected to smash hard into it. Instead, when he felt cold air on his bare feet, he realized he was outside and descending fast.

There was a movement above him. The Necroatheling dove after him.

Was Kalt crazy?

The purple robe snapped at the ends as Kalt chased in him in a rush toward the ground. "Shi'baten to'a helcord," the Necroatheling shouted.

The blast pushed Rivic faster. He was going to die. Right here. Now.

"Talcor dun," Rivic said again. He landed in the alleyway outside the dormitory tower, wobbling on his unsteady feet.

The Necroatheling appeared in front of Rivic. "Shi'baten to'a helcord."

Rivic blew backwards into a stone wall. Senseless, he dropped to the gravel.

"Shi'baten to'a helcord."

Rivic's body slammed against the stone wall for the second time. He felt a couple of ribs break. Grit from the stone sifted down over him. Kalt raised his hand and Rivic's body lifted up, scraping over the wall.

Holding him there, Kalt brought back his other hand. "Do I push you again, acolyte, or are you going to fight back?"

"I don't know how?" Rivic responded, his mouth feeling swollen.

"Porta'mentay totalitis." Lowering his hands, Kalt walked up to Rivic. "Isn't that why you were supposed to be in class yesterday?"

"I have no interest in fighting back. I don't want to hurt anyone."

"People get hurt all the time. You either let them walk all over you or you fight back."

"I don't know how to."

"Then you are weak and not worthy of being a Necroatheling."

Anger flooded through Rivic as he strained against the invisible bonds holding him against the stone wall. "I don't want to become a Necroatheling." Wasn't that the path

Nyree's foreboding words always alluded to? Wasn't that exactly what he had to do?

"Then why are you wasting our time?" Kalt shouted back at him with an equal amount of venom. The Necroatheling took several steps back, then picked up a couple rocks. He physically threw them at Rivic. "Defend yourself."

The rock smacked Rivic in the cheek. He felt a cut open and warm blood drip down his jaw. Kalt hurdled a second rock, which hit Rivic's stomach. "Miex'balish," Rivic said before the third rock hit him. Instead, the stone bounced off the shield spell.

"At least you can defend yourself somewhat once you finally decide to," Kalt said. "But what good does that do for the people around you?" He began to pace back and forth in front of Rivic. "I could go get Nyree right now and have my way with her right here, and you wouldn't be able to do a thing."

"Don't." Rivic felt teeth and claws pressing beneath the surface as his senses heightened. He smelled the musky soap Kalt had washed with this morning as if it were an abrasion on his own skin. He struggled, knowing that he mustn't let his aspects take over yet. This might be a test, a way of Cirvel pushing him to discover Rivic's true power. He had to keep concealing them until that moment when he could combat Cirvel face to face. The time wasn't yet right.

"Then fight me. Stop me. Keep me from getting her."

Anger changed to fear. Rivic knew the Necroatheling's words were all too true. The thought of Nyree in Kalt's hands, even more defenseless without exception against the Necroatheling's magic, wiped logical thought from his mind. At least Rivic knew he could evade some of Kalt's spells, but Nyree had no protections. If he pretended to be as weak as Kalt thought, maybe Kalt would release him. "I can't."

"Nay, you're too afraid." Kalt got right up in his face and growled, "Break free."

"I can't."

"You must." Kalt's voice quivered, but Rivic found no cause for it.

"I can't," Rivic repeated, his voice flat with desperation.

Kalt's eyes glared at Rivic with forceful anger. "Talcor dun."

As the Necroatheling vanished, Rivic realized his opportunity. "Radin lukion."

The spell didn't shatter. He remained hanging where he was. Rivic repeated the words to dispel the magic, but he didn't drop to the ground. He steeled himself with a deep, steadying breath and closed his eyes. "Nah'landa rekshant ali'tarsa," Rivic spoke, his voice deep. He stayed firm against the wall. That should have worked. What made the Necroatheling's magic so much stronger than his, and even mightier than his dragon magic?

Kalt appeared a moment later with Nyree by the arm. She looked sleepy-eyed and fearfully confused, as though Kalt had pulled her right out of bed.

"Rivic?" she asked. But as she tried to go to him, Kalt hauled her around and brought his mouth down hard on hers. He grabbed at her nightshirt and yanked it up around her waist.

"Nay!" Rivic screamed. He fought against the Necroatheling's magic holding him fast to the wall, but he couldn't break free. He struggled to release the dragon within him. It wouldn't come.

"Stop me!" Kalt-na shouted.

"Rivic," Nyree shrieked as Kalt lifted her up and pressed her back against the wall just a short distance away. "Rivic!" Her voice broke.

As if it were happening to him, Rivic felt Kalt push

himself into Nyree. She squealed. There was pain. Rivic wanted to wither, but the Necroatheling's magic wouldn't let him move. He tried to close his eyes or look away, but he could do neither with the spell holding him. He watched helpless as the Necroatheling shoved into her again and again, seeing only the steady sway of the dark purple cloak, but feeling the thrusts over and over. The world seemed to slow down. Her tears flowed hot down her cheeks, and Rivic felt each one fall from her face.

At last, the Necroatheling dropped Nyree to the ground and turned toward Rivic. "That's what happens when an acolyte skips class; their worst fears are realized. Don't do it again."

The magic securing Rivic against the wall unshackled and he slid down as Kalt walked away. Rivic grabbed a rock and threw it toward the Necroatheling, but by the time it reached where Kalt had been, he had vanished. Rivic scrambled across the gravel to Nyree and tried to take her in his arms.

She screamed and shoved him away. "Don't try to make this better," she yelled at him with tears streaking down her cheeks.

"Let me take you back to your room," Rivic said.

Nyree slapped at him a couple of times in frail defense, then used the wall to stand up. "I don't want you around me right now." She hobbled along the wall for a moment, then limped barefoot down the alleyway. "I knew this was a possible outcome. I didn't know it would be because of you."

He wanted to remind her that she had pressed him to visit the city with her, but it was better to let the blame fall on himself. After all, he had been the one to skip class and he hadn't been strong enough to stop Kalt. That was enough.

Rivic watched her limp along using the building for support until she reached the street. Then she turned around the corner and disappeared from his sight without ever looking back. He put his hands on the castle wall, struck the gray stone a couple times with the side of his closed fist, and then vomited against the building, making his chest throb even more.

With all his might, Rivic hated Gohaldinest.

CHAPTER 18

*T*he sickness inside Rivic wouldn't leave. He had no bed to sleep on in the dormitory, so he sat back against the wall with his knees up to his chest. He didn't know what to do next, but he wanted revenge. Vengeance against a Necroatheling seemed like a death sentence, even with his added protections and magic. How was he to fight a Necroatheling?

A girl with mousy brown hair knelt beside him to hand him a moist cloth. Several others scuttled along making a wide berth as they headed for their beds. "Your face is badly bruised. This will help soothe it," she said. "You should probably still go see the apothecary."

Rivic mildly nodded. That was all he could manage to acknowledge her kindness. He cast his gaze away from her and waited until she stood up and followed the others to get ready for bed.

His heart hurt, but he wasn't sure how much of that was actually the cracked ribs. Rivic just couldn't bring himself to get medical help. His body would heal. His memories, his relationship with Nyree, those were things that couldn't be repaired. Nothing could ever undo Nyree's violation.

Alityka entered the dormitory and took up a spot of floor beside Rivic. "She's refusing all visitors. I'm sorry I couldn't talk to her for you."

Rivic stared across the room with dull realization that it was only a third of the way full. More acolytes would return, each one glancing at him with empathetic sorrow at his shame. He wasn't certain how much more he could take.

That wasn't true. His emotions were numb. He hadn't felt this void since breaking free from the dragon pearl and realizing his life prior to that moment had been a dream. He wondered how he'd ever fill it again, if he'd ever feel whole. "Thank you for trying."

"What are you going to do now?" she asked him.

"Sit here. I don't want to move." His words held some truth. He hurt all over, but he knew if he had an outlet for his rage right now, he'd take it no matter how much pain he endured. "I did my chore rotation and attended class. I paid my price and served as warning to the others. The Necroathelings will leave me alone now, right?"

Alityka reached out and gently laid her hand on his arm, but she didn't give him a direct answer. "Oren's bed is still open."

Rivic thought about the boastful boy who had been pulled out by the Necroathelings. Oren had never reappeared, and rumors were that he'd failed the tests and died. He'd had an easy escape. "I'll stay here."

Alityka got up and pulled the blanket off Oren's bed. "At least cover up. That floor is cold."

Not as cold as he felt inside. He closed his eyes, ignoring Alityka as she threw the blanket over him. He felt her kneel down beside him. "I am really sorry," she said.

"You tried to warn me that something bad would happen."

"I never thought they would do that though." Her voice was barely more than a whisper. "I know how much you are hurting, but please don't try your hand at revenge."

Rivic doubted that she could see him casting his gaze away in the darkness of the shadows where he sat. "I won't go after the Necroatheling." Not yet at least, but he wasn't going to admit that to Alityka.

More acolytes returning from chores and studying came into the dormitory. He heard the whispers start as soon as they saw him sitting on the floor.

"All right, everyone. Time to get to bed." Alityka stood up. "No chit-chat tonight."

Soon after Alityka's issued command, the lights went out and all fell quiet. Rivic waited as the sounds of breathing throughout the room deepened. It brought him no comfort. He suspected it would be a long time before anything ever did again.

After several more moments, Rivic got up and left the room.

He crossed over the courtyard to the tower and went inside. He really didn't care if Lord Cirvel was there or not. At the stairs, the second step lit up as he placed his foot on the first.

Those who know shall show their reverence.

Rivic knelt before the image of Lord Cirvel as it appeared. This time, it didn't even speak the spell; it just faded out. Something inside Rivic had distorted. Aye, he would bow. The Lord of Gohaldinest had power and Rivic now wanted to rival that. He wanted to destroy them all. That indeed was a change.

He tried to remind himself that he was here to defeat Cirvel. The dragon had ordered that as his mission here. Yet to get to Cirvel, he would have to learn to defeat a few Necroathelings along the way. Why not start with Kalt?

The second test lit up about halfway up the staircase. *Too many to speak, too many to name, but all with equal opportunities.*

"Spells," Rivic said flatly. That had been Kalt's main lesson to him today. When you knew the magic, the playing field levelled. But if you didn't have the spells, your side was weak.

Why not strike back at Cirvel too, because Kalt only did what the Lord of Gohaldinest instructed him? Rivic just had to prove that he could be as ruthless as they were. He had to match their power, exceed their abilities, and finally annihilate them. A simple three step plan.

He proceeded cautiously, waiting for the spray of steam that never came, nor did the stairs turn into a chute.

Near the top, a third test began. *This is the only thing you have of value to give.*

It was the one thing he still might have. "My soul."

Rivic reached the top. "Vocha chia cada'dada." The silver column came down. "Vochey." All the pictures lit up inside and Rivic picked the one to Lihn's secret room.

He entered to darkness. "Laza'pre ren," he said, creating a small ball of light in the room which cast enough to see Lihn sound asleep in bed.

Anger gripped him hard as he stalked over to her. Nothing about her soft breathing indicated that he'd awaken her. He wondered how Lord Cirvel would react to find out that his precious Lady Lihn had been violated. How much wrath could the Lord of Gohaldinest bring down upon Rivic's head that he didn't already feel? Would Cirvel even care what had happened to Lihn or would he just cast her out as broken? Did Rivic even care?

Nay, the Lord of Gohaldinest would know that he couldn't tamper with the feelings of his acolytes. Retaliation must be made.

He slid his feet slightly apart as he curled his hands into tight fists at his side. Tears stung in his eyes. He had come this far. He would rape Lihn. Aye, he might as well admit the word. Rape.

Dragzel, sleeping on a pillow beside Lihn's head, opened his eyes. "Rivic?"

"Cahaster, I suggest you get out."

Dragzel moved carefully on the bed so as to not waken Lihn. "We've heard about Nyree. I won't let you hurt my mistress as a means of revenge."

"I just wanted to be left alone, to live in peace, and your people couldn't let me have that," Rivic raged. He reached for the blankets covering Lihn.

Dragzel hissed as he jumped across Lihn, now waking her up. Rivic drew his arm away fast from the cahaster's sharp teeth.

"Rivic?" She blinked the sleep from her eyes. "What are you doing here?"

"I've solved the tower," he said, dropping his head to his chest. Summing up all the angry energy he could, he snarled, "I can come up here any time I want." He felt tears stinging in his eyes and as he fought it, his mouth pulled uncomfortably in trying to speak clearly and without the overwhelming emotions.

Lihn tried to smile, though she clutched the bed sheets up to her throat. "I wish I could say I was glad, but you're scaring me. Why are you here tonight?"

"Vengeance."

Lihn shifted to get off her side and sit up a bit more. "About Nyree –"

"What about her?" he screamed. He started to reach to pull her from her bed, but Dragzel jumped at him. "Royka piryeian."

Vines sprang from the stone floor to tangle around the cahaster.

Rivic grabbed Lihn and pulled her up. "You knew something bad was going to happen. Why didn't you tell me?"

Her bare feet slapped on the wood floor as she regained her balance. She held her hands up defensively between them as Rivic held her close. "I knew something bad was going to happen to you, but I didn't know the cause. If I had known, I would have warned you."

"My own powers failed me against the Necroatheling. You said you could make me powerful, potent enough to be recognized and stand out. Formidable and feared!"

"That should never be anyone's aspiration." Lihn shook her head hard while her eyes filled with tears.

"That's Cirvel's desire," he spat back. "How can I go against him if I don't have the same intentions? I have to be as commanding and as determined as he is."

Lihn's eyes widened as she gasped. Rivic noticed that she was staring over his shoulder. With an accompanying ripple of magic from behind him, he realized what had unexpectedly shocked her.

"One would think that your time among the tribe might have taught you that there is one thing I do not tolerate," Cirvel's calm voice came, "and that is anyone challenging me."

Lihn ducked her head, bowing toward Cirvel. "As I have been trying to explain, my lord."

Rivic turned, knowing that he should also bow, but the sight of another figure stepping from the shadows behind Cirvel froze him in place. Nyree. His breath caught. She wore a black dress which hung in layered waves of lace all the way to the floor.

"How did you get in here?" Cirvel asked.

Rivic opened his mouth to answer, but Lihn spoke first. "I brought him, my lord. I felt his anger and heard what had happened today. I knew he'd want revenge. I brought him here to try to talk him out of it."

"I'll deal with you later." Cirvel raised a hand, circling his fingers around in the air, and then he snapped.

Lihn evaporated from beside Rivic.

"Revenge on one of my Necroathelings?" Cirvel asked, but his question was directed at Nyree, while he kept his eyes on Rivic.

"I did warn you," Nyree spoke beside Cirvel.

"Aye, you did." The tone indicated the Lord of Gohaldinest was pleased with her.

Rivic saw that Nyree's eyes were black with the yellow slits. What else was she seeing?

Nyree made a soft murmur. "And your mistress lied about how he got here. Rivic's own anger did that."

"I know."

"Nyree?" Rivic asked, taking a small step toward her and reaching his hand out, but not quite able to close the distance between them.

"Let's take this to more comfortable quarters, shall we?" Cirvel asked.

The world spun beneath Rivic's feet and everything blurred. A wave of dizziness swept over him. He staggered, falling against the long table in the room where he'd first met Cirvel. One of the strange pots, the genie lamp as Cirvel had called it, rattled in the center of the table as Rivic bumped the wood.

"I'd ask you to take a seat, but I suspect you don't want to sit," Cirvel said.

Rivic rushed over to Nyree and grabbed her gloved hand to draw her near. "What's going on?"

Nyree dragged her lace-covered fingers from his grasp. "We must walk the paths, even in misfortune," she informed him harshly. She turned and walked back toward Cirvel. "The good Lord of Gohaldinest brought me justice."

Rivic felt revenge slip through his grasp. Once again, he had failed.

"Are you curious about what happened to Kalt?" Cirvel asked.

Rivic nodded, unable to help himself.

Cirvel pointed to the lamp on the table. Nyree stepped around and picked it up. The shine of the metal reflected a strange, distorted pattern of her black, lace gloves.

"He's trapped for as long as I please," she noted with a wry smile and cold harshness in her black eyes.

Cirvel took the lamp from her hands and turned to place it on one of the tables by the nearest door. "In the meanwhile, your sister has agreed to stay and be a seer for me. Isn't that great news, Rivic?"

"Nay," he choked on the word. He couldn't imagine Nyree ever agreeing to it. But she obviously wasn't the Nyree he knew. She had changed.

"Now, how about a seat so we can discuss what Nyree's latest vision has told me?" Cirvel sat, seeming to believe that Rivic would follow his lead. Nyree stood behind Cirvel, placing one hand atop the other on the curved back of the chair.

Rivic couldn't take his eyes off of Nyree, wishing he could have a moment to speak to her alone. There had to be more going on than he knew. What was her plan? Aye, he had failed her. But betrayal like this…? He just couldn't believe it.

"Nyree tells me that you have been going to see Lihn, that the two of you are making plans to overthrow me." Cirvel leaned forward and folded his hands together on top of the table. "Now, would you like to tell me how you got into the tower?"

"Nay."

Cirvel snorted. "But you do not deny conspiring or sneaking around, not even that you got yourself into the tower."

"Why are you doing this? What spell do you have on my sister?"

"Oh, she's here of her own free will," Cirvel assured him.

"'Tis true, Rivic," she echoed.

"She likes it in Gohaldinest. She even told you as much. You weren't listening to her, or realizing that she wishes for you to stay. So, I asked how best to get you to become one of my Necroathelings and she said it would take great anger to push you that far."

Had Nyree really turned against him? How much had she told Cirvel? Had she mentioned that Rivic had been given the power to destroy Cirvel? "Excuse me," Rivic said, raising a hand, "with your permission, I'd like to speak to my sister for a moment. After that, I will submit myself to your punishment for being in Lihn's tower." He dropped his head subserviently while not taking his gaze away from Cirvel.

The Lord of Gohaldinest gave a nonchalant wave of his hand. "As you wish. You want to hear it from your sister's lips. Go right ahead." Cirvel made no movement to leave.

Rivic stepped close to Nyree and whispered, "Miex'-calidori."

He waited, feeling the bubble go up around them. Then he stared down at Nyree. "I won't be fooled into thinking that we are completely unheard in this bubble, but I have to know: what are you doing and why?"

"Oh, brother, I told you to walk the path no matter how dark it got. I knew we would come to this."

Rivic searched around her for traces of magic. She didn't have any spells influencing her. That left him with one inescapable conclusion. "Are you really working with him?"

"I asked for justice. He gave it to me."

"But you didn't even come to me."

"'Twas part of the plan. You knew this. I told you. Why can you not accept that?"

"I want to talk to my sister," Rivic said, grabbing her upper arms and shaking her lightly. "Get out of the visions and come talk to me."

Nyree blinked and her eyes returned to normal. "I'm always here, but is that better?"

Rivic noticed her shiver, yet he still held firmly onto her. "Why didn't you come to me first?"

Nyree turned away, twisting out of his grasp and putting her back to him. "How could I?" She covered her face with her hands. "That was embarrassing. It's hard enough standing here with you now. I can't think about what you saw, and I certainly don't want to face you."

Rivic hadn't really thought about how she felt in regard to him having witnessed it. She shouldn't have had to consider him at all. "The punishment of watching was my burden, not yours. Don't carry that weight too." His voice cracked too many times and each time it felt like a strike to his soul. How many failures must he endure?

"How can I not?" she screamed at him. She continued to shriek.

Rivic slapped his hands over his head as Nyree crumpled to the carpet, curled over, and began to wail. He felt the magic bubble come down around them and realized too late that Cirvel had moved in. His arms around Nyree, Cirvel gently lifted her off the floor. While the actions were full of concern, his dark eyes held a smug, satisfied look.

"I think you need some time away from your sister," Cirvel said.

Nyree leaned against Cirvel, weeping.

"I know you've done something to her," Rivic accused. "Remove whatever spell you've put on her." He strove to keep the dragon voice from vibrating within his growl. He wanted to attack Cirvel now, but if he did, he would lose. There was no way Rivic could successfully stand against Cirvel alone, and he was truly abandoned now that Nyree had placed her trust in Cirvel.

"Come now, boy," Cirvel said. "Your sister has had a trying enough time without you slinging allegations at me. I must look after all my people."

"We're not your people."

Cirvel's look of displeasure quickly turned to anger. "Is that the way you would have this? I dare say you'd hate to see what I do to my enemies."

"I know what you do. You send your gargaxes and your Necroathelings out to terrorize them." Rivic took a bold step forward. "You don't even do your own dirty work yourself."

Cirvel settled Nyree down into a chair and moved closer to Rivic. "I think it's time we commence your punishment and give your sister a break from your presence." Cirvel snapped his fingers and a framed canvas appeared on an easel nearby.

The amount of magic oozing off the blank canvas tore through Rivic and he had to fight to remain calm. Part of him wanted to extend claws and rip the canvas to shreds. Instead, he took deep breaths and pushed the fighting magic down within him. He swallowed past the lump in his throat and raised his head. "What is that?" he dared to ask, knowing that he had to say something, and knowing the getting any information would be better than remaining ignorant about what he now faced.

"I think we shall make it your home for the next little bit." Cirvel reached out and slapped one hand on Rivic, the other he put on the painting. Rivic felt his energy transfer and without warning he realized that he was looking at Cirvel from behind the fabric of a painting.

"I shall keep you here until I am bored with you," Cirvel said, his voice sounding a little muffled. "Enjoy the sights you see while you are here. You may learn many interesting things."

Rivic tried to turn to see what was behind him but couldn't. It seemed as if he could stretch some, but other than that minimal shift he could not move; he was locked firmly in place. Speaking also proved difficult.

Cirvel looked pleased and his smiled deepened. After a short moment, Cirvel turned and returned to Nyree. He helped her dry her eyes, then assisted her to her feet. With an arm around her, he began to usher her from the room. Rivic strained against the canvas trying to see where they went, but he quickly lost sight of them.

A few of the lamps used for lighting the room darkened as their wicks burned short or the oil ran out.

After a bit, a couple lanky Domini in red armor came in, filled the lamps, and relit the wicks.

A long time later, Cirvel returned and walked through the room without a glance to the painting. The door to the bedchamber closed behind him.

A Necroatheling stepped into the room later and blew out the wicks.

Briefly, another Dominus came along and revived the lamps.

When Cirvel's chamber door opened again, pale morning light spilled into the salon. Cirvel walked in carrying a book in his hands, much as the time Rivic had first seen him. Cirvel looked startled at the painting as if he'd forgotten that it was there, then with a grin, he sat down at the table and returned to his reading.

A Necroatheling entered and stepped close to speak to Cirvel. Rivic couldn't hear what was being said, but Cirvel stopped reading long enough to gesture the Necroatheling's attention toward the painting. The Necroatheling's gaze widened, then he nodded to Cirvel and left.

A new fear rolled into Rivic's stomach. Certainly, this time in punishment didn't count toward missing his classes. It wasn't like he could attend while being cast into this prison. Could Cirvel do anything worse to Rivic than what had happened to Nyree or the claustrophobic feeling of being in this painting?

Over the next few days, Rivic did not feel tired, though he didn't blink, nor did he feel hungry. For the most part, he felt exactly as he had when he been put into the painting. That state did not change for him even as he watched time go by, which he marked by the refilling of the lamps, their extinguishing, and relighting.

Cirvel came and went from his chambers, occasionally stopping before the painting and giving a wave. Rivic wondered how long until Cirvel got weary of this game. But Cirvel never seemed to tire.

To worsen the matter, a Necroatheling came by one day and moved the painting. Carried by the string wired across the back, Rivic watched helplessly as they travelled through the door Cirvel exited every morning and retired every night.

Two large double doors were opened to a balcony. Light streamed through along with a breeze that made the curtains stir on the huge bed centered in the room. The Necroatheling hung the painting on the wall and since it had no need to be mounted, Rivic suspected this or a similar painting had been placed here before.

A grand desk sat against the wall off to Rivic's left. The ostentatious furniture of the room made the chair sitting pushed in beneath the desk look small and simple.

Cirvel acknowledged the painting when he returned later that day. He reached out and straightened it a tiny amount before stepping back and looking pleased at the hanging.

After that, it seemed to depend on his mood. Some days he noticed the painting and others he did not. Rivic quickly saw a regular pattern of sorts in a daily routine. Cirvel would wake in the morning, sit in bed and read for a while, then ring the bell for servants. When they came, he rose and allowed them to dress him. Once he was outfitted and properly groomed for the day, someone brought him a light breakfast and tea. Halfway through his meal, another Necroatheling would appear and give him a report. It seemed to be about the acolytes and their progression, but the words always got lost among the weave of the fabric, leaving Rivic to hear nothing.

Sometimes, shortly after that, an acolyte was sent before Cirvel. While the student got a glimpse of Cirvel's chamber, they normally moved off to the salon. Cirvel often read while taking his midday meal on the balcony. The afternoons meant he would study a lamp or thick tomes set before him at his desk. He would make notes and slide them away magically to another dimension.

Cirvel carried many pieces over toward the painting and set them down as if on a table below the painting. Rivic couldn't tell, but he felt as if Cirvel had brought these directly in front of him on purpose. It was at these times that Cirvel always met Rivic's eyes directly and gave a little smile. Sporadically, he would speak to the painting. Rivic heard no words.

And then there were the evenings in which Cirvel dined alone or, on occasion, he brought in Lihn. Every time Lihn came into the chambers, Cirvel waved his hand in front of the painting prior to Lihn seeing it, and Rivic felt the surface of it change. Rivic learned how to avert his gaze when they moved toward the bed and Cirvel drew the curtains closed. It was never quite enough to hide the shadows though as their figures moved behind the drapes. At least here, he could gaze to the top rail of the poster bed.

Then one day, Rivic found himself no longer caring. He stared blankly forward as Cirvel went about the day and felt as if he would be here forever.

He barely noticed when Lihn stepped up to examine the painting, then turned toward Cirvel, hurriedly talking to him and gesturing. Cirvel merely smiled and led her away from the wall.

But later that night, Cirvel stepped before Rivic with a dagger. He sliced open the canvas and dragged Rivic from inside. Rivic's tenuous legs gave out and he dropped to the floor at the feet of Lord Cirvel.

"I had nearly forgotten about you, acolyte," Cirvel said. "I suspect you were very close to forgetting about yourself. Back to the dormitory tonight and your classes tomorrow."

Rivic started to speak, but he wasn't sure if his words would be to ask for help, a thank you for his freedom, or a rebuttal to what Cirvel had said.

Cirvel turned away before Rivic had the chance. "Go now, before I change my mind."

Trying to crawl, but mostly dragging his weakened body from the room, Rivic made it to Cirvel's auxiliary room before collapsing on the carpet. He closed his eyes, wanting only to sleep. "Talcor dun," he whispered, knowing he had to get far away from Cirvel before Rivic was discovered lying here. Then he found himself on the cold, harsh wood of the dormitory floor. He wasn't certain it had been his own magic carrying him here.

"Rivic!" Alityka shrieked.

He heard her bed creak, then heavy running footsteps toward him.

"Help me get him up," she demanded.

Several hands came to lift him. They awkwardly carried him, arms and legs all at different heights and angles to a nearby bed. They set him face down on the mat and Alityka, along with the help of several others, rolled him over. Alityka pulled a blanket over him.

He knew it was cold in here from the feel of air on his exposed skin, but he couldn't bring himself to complain. Even the splinters gouging into his shoulders from when he had appeared on the floor didn't bother him. Hunger began to gnaw in his stomach and his mouth felt dry, his tongue like a piece of canvas in his mouth. The rest of his body felt as if it were covered with wet, gelatinous goo, much like he felt when he'd first emerged from the pearl. He needed food, water, fresh clothes, and a blanket. Yet he couldn't bring himself to ask for anything.

The sounds of curious voices grew around him and he wished they would stop. He slowly became aware of Alityka asking him something, but her question seemed like a jumble of unintelligible words.

"I don't... I can't.... I'm numb, Ali," he answered, hoping the words made sense to her. He rolled onto his side and closed his eyes against the tears that wouldn't come to moisten his eyes. "He's broken me."

CHAPTER 19

*A*lityka shook Rivic conscious the next morning. "Wake up," she commanded. "We have a day off. Which means we have a lot to get you caught up on."

Rivic still felt numb and his tongue lazy. Speaking came only with great effort. "What's the point, Ali," he asked. "I've lost so much study time."

"I dare say 'tis only been a fortnight. You're not that far behind if you start now."

"A fortnight?"

"Aye. How long did you think it has been?"

Rivic felt himself sink deeper into the mat as this new information processed through him. "I don't know. The time felt like forever."

"Come on and get moving. We can bring you current, but only if we get to it." Alityka turned away and started moving toward the dormitory door.

Rivic struggled out of bed and followed.

They made it to the base of the stairs of the tower when two Necroathelings stepped out before them.

"About time you come down," one said, reaching out and grabbing onto Rivic's arm.

Rivic jumped sideways out of the man's grasp. Alityka turned and saw the confrontation. Hurrying back over, she put herself between Rivic and the Necroathelings. "He's got a free day. We're going to do some training."

The Necroatheling leered at her. "Training is what we had in mind too."

"Looking to work off some aggression toward some Necroathelings, are you, boy?" the second asked.

Rivic hated having Alityka shielding him. He stepped to her side. "You looking to help?" Rivic asked, raising his head.

"Oh, yeah," the first one laughed. "Let's go." He reached out and seized onto Rivic's arm again.

"Wait," Alityka protested. "He's going with me."

"Not any longer."

The second Necroatheling rubbed his hands together. "Should I take her? She's got spirit."

"Nay," Rivic answered. "Leave her out of this." He hated that he couldn't make his voice more forceful, and that he didn't have more fortitude to stand against them even for her sake.

Alityka's face scrunched up as she glared at Rivic in protest. "Nay, take me along. Rivic and I were going to train. We stay together."

He looked to the Necroathelings. "You said I could work off some aggression toward Necroathelings. I want to face Kalt." He had to keep Alityka away from these men. Didn't she understand that? Didn't she know just how dangerous they were?

"Kalt is a little preoccupied at the moment," the Necroatheling holding him said. Then, to the other Necroatheling, he said, "Take the girl. We'll pit the two of them together. It could be interesting."

"Nay, too predictable," the other sneered as he shoved Alityka aside. "Go on. Get him ready. I'll be along shortly, after I find someone suitable."

Alityka started to protest, but both Necroathelings had turned away from her. Rivic moved with them, knowing he had to direct them away from Alityka at all costs. She obviously didn't know them like he did.

Then Rivic felt the world spinning around him. The next moment they were standing in a dark room made from a stone unlike any he'd ever seen inside the walls of Gohaldinest or outside.

The Necroatheling took him downstairs into a long, sloping tunnel which seemed to go on for several lengths before leveling out. It felt like they were walking forever through this cold, clammy section of walkway. There was an occasional puddle of water on the floor where the stones above were dripping.

"Where are we?" Rivic asked. "Are we still in Gohaldinest?"

The Necroatheling snorted. "Aye, but deep below it. Soon however, we'll be in The Playground."

"The Playground?"

"An alternate dimension that Lord Cirvel set up as a training arena. I suspect you'll come to like this place, just like the rest of us."

Set up? Rivic thought. The Lord of Gohaldinest could just create an alternate dimension? Imagining the amount of magic that it would take made Rivic tremble. But wasn't that exactly what the painting had been: a small alternate dimension?

At the end of the tunnel stood a closed door with a lion-head knocker on it. The Necroatheling knocked three times and the lion opened its eyes. "Seelihest vadica," spoke the Necroatheling.

Rivic expected the entrance to unlock, but instead there was a bright flash of light and they were teleported. He glanced around, taking in a circular room with several sets of chains hanging from the walls. Behind him was a door like the one with the knocker, but Rivic couldn't be positive it was the same one.

The Necroatheling walked him across a black circle in the center of the room.

"Is this The Playground now?" Rivic asked.

"Not yet. We're in the staging area. Tonight, I'll be your Necronosti and you'll be the Necroatheling," the man said.

He pushed Rivic against the wall and chained up his arms.

"I'm not a Necroatheling," Rivic said.

"This is only a practice tournament. We want to assess if you're even Necroatheling material."

"If I'm not?"

"You'll die here."

"How am I supposed to fight chained against the wall?" Rivic asked.

"Actually, 'tis for me to know where you are at all times in case I need to pull you out and slam you back in your body."

Rivic knew he still wasn't quite feeling like himself. Maybe he wasn't hearing correctly either. "Slam me back into my body?"

Another hooded Necroatheling entered with a trembling girl beside him. She put her back to the wall and raised her arms as if she knew the routine. The two Necroathelings didn't acknowledge each other, but rather kept minding those they were chaining to the wall.

The Necroatheling with Rivic sighed. "Kalt told me that you didn't know anything about Necroathelings. To partici-pate in this fight, I'll be pulling your life force out of your body and transporting it to another dimension where you will fight under my command. If you take too much damage, I'll have to return you to your body to heal."

"So, I have to be chained to a wall for that? I can't have a chair or something?"

"You won't need it. You'll see."

Rivic could hear the delighted smile in the Necroatheling's voice as he moved back into the black circle and faced Rivic. "'Tis a great party already going on, I hear," he said as he raised his hand toward Rivic. "Hope you're ready for this. Rocktardien swalon sudinada vakarate lamishoon. "

Rivic saw what looked like a silver thread reach out of the Necroatheling's hand and hook into him near the belly button. His silver thread pulled a similar one from Rivic, except that this one was blue.

"Remember: a Necroatheling's weapon never misses," the man said as he slowly sank into the black area as if being lowered down into a pit.

Towed into darkness, Rivic felt himself go faint.

"Acolyte, wake up!" Rivic heard someone scream at him.

Rivic's eyes shot open and he found himself on a cold stone floor with the Necroatheling bending over above him. "Get your sorry ass up," the Necroatheling yelled at him again.

Rivic looked down at a white glowing aura which surrounded his body and seemed to restrain his energy to this form. Worse was that he wore only a white loincloth and leggings, leaving his chest bare and exposed.

The Necroatheling also glanced him over and sneered. "White! Might as well have put a target on yourself, boy."

Rivic got to his feet and saw that he was in some sort of arena. Right now, all the combatants were moved off toward the walls. Some of the participants had markings over varying colors on their bare chests and on their faces, down their arms, backs, and necks.

"How do you feel?" the Necroatheling asked.

"Terrible," Rivic answered as he bent over and put his hands on his knees. For a moment, he thought he might throw up.

"Good. I'd worry about you if you didn't." The Necroatheling grabbed onto a ladder and started to climb. Rivic wanted to follow, but suspected he wouldn't be allowed to. Especially as the ladder began to dissolve behind the Necroatheling.

Rivic stepped away from the rock wall and looked up to see the Necroatheling in a box-like structure several feet above him. "What am I supposed to do?" Rivic asked.

"Fight. I thought we had an understanding on that point! Take your anger out on a Necroatheling."

Rivic turned as he heard a bell sound above him. Several Necroathelings advanced toward the middle of the circle, many of them with their hands raised like claws. As some started to growl, Rivic realized they weren't proceeding to the center, but were coming toward him. Sack the new guy first. But were they really Necroathelings or just more scared acolytes like himself who were now cloaked to appear like Cirvel's dark maeges?

Rivic crouched. As he did so, he raised his hands. That wasn't what he intended to do. "Malkibar," he said, the power of the spell coming through his mouth, but not from him. Completely unfamiliar with the spell, he braced for backfire. It came shortly after the spell left his hands and blew him back against the wall, even though he resisted it with every muscle in his body. When he shook his head to clear it from the jarring impact, Rivic saw that only one participant was still standing and holding a shield spell.

The combatant rushed forward, charging at Rivic with the shield spell.

Rivic ducked and rolled, this time feeling more like himself as he moved.

"Coward," his opponent yelled as he hit the wall and turned.

"Shakalal," Rivic said, lashing out with his arm toward the other man's legs. A red line formed across his ankles and blood began to swell from the cut. A moment later, the combatant fell right off his feet. Rivic stared in horror as blood spewed from the man's bloody stumps still planted on the ground.

More enemies were now standing, retaking their ground.

"Vendicus," another competitor yelled.

Rivic's arms lifted. "Miex'balish palikiem a't," he said, creating his own shield spell.

"Cazidor palikiem," a third participant hollered.

Feeling a rise of heat coming from beneath him, Rivic threw a shield spell down beneath his feet and rose up on the rising flames. As Rivic lifted off the ground from the heat of the fire spell, a cry of surprise issued from the crowd. Quite against his will, he raised his hands, leaving him to balance through his hips and legs on the magical shield. As he listed to the side, Rivic somersaulted off and came up on his feet to the spectators' merriments.

"Vendicus," the second competitor yelled again.

"Talcor dun," Rivic fired back, intending on not being at the center of that repeated spell. Obviously the maege thought very highly of his one-hit wonder and Rivic didn't want to find out why. He teleported to the other side of the ring.

"Shalish," he said as he reappeared. The ground became like mud under the other battling participants. The few still unconscious from Rivic's first spell sank beneath the surface.

Those who were able fought to get out of the mud now rising up around their knees.

Rivic noticed that each of the contestants had an aura of a different color, some darker than others, but none had a glow as bright as his. The others seemed to fade within the murky light filtering down from above, but not him; as the Necroatheling had told him, he looked like a target.

"Talcor dun," one of the stuck combatants yelled.

A jagged lightning burst tore from the darkness above them and zapped the competitor squarely in the chest. Collapsing, he hit the floor and vanished, draining away like the curling tendrils of magic that had reached Rivic during his first night in the dormitory. Rivic involuntarily flinched as the air surged electrically around him. His magic felt out of alignment.

Unfortunately, the third fighter didn't feel the same way. He grabbed onto Rivic's leg. "Wiklodia,"

Talons shredded into Rivic's leg as though he were being attacked by five gargaxes all at once. Invisible claws tore down the length of his thigh and calves. Though the leggings didn't have a rip in them, the material quickly gathered the blood dripping from Rivic's leg.

"Royka piryeian," Rivic said. As the combatant tangled in the vines sprouting from the mud, Rivic felt another spell enter his mouth. "Shi'baten to'a helcord."

The entangled competitor disappeared under the surface. A moment later, a suction noise accompanied a gurgle of bubbles, and the sliding of mud cascading into a newly formed hole told of the combatant's Necroatheling pulling the man's life force out. Rivic was certain that some of the other contestants hadn't been so fortunate.

"A new winner!" a voice called out from above. Rivic realized he was the last participant standing.

A helm appeared in the middle of the ring on a marble

pedestal. Rivic walked toward it, even though that felt like the last thing he really wanted to do, picked it up, still against his better judgement, and raised it into the air above his head. He turned in a circle and saw the box where his Necroatheling stood. Beyond that, even higher up, crowd of people cheered to his victory. With dread, he realized that every single one of them was a Necroatheling.

"Receive your marking," the voice boomed out as the applauding horde hollered louder.

Rivic really didn't want to put the metal cap on his head, but his arms acted of their own accord and lowered the helm down. There was no face plate over the helm, only a section of nose guard which protruded out. As the curved metal slipped into position, he felt a cold, dark magic grab onto him from inside. His white aura snapped and crackled to the point it became gold as if reacting in defiance to the magic of the helm.

Then the pain began. It gripped him, tearing through him with such force that he thought he'd drop to his knees. The hot, searing ache landed in his shoulder.

The crowd seemed to go wild.

Rivic screamed. He shuffled back and forth trying not to fall and knew that it wasn't his own strength holding him up. Through a swaying haze of red, Rivic saw his Necroatheling glaring down at him.

Finally, Rivic's hands went to the helm and he threw it off. Before it hit the ground, the helm vanished. It took a moment to stop his stumbling, scattered steps. Rivic looked to where his skin still burned, a silver torch now emblazed on his arm near the shoulder.

"His first win and a new light in our arena," the disembodied voice from overhead continued.

Rivic swayed on his feet, but remained standing.

"Round two!" the announcer said.

Six more combatants rushed out onto the field, all of them running toward Rivic. The girl he'd seen being chained in the room was one of them. No longer did she look scared, but rather possessed and determined for a kill as she raced for him.

Rivic's tender skin refused to move as he raised his hands to defend himself. He only got his arm about halfway up before his voice, though not his words, shouted, "Kil'marc destiharye."

A three-foot circle of the ground opened up around him and acted as a platform to shoot him straight upwards.

"De'trada roktion halish ma pryne," a foe yelled and Rivic felt the column shatter beneath him.

He began to fall. "Porta'mentay." The levitation spell caught him, but another rival punched him in the face. Senses reeling, Rivic lost concentration on the spell and fell to the ground. His ribs cracked, doubling the injury that had been inflicted a fortnight ago when Kalt had thrown him against the building in the alley, and they snapped under the stress. Rivic screamed again as a kick landed in his chest.

"And the light goes dark," the voice proclaimed from above.

"Rok'shada tu-may vakara," Rivic heard someone beside him say. The ground opened up beneath him. He tried to grab onto something as he spun helplessly.

The arms and legs of another challenger slammed into him as they were swept along together. Dirt closed in all around, crushing down on his injured ribs, filling his nostrils with damp scent, and pressing moist loam against his mouth. He felt like he was drowning.

"Praka'shay," a voice said and Rivic felt himself pulled out. For a moment, he felt floaty and disassembled. Then, with a rush, Rivic slammed back into his own body. The force sent him scraping against the rock wall behind him. Being chained directly to the stone kept the blow from being more intense, yet it didn't stop his world from being filled with darkness.

"Hey," shouted the Necroatheling as he began to unchain Rivic, "not bad for your first time. You made it to the second round and even got your first brand."

Rivic opened his eyes. "My ribs?"

"Feels good, doesn't it? Fighting like a Necroatheling, 'tis nothing quite like it, right?"

Rivic nodded, sorely admitting that his chest didn't hurt like he had expected it to. "Aye, 'tis pretty..." He wanted to admit how wonderfully powerful it felt, but the memory of Kalt holding him and his sister immobilized with Necroatheling magic wiped the triumph from his mind. It might be best to change the subject and gain the answer to his other question. "Why doesn't my body hurt more?"

"You're fighting with your life force, not your body. It remembers the injuries in your body, but doesn't hurt you any further. Except for your winning brands."

As Rivic stretched his arms, he raised the sleeve of his tunic to look at his arm. "The torch is there."

"Aye. Your trophies you get to keep."

"'Tis a reward?" Rivic asked, not sure he found it acceptable. The Necroatheling tossed aside his outer purple cloak and raised his pant leg to show Rivic the back of his calf. He pointed to a sparkling diamond tattoo there. "'Tis my first one," the Necroatheling said proudly.

From the looks of the other marks on his leg, the dark maege had won several more battles.

"I didn't always feel like I was in control of my actions," Rivic said. "Were you manipulating me?"

"'Tis a joint effort between the Necronosti and Necroatheling, both in movement and spells. You did really well, especially for your first competition. 'Twas a beginning match, but most of them had more experience being in the ring."

"Why was the man in the first round struck by lightning?" Rivic asked.

"Because he had cast a spell that had already been successfully cast. This tests the memory and skill of Necroatheling and Necronosti."

"But one opponent kept trying to hit me with 'vendicus.' Why wasn't he hit by the lightning?"

"Because he never cast it successfully against you. You blocked it every time."

Rivic still disbelieved the whole experience. He looked down at his pants and touched his thigh to make sure it wasn't torn and bleeding still. It felt perfectly whole. Then he pressed lightly on his ribcage. Still tender, but that was probably his injuries from before.

"Let's get you back to the dormitory. You drained a lot more of your magic than you probably think you did, and you'll want to fall asleep soon. I have a report to go make to Lord Cirvel," the Necroatheling said. "Your skills are most impressive."

Those words brought events crashing back into Rivic's mind. He still hadn't been strong enough to help his sister. He hadn't been powerful enough to break free of or even survive the painting. Instead he had surrendered. He tried not to think on it. "So, The Playground lets Necroathelings train their magic as well as how to manipulate the energy of others?" Rivic asked, wanting to make sure they were on the same page.

"Very good, grasshopper," the Necroatheling smiled.

A chill went through Rivic as he realized the Necroatheling he stood by was the one he'd beheaded in the forest.

The Necroatheling's hand dropped on Rivic's shoulder,

sending the world spinning. When it settled, they were back at the staircase to the dormitory.

The Necroatheling followed him up the stairs, stopping him just before he got to the door. "Be as quiet as a mouse when you go in there. Very few of them have been where you have been and returned. I will follow you and help give you something to sleep because I think you need it. 'Twill help you sleep the remainder of the day and through the night. It has been an interesting time, has it not?"

Rivic had to wonder if the Necroatheling's discreet comments had been a way of explaining what had happened to Oren.

Stepping inside the dormitory, Rivic took a quick glance around. A few acolytes sat on their beds reading or practicing small spells. Only a couple actually looked up to see who was entering.

The darker, arcane magicks crowded along the walls near Rivic, the powers seeking him out. To his dismay, he discovered he had a taste for it and he wanted to indulge their decadent yearnings. He started to raise his hand to the tendrils stretching toward him.

The Necroatheling's potency nudged against him and the dark maege lean in to whisper in his ear, "You know you don't belong here anymore, don't you?"

Rivic felt discontentment rising within him. He had the juxtaposition of his desire to go back to The Playground fighting against the need to avenge his sister's rape, along with his mission to defeat Cirvel.

That knowledge galled him. He wanted to scream in rage.

Rivic started walking toward the spot where his bed had been. Remembering that it was only a patch of floor now, he glanced at Oren's bed, still empty. After the power he'd felt tonight, he didn't want to sleep on the floor. He deserved better than that. He had returned when, as the Necroatheling had admitted, others had not.

Rivic took the blanket off the floor and did a quick spell to shift Oren's bed to his spot. He flapped the thin covering over the mat before climbing on.

The Necroatheling chuckled softly behind him. "Very good, grasshopper. I think you're beginning to understand."

Rivic laid down with his back to the dark maege. He felt the Necroatheling lean over him and come close to his ear. Rivic wished the Necroatheling would, could, drive a dagger into his back beneath the rib cage and just end his torment now.

"Mezzipalor," the Necroatheling whispered, his breath hot against Rivic's ear.

Rivic allowed his eyes to drift closed, wishing he would never have to wake up.

CHAPTER 20

"*A*re you all right?" Alityka asked him the next evening when she finally cornered him in the meal hall, getting right in his face to do so. "What did they do to you?"

"I was at a Necroatheling match," Rivic answered, spooning another mouthful of stew into his mouth. He wondered if any of the batches he'd made had ever tasted this good. As strange as it sounded, he thought they might have added some fruit to it, strickleberries perhaps.

"A Necroatheling match?"

"Aye. 'Twas not a distraction I wanted," Rivic said, still leaning over his bowl.

Alityka slammed her hand down on the table. "I've been hoping that they'd choose me for some time." She sat down beside him. "I can understand why you took the opportunity. What was it like?"

"I won my first match," he said offhandedly.

"For real?"

"Aye. I have the mark to prove it."

"What is it? Can I see it?"

He reached over and pulled up the short sleeve of his

tunic to show her the torch brand there. His fingers grazed it slightly and he grimaced. "Still hurts a bit."

"I wish they would've taken me too. I've been here longer." She looked frustrated, especially as her gaze dropped to the table, then circled around the room. "I've proven myself. Why won't they put me in a Necroatheling match?"

He's seen Alityka fight the weapons master and knew she was good enough. Maybe she had a point. Could they intentionally not be choosing her? "How long have you been here?"

"Nearly three cycles." She placed her chin on her hand and looked off toward a distant corner of the room.

Rivic ate several more bites of his stew before Alityka interrupted his silence with another of her thoughts. "Maybe my lady Lihn is right. My magic is too gentle. Maybe Cirvel suspects. Why else would he hold me back?" Her last two sentences were mumbled as if she were speaking them to herself.

"He craves power," Rivic said around his spoon. "You've got to do something to prove yourself as outstanding."

She nodded thoughtfully. "You're right. I've been playing it mediocre. I think I need to see if anything can be done about that." She got up from the table. "Thanks, Rivic."

He watched her release her reddish-blond curls from her braid and shake out her hair as she walked out. A nervous tingle shook its way up Rivic's spine.

"Damn," he whispered. He certainly didn't need Nyree to tell them that whatever inspiration Alityka had, it wasn't good. He quickly scraped the bowl and swallowed the remaining stew before sliding off the bench to follow her. He dropped his dish into the wash bin.

By the time he got to the hallway, she was nowhere to be seen.

He attempted to feel for her magic and located her at the

tower to Lihn's. She'd gotten there fast, so she'd probably used magic. But maybe going to cry on a friend's shoulder would release her anger.

A heavy feeling rested in his gut. That was not the case.

Plus, he sensed others moving in around her. He couldn't say why he felt that way, but he did. It was enough to make him rush. He ran through the hallways, knowing he had to get across the courtyard.

Then it happened.

Rivic no longer sensed her. It was as if she'd disappeared from Gohaldinest.

Of course, if she'd gone to Lihn's, that would make sense. The tingle running up his arms made him feel like something else was going on. Unable to shake the feeling, he exited the castle and started across the grass of the courtyard.

"Acolyte Rivic, where do you think you're going?"

Rivic spun at the sound of the deep male voice and found a Necroatheling stepping from the shadows. He had no good answer to give. "Just walking," he responded, hoping it wasn't a terrible one.

"Then you should walk on to Lord Cirvel's chambers. He has requested your presence immediately."

"Why now?" Rivic muttered under his breath. He knew better than to inquire why Cirvel had asked for him. He'd probably get smacked with a statement about when the Lord of Gohaldinest called for you, you didn't need to know why; you just showed up. Rivic nodded. "I will head there immediately."

As the Necroatheling turned, Rivic gave one last longing look toward the tower. If only he could get over there and follow Alityka. But he'd never be permitted to go off on his own now. The Necroatheling would follow him all the way to Cirvel's salon.

True enough, the Necroatheling never left his position,

remaining one step doggedly behind Rivic until they reached the door to Cirvel's room. Two domini in their red and gold armor stood guard at the entry. One reached over and knocked before opening the door for the Necroatheling, who motioned for Rivic to enter.

No one sat at the long table, however there were two Necroathelings in the salon. One guarded the door leading to Cirvel's quarters while the other stood beside the door they had entered. Between the trio of Cirvel's dark maeges, Rivic felt pressed into the room as if it were a cage.

He started to take a seat at the table, but the Necroatheling dropped his hand on the back of the chair and kept Rivic from pulling it out. "Lord Cirvel will be along shortly."

As he finished the words, the door to Cirvel's bedchambers opened and Cirvel strode out, book in hand. He looked up, possibly a little startled that there were people in here. "My, that was fast."

"I found the acolyte walking through the courtyard."

Cirvel raised an eyebrow in interest. "The courtyard? Going somewhere interesting this evening?"

"Just walking," Rivic found himself repeating.

Cirvel paused, his eyes shifting upwards slightly. "Aye, walking. Very well then. Let us discuss what we need to and let you get back to your... walking."

"Aye, sir. What do you require of me?" Rivic watched as Cirvel crossed the salon and opened a doorway neatly concealed in the wall.

Cirvel glanced to the Necroatheling standing behind Rivic and gave a quick nod. Rivic felt the Necroatheling turn from his position and head out the door.

"'Tis time to surrender." Cirvel answered before stepping inside the hidden chamber.

A flash of fear moved through Rivic. Did Cirvel know

about Rivic's mission as given to him by the dragon? Or maybe that Rivic and Alityka were working against him. How had Cirvel found out?

Cirvel's voice floated out. "Don't look so frightened, lad. 'Tis only a mere drop of blood. Remember our bargain?"

Rivic tried to rein in his screaming emotions. He knew the day would arrive when Cirvel would come to collect. "Aye, sir. I remember our bargain and I am ready." He leaned to the side, trying to see deeper into the room where Cirvel had gone. It was dimly lit, casting off a bluish light. Rivic couldn't view much more than a countertop and some cupboards from where he stood. He listened for Cirvel's movements inside. The echoes of the room told him it wasn't very big.

"Unfortunately, I am not," Cirvel said from inside the chamber. "Come on in here and have a seat while you wait. That way we can converse without me having to shout."

A Necroatheling, the one who had been guarding the door to Cirvel's quarters, appeared with a wooden, black chest in his hands. Rivic startled, because he hadn't even realized the Necroatheling had left. He quickly searched for the other Necroatheling and found him still standing by the doorway.

Cirvel set out what looked like a long metal trencher and waved his hand over it. "Cazidor." The length of the trencher lit with magical fire. "I apologize; I should have been better organized before summoning you. An important concern arose and I didn't have time for preparation."

Rivic followed the sound of Cirvel's voice into the chamber and he took a seat while wondering what affair had required the Lord of Gohaldinest's attention. He hoped it had nothing to do with Alityka or her abrupt vanishing.

The Necroatheling placed the chest down on a small, round, black table with silver etchings in it. Rivic knew the writings were magical in nature, but he couldn't read what they said.

Cirvel held out his arms again and his clothes instantly changed to black and silver robes over a dark tunic and pants. A silver crown appeared on the top of his head. Several silver helixes came down over his forehead and around the sides interspersed with clear and silver beads linking together into a fancy headdress covering his magnificent black hair. The silver writings on his robe flashed with gold and blue, partially reflecting from the magical fires burning, but mostly exposing the power they contained.

To Rivic's surprise, Cirvel manually opened the black chest and began picking jewelry from it to put on. There were golden and silver rings. One, when he slipped it on his finger, began to stretch and coil over the back of his hand and came to wrap around his wrist. He placed a thick collar around his throat and silver writings appeared in it. The magical scrolling disappeared before Rivic could read it, though he thought it said something about being trapped in a bottle.

The Necroathelings approached with silver cords they buttoned onto his robes and draped down his back.

The ornamentation on Cirvel began to jangle and clink as he moved. Rivic caught Cirvel smiling as he went about preparation, until Cirvel saw Rivic looking at him. "Preparation for a bloodmarker spell is usually done in private," Cirvel said. "This is a rare treat you are getting."

"Bloodmarker spell?" Rivic asked.

"Aye. With your promised drop of blood, we shall also locate your position. If you should ever concede to your desire to become a Necroatheling, knowing your exact markers on the bloodwave is imperative."

Rivic nodded, pretending to be as honored as he knew Cirvel felt he should be. In some ways, Rivic did feel privileged because he already sensed his magic growing stronger with the training he'd done. What worried him was Cirvel's knowing that he desired to become a Necroatheling. He'd barely begun to acknowledge it himself since his visit to The Playground.

But Rivic knew this show was meant to impress him. Cirvel had never had any intention of preparing for the bloodmarker spell in private, no matter what he claimed. He wanted Rivic to watch, to feel the potency, and to be spellbound.

It worked.

Cirvel leaned over the trencher and dropped silver sand over the magical fire. "Raysha lin malahest klivien moka'vo cha." Black and silver threads of magic arose from the flames. Cirvel breathed in the threads through his nose and mouth. His eyes rolled back as he straightened his posture. Black and gold scrolling marks appeared on his face and neck. Rings of flashing gold circled his dark pupils as if a fire were lit behind them.

"Let us go back out to my salon where we will all be more comfortable," Cirvel said, motioning with a hand. His voice was deeper now and Rivic heard the magic resonating through it.

Rivic hurried from the workroom out into the salon where he turned to watch Cirvel enter. He wanted to see Cirvel without the darkened lighting of the hidden chamber. The Lord of Gohaldinest looked splendid in the full light of the reception area.

The sound of the door opening behind Rivic made him turn. Nyree entered and curtsied. "You called for me, my lord?"

Rivic's breath caught as Nyree's gaze briefly came to him and dropped away. The dominus who entered with her stepped back out of the room.

"Please take a seat, Nyree," Cirvel said, his voice deep with magic.

The Necroathelings retook their post by their assigned entryways, folded their arms over their chests, and bowed their heads. They looked as if they were praying, but Rivic wondered what spirits of the Onesong would dare to take their prayers.

Cirvel approached the table near where Rivic stood and placed two small glass vials upon the shiny wood. He took a long, slow breath to deepen his concentration, then raised his hands toward Rivic. "You have given permission for me to discover your markers upon the bloodwave. Do you submit your will to my sight?" Cirvel asked.

"Aye," Rivic nodded, placing his hands into Cirvel's. "For myself only. My sister is my twin and will have the same placement. She does not need to submit to you." Rivic looked at Nyree for some indication that she understood he was trying to keep her away from all this.

"Is your parentage known?"

"Aye, yet they died when we were young."

"Do you remember their names?"

"Nay." Rivic couldn't even say he remembered their faces.

"Then, with your parentage unknown, we shall seek to determine your place upon the bloodwave and your twin sister's will be assumed on the same thread. Having been granted your permission, I take your blood." Cirvel turned Rivic's hand so the palm was up and placed one hand below and one on top of Rivic's.

Rivic felt a cut being made on his palm.

Cirvel reached for a vial, then placed it to gather the blood surging from the incision. As he did so, Rivic saw a translucent purple stone with white smoke twisting around inside it held close in Cirvel's other palm. Once the vial was half filled, Cirvel raised the container and said, "Kalmar prosen." Rivic watched his name being written in magic along with a string of additional words.

Cirvel placed the jar on the table. "Vapidious."

Magic drew over Rivic as the cut on his hand healed, wiping away all traces of his blood with it.

Cirvel held the purple stone between his thumb and index finger as the white swirls inside the gemstone turned red.

"Blocadious tor'na vakan primidious tooka," Cirvel said as he looked toward the ceiling. Even though he had his eyes closed nearly all the way, Rivic could still see the black fire beneath. When Cirvel opened his eyes to look to Nyree, his eyes were completely red. "And now you, my lovely," he said reaching for Nyree's hand.

"Nay, you said you would assume her to be on the same thread. Don't make her go through this," Rivic protested.

Cirvel smirked. "You promised me a drop of both of your bloods. I cannot have you rescinding that bargain now."

Nyree rose from her chair and stepped over to Cirvel, extending her hand. "I submit by my own choice."

Cirvel appeared pleased as he took her hand and made a cut across her palm. He filled the second vial, then said "Kalmar prosen," before setting it aside. "Vapidious," Cirvel added.

Nyree pulled away and inspected the area that had been cut, smiling when she saw it completely healed. She tossed Rivic a challenging peek as if to say triumphantly that it hadn't been that bad.

"Blocadious tor'na vakan sada'har mardo," Cirvel said, now turning in a circle. His red eyes flickered and moved as if he were studying the stars on a moonless night. He turned around a second time.

The red color vanished as the spell dissipated. He blinked and a yellow covering came down as he glowered at Nyree, then at Rivic. "How have you accessed the secrets of the Onesong?" he asked Nyree.

"'Tis a talent I was born with," she answered.

Cirvel's upper lip snarled as he faced Nyree. "She's opened the secrets of the Onesong to you! Didn't she?"

"Who?" Nyree asked.

Rivic stepped closer to Nyree, afraid that Cirvel would attack her. His fingers twitched, bracing to throw up a shield spell in front of Nyree.

Cirvel shrieked with rage as he turned to his Necroathelings. "Get Lihn now!"

Their cloaks turned to mist and spun like a cyclone upward around the Necroathelings as they disappeared.

"Has Lihn shown you the secrets of the Onesong?" Cirvel asked, turning to Rivic.

"Nay," he answered honestly.

With his head down, Cirvel raged toward Nyree. "Show me what she has revealed to you."

Rivic moved to intercept, but Nyree stepped in front of her brother and kept him back with an outstretched arm. "Lihn has shown me nothing, my lord," Nyree answered. "Even if I wanted to, I have no magic to open the Onesong to you. I was simply born with the ability to have glimpses, as you are fully aware."

"How could a magicless twin end up with magic?" Cirvel went to smash his hand down on the table, but when he saw the vials sitting there, he gingerly picked them up as if they were the most precious things he owned. Looking at them in his palm for a moment, he curled his fingers around them. "I have what I need," he said. "You may go." He waved his hand dismissively.

The next thing Rivic knew, he was standing out in the hallway with Nyree. With pain stabbing at his heart, he started to walk away from her. She had made her choices.

"Rivic," Nyree called out behind him, "may I have a word with you?"

Rivic pivoted around. "I don't know what's left to talk about. You seem to have made your decisions pretty clear."

Nyree made a motion which indicated she wanted him to put a bubble around them. He obliged her.

"I am sorry that you see it that way," Nyree began, "but this really is best for both of us. We've both seen what he will do to punish you. What if he decides to punish me? Aside from my visions, I am worthless to him."

"That doesn't mean you have to work with him, Nyree. If you just avoided him, he'd forget that you were even there."

"Aye, I do have to work with him. If one of us does something that displeases him…"

Rivic thought for a moment she might not finish her thought, but Nyree continued, "Don't make me say it."

"You're worried about what he might do to me."

"Nay!" Her face furrowed with soured confusion. "I don't want to be in the line of fire again. Twice now, you have killed everyone around us. I sometimes wondered if I survived because I clung to you. Or maybe I survived because I have no magic for you to devour. After being so violated and disgraced, what could possibly be worse? He can inflict nothing more upon me other than to kill me. I side with what keeps me alive, and that is by proving myself valuable to Lord Cirvel."

"'Tis your own life you value more than your brother," he said with a downward glance. "'Tis understandable."

She said nothing.

"I'm sorry I couldn't protect you," he muttered, wishing desperately that he could speak the words more clearly, but his own shame muddied them. "I'm sorry that you feel that I can't keep you safe in the future. I don't want you to get hurt again."

"Every day that Kalt is imprisoned within that lamp, I am hurting."

"Why? It should make you feel vindicated!" Rivic shouted, pointing a finger at her.

"He was a friend, Rivic. I wish you would understand that."

"He was the man who assaulted you."

"Walk your path, Rivic."

"You keep saying that to me, but what are you trying to tell me? What is it I need to do? What am I not getting?"

"You must do what you need to do just as I need to do what I must do. Let us not bicker about our methods." She blinked and looked up at him with her strange black and yellow eyes. "'Twould be best if we did not take notice or objection to what the other is doing and just let our paths fork here." Nyree motioned for him to break the spell.

His heart felt so torn he wasn't certain he could utter the necessary words to end the magic, yet he did so.

Nyree glanced at him one more time as she stepped around him. "Walk the path, Rivic. Walk the path."

CHAPTER 21

"*R*ivic!"

The shout behind him jerked him from his thoughts as he walked down the narrow streets between buildings. He turned to see Alityka running toward him.

"Where have you been? I've been looking all over for you," she said, stopping beside him.

"Wandering," he answered. He felt the impulse to expand on his explanation. "I needed some time to think."

"About?"

"Cirvel wanted a drop of mine and Nyree's blood. He said 'twas to find our markers on the bloodwave, but I'm not sure there wasn't more involved. Something about it 'tis bothering me and I wish I could place it."

"'Tis certain that he wants you here for a reason." She glanced to the ground as they walked, her lips tight.

He knew that, but he didn't understand why she also had similar thoughts. "Why? He's got Necroathelings that are way more powerful than me. I feel weak compared to them."

"Weak?" She scoffed. "Cirvel sought you out, hunted you down. If you think we all didn't feel your arrival in

Gohaldinest, you're wrong. There's also a reason I was the one Cirvel called for, that you ended up in my dormitory. Lihn and I both worked hard to make that happen."

He had never imagined that she might have motivations for being his friend. "You're a fool for thinking you can take him down."

"I take it that you're not going to join us in trying to overthrow him then."

"Nay, I cannot."

"Won't!"

He glanced at her, but she was still watching her feet moving beneath her, as if they would stop walking if she stopped staring.

"Your sister is in his clutches. Are you just going to let that be?" she asked.

"What else can I do?"

"Fight him."

She sounded so sure of herself, like they could win right now if they had to.

Rivic knew differently. "As you stated, my sister is in his clutches. Too many bad things have happened to her already. I can't let her get hurt again. 'Twould be best if I just was the acolyte for now, learned what I can, and hope that I can get myself and my sister away from Gohaldinest when growing season comes. Maybe in a few cycles, I'll be capable of taking on Cirvel."

"Cycles? You would wait? Do you realize people are out there dying every day because of Cirvel's conquest for magic?" she snapped.

His fears of Ellonia being hurt or killed rushed back in. In some ways, Alityka was correct, yet this was so dangerous to be plotting against the Lord of Gohaldinest and the powers he had built over countless cycles. Why should they be the ones to start the rebellion? "You should come back to your tribe too. That would help everyone so much more than you staying here trying to deceive Cirvel. Your sister and Krithstand-chief worry about you."

Now she looked confused. "My sister? How do you know I'm from Krithstand's tribe?"

He lifted his tunic and untied the opening of the pouch. Reaching inside, he pulled out the package of folded cloth and yielded it to Alityka. When she extended her hand, he dropped it into her palm. She stared at it for a moment, then back up at him. "I didn't want to say anything earlier, in case we were being watched," he said.

Alityka unfolded the cloth to reveal the blue gemstone. She held it up to the moonlight. "My father says I was born with this in my mouth, that I had carried it through from another dimension when my soul entered this body. I don't know if 'tis true or not, but it always made me feel special, as if I were destined for something."

"And you are," Rivic said, placing his hands around hers holding the gemstone.

She nodded, yet something hid behind the shadow of her gaze. He didn't ask about it, though he knew she was keeping something from him.

Alityka twisted the stone in her fingers. "Are my father and Ellonia all right? She wouldn't send this if she weren't worried."

"She's worried."

"Yet she trusts you enough to bear this to me." Her widening eyes lifted from the stone to him and her mouth dropped open. "You're the one of her visions, aren't you?"

There seemed no point in denying it. Rivic nodded. He wouldn't speak the words though and admit it; that made it too incontrovertible. Regardless of how strongly Ellonia felt that he was the one, he didn't want to claim it in case it came under dispute later.

Alityka hid the stone away, anger settling on her face as she did so. "Nay, you cannot be." Before he could ask why she spoke so harshly, she continued, "The man of her visions had not an ounce of fear to him. You do not trust the magic you've been given and you let it control you rather than the other way around. You would rather go back to the tribes and hide among them than stand your ground here."

"You're right," he said, still trying to stay at her side. "I don't have control of my magic and I'm afraid someone I care about might get hurt. But I don't feel safe at the tribe either. At least here, Cirvel might be able to help me if I get into trouble."

Her blue eyes narrowed. "I can't believe this. Why would Ellonia believe that you are the one?" She started to walk away from him.

"Wait," Rivic called out, trying to catch up to her.

Spinning around, she pointed her finger at him. "Nay! I only hope that you are honorable enough to not confess my plans to Cirvel." Pushing through a door, she sprinted across the courtyard grass and threw open the doorway to the section of the castle where the dormitory was.

"Ali!" he shouted, but she kept running.

He didn't try to keep pace with her. Alone, he came to the stairway leading to the dormitory and began the ascent.

Alityka stood on the steps near the top. He stopped as he saw what had made her halt: the closed dormitory door. Alityka looked back at him bearing an expression of curious tension. "'Tis too early to be closed," she said, verifying his thoughts.

Rivic tried the door and found it unlocked. He pushed it open and stepped inside.

"Been somewhere together," a Necroatheling asked as they entered the dormitory. He glanced around at the other acolytes in the room. "Where do you children think the little lovers have been?"

A few of the acolytes issued nervous snickers while some of them looked terrified to be in the presence of a Necroatheling. The only one who seemed unfazed was Melodin, who stood near the head of the group nearest the dark maege as if guarding the members of the dormitory in Alityka's absence.

"Well?" the Necroatheling pressed.

"In the courtyard," Rivic answered, knowing that he had to answer before Alityka did.

The Necroatheling made a rude thrust with his hips. "Up against the marble columns, eh?"

The memory of Kalt holding Nyree against the wall assaulted Rivic's mind. "You son-of-a—" Rivic said. Alityka grabbed his wrist and pulled him back as he rushed forward.

"'Tis not worth it, dearest," Alityka said with careful annunciation on the last word. "Our tryst has been discovered. 'Tis not a shame to reveal it."

The Necroatheling laughed, the pleased smirk the only thing visible beneath the dark hood.

Rivic allowed the anger to go from him. He didn't know what Alityka was planning, but perhaps she knew something he didn't.

"What do you want?" Alityka asked. "Why are you here?"

"To deliver a message." Lowering his hood, the Necroatheling stepped closer to Alityka. His eyes were narrow and his lips curled into a scheming grin. "But before I do, why don't you show us all a little bit of the sugar you got?" His green eyes glanced to Rivic as if daring him to say something.

Alityka smiled and stood just a little taller. "Sugar, huh?" She turned toward Rivic.

"We're playing in dangerous waters," Rivic whispered,

trying to hide the movements of his mouth by shielding himself with Alityka.

"Then you better make it look good," she muttered as she leaned in and kissed him.

The room erupted into oohs and giggles all around them.

"That doesn't look like a couple who are very familiar with each other," the Necroatheling mocked. "Looks more like untamed first love to me."

Rivic let his hands come to Alityka's head and back as her warm mouth pressed against his. All the while, he saw Ellonia behind his closed eyelids.

His magic surged.

She pressed harder against him, forcing Rivic to step backwards until he fell against the wall, taking her stumbling along with him. His bent knee slid between her legs and she pressed forward with her hips and dragged her thigh over his.

"Woah, let's not go too far," the Necroatheling said. "'Tis not any need to give the young ones too much of an education."

Rivic felt Alityka's magic encompass him, choking back his magic.

"Enough!" the Necroatheling shouted. He pushed Alityka and Rivic away from each other. "I hear you've taken Oren's bed."

The room seemed to fall dead silent as Rivic regained his balance and faced the Necroatheling. "Maybe," Rivic replied.

"Oren is dead, you know."

Someone near them issued a surprised sob.

Rivic forced himself to shrug as if the news didn't bother him at all. "I kind of figured when he didn't return."

"He didn't make it through his first tournament and his Necroatheling didn't feel like pulling him out in time."

The subtle threat in the Necroatheling's words made Rivic pause before he asked, "So?"

"I just wanted you to know. You're the new up and coming star, you've had your first win, and there are some that might not like that." The Necroatheling leaned close enough to whisper in Rivic's ear. "Like me."

"Duly noted, but you have nothing to fear from me."

"Fear? You think I fear you?" the Necroatheling asked with a laugh.

Rivic continued, cutting across the Necroatheling's words. "There's only one Necroatheling I want to take down. Everyone else is fine by me."

"We'll see about that."

"Why are you here? Surely you have better things to do than come and taunt me."

The Necroatheling gave a wry smile and a curt nod. "Lord Cirvel wishes to see you tomorrow night at sundown. Don't be late." The Necroatheling disappeared in a swirling cloud of purple smoke.

Rivic turned away from Alityka as he tried to rein his tumble of emotions. All sharp and confused, he needed a moment to get away from everything so he could sort out his own thoughts. He had just come from being with Cirvel. What could the Lord of Gohaldinest want from him now, so soon?

"You're right," Alityka whispered, touching his arm as she leaned in close beside him. "You're not ready. You might never be."

CHAPTER 22

*T*repidation followed Rivic all day. He found himself continuously wishing that Cirvel would come and pull him away from his classes or chores in order to talk to him. Every time he saw a Necroatheling or a Dominus approach him, he hoped that the moment had come.

Rather, sundown came before the early summons.

Having had his fill of waiting, Rivic went down the black and white tiled hallway. Two Domini stopped him at the door.

"I am here to see Lord Cirvel," Rivic explained. When their faces showed no sign of letting him pass, he added, "At his request."

To this, the Domini admitted him to Cirvel's salon. Surprisingly, it was empty; not even a Necroatheling or two guarding the doors. Rivic used the moment of privacy to inspect the genie lamps. He briefly wondered which one held Kalt. If he knew, he might be tempted to throw it from the highest tower closest to the sea. Would Kalt come streaming out of it as he fell toward the water?

Closing his eyes, Rivic did his best to shove away those thoughts.

He knocked on the door to Cirvel's quarters. Though there was no answer, Rivic heard a giggle coming from inside. Rivic waited, then when all was silent once more, he knocked again. Still no answer. He rapped a third time, louder.

The door opened revealing Lihn. Her tousled hair and flushed face surprised Rivic as much as the sheet wrapped around her did. Moist brown strands clung to her skin. She gasped and slammed the door in his face, leaving only a tangy scent hanging in the air.

Rivic turned, his body suddenly so numb that all he could feel was his hands beginning to shake.

"Disgusting, isn't it?" a high-pitched voice came from the shadows.

"Dragzel?" Rivic asked out of a dry throat.

The cahaster slipped out from under one of the nearby tables and revealed himself. His blue eyes glared at the door as if the creature could disintegrate it with a mere thought. "Humans, tangling together. Yuck!"

The door creaked open and sent Dragzel diving back for cover. Rivic wished he'd recalled that he could've teleported himself out of there sooner, but now it was too late. Lord Cirvel stood in leggings and a dressing robe which hung open revealing his bare chest. His hair was not tidily combed as it normally was, but it wasn't as messy as Lihn's had been either. He tried not to smile, tried, but he also couldn't keep the sly look back over his shoulder as he began to speak to Rivic. "I'm sorry, lad. I'd forgotten that I'd requested your presence tonight."

The words felt false. Rivic wanted to scream that there was no way that Cirvel could have simply forgotten that he was coming, but he knew that it could be true. It wasn't, but it could be.

"Give me a moment, Rivic, to make myself presentable," Cirvel commanded. He pointed to the door of to Rivic's left. "Why don't you head into my private library and I'll be there shortly."

So many things rushed through Rivic's mind: what Cirvel wanted, Necroatheling magic, the training room where Rivic had fought, Dragzel's irritation, Alityka, Lihn's breathless shock. He didn't even know where to start. The words wouldn't come.

The entry to the library clicked open.

Rivic's feet turned him and began dragging him, but he couldn't make the short distance from one door to the other. Instead, he staggered against the long table in the salon where he flopped down, half-numb, into a chair.

Why had Cirvel requested to meet with him tonight? Rivic knew the answer to that: Cirvel wanted Rivic to see Lihn in Cirvel's bedchambers! He knew they were sleeping together. He'd discovered that while he'd been trapped inside the painting. Why did it feel like such a surprise now?

Because before, everything had been darkened and shrouded, making it seem unreal. Her appearing in the doorway, panting, disheveled, and sweating, had been completely in his face. She was part of the group to overthrow Lord Cirvel, but how could she act in that function if she were also sleeping with him at the same time? Was it something she had no control over?

Then why had she been giggling and appeared so flushed from activity, unless she'd been enjoying it?

Dragzel slipped around Rivic's feet as he continued to muddle along. The cahaster let out a sorrowful mewl that matched exactly what Rivic felt in his heart. In some ways, the sound forced Rivic to pull himself together and he realized that he needed to move to the room Cirvel had indicated.

He slid from the chair at the long salon table and started toward the entry that had opened at Cirvel's magic. He'd never seen behind this door before, though he had known it was there.

His gaze drifted to the hidden chamber he'd learned about yesterday.

To his relief, the wall concealing the magical room behind was closed. He wasn't certain he wanted those arcane magicks oozing toward him in his current state. He might not be able to resist their call.

Rivic entered the library. Shelves lined every wall from floor to the high ceilings. In one corner, though set away from it to allow someone access to the books behind, sat a small desk with writing utensils lay out along the flat top. A closed book rested on the slanted surface, with a piece of parchment tucked to the side as if someone had been writing, then got called away, leaving in the middle of the work. Rivic collapsed into one of two rather large, padded chairs, which also sat away from the walls, with his back to the entrance so he wouldn't see when Cirvel arrived. Between the chairs, a small round table held a brightly lit lamp.

Dragzel jumped on his lap and curled up. He absentmindedly stroked the cahaster, knowing that Dragzel probably needed him as much as he needed the cahaster right now. "What is she doing?" Rivic whispered.

Now Rivic's worried thoughts turned to his sister. Had Cirvel been hoping that Nyree would cross over to his side, maybe even take to sharing his bed too? Was that why Kalt was trying to get close to her? Had Cirvel always been planning to hand her over to his Necroathelings?

The ground rumbled under Rivic's feet.

"Woah, boy," Dragzel muttered.

Rivic caught himself and stopped the magic flashing through him. The cahaster was right. He had to remain calm, at least for the moment. Destruction could come later.

Lord Cirvel, now fully dressed, entered and took a seat in the other chair. Rivic felt like he was too close. Cirvel leaned slightly to the side while he put his right hand to his head, index finger on his temple, thumb on his jaw, and the other fingers curling down over his lips. He stared pensively at Rivic for several moments, his dark eyes merely watching.

Rivic looked down at Dragzel as that seemed easier than staring back at Cirvel.

"Something bothering you, lad?"

"Nay," Rivic answered hesitantly. "Just not sure why you summoned me."

"I hear you did exceedingly well in your first Necroatheling match."

Rivic shrugged, still feeling moderately numb over seeing Lihn. "Pardon me, but I don't understand. You could have talked to me about this yesterday. Why call me back here?"

"My Necroatheling said you had promise."

"I did what I was told to do." Rivic glanced up, feeling strong enough now to meet Lord Cirvel's stare. It still felt weird and he felt like an interloper intruding on Cirvel's moment with Lihn. He didn't know how to say it though, not in a way that wouldn't appear crude. "Am I here to talk to you about the match?"

"That, among other things." The old wood of the chair creaked as Cirvel shifted. "I know you are anxious to get back to your tribe, but I am just wondering if I can say or do anything to compel you to reconsider."

Dragzel got up and jumped from Rivic's lap.

Rivic watched the cahaster leave the room, feeling envious that Dragzel could escape so easily. "Nay, I do not think there is anything which would make me change my mind."

"I can't tell you how disappointed I am to hear that."

A woman appeared in the adjoining doorway and Rivic looked over to see Lihn standing there, her hand on the doorframe. She was dressed and her hair combed, but her cheeks still held a flushed look, brightening even deeper pink as she saw Rivic staring at her. Dragzel danced around her feet.

"My lord," she said, breaking her gaze away from Rivic's, "I'm sorry for the intrusion, but I would like to take the book I requested back with me."

Cirvel smiled deeply and he waved her in. "Of course, my dear. I had forgotten. It would seem I am quite inattentive tonight. Please, come and get it."

Rivic doubted that Cirvel's thoughts were really as scattered as he pretended. Preoccupied maybe, but probably not, Rivic thought as he watched Cirvel rise from his chair.

Lihn's slippers whispered over the rugs as she rushed to the bookshelf and righted a stepstool which had been overturned. Cirvel went to her side and placed his hand on her hips. He leaned in close and whispered something in her ear.

"You've already distracted me from this once," she said. As she tried to push Cirvel away from her, she saw Rivic watching them and she returned her attention quickly to the bookshelf.

"You don't need to rush off though," Cirvel said, his voice not quite as low any more. "You could take the book back to my bed with you."

"Then I wouldn't get any reading done tonight and my assignment would be late."

Cirvel nuzzled his face against her hair and neck. "I think I can send the teacher your excuse."

"Lord Cirvel, you have company in your presence," she chided.

The smile fell off Cirvel's face as he pivoted and returned to the chair. "As you wish it." He sat down. After an awkwardly silent moment, his head, but not looking back directly at Lihn, he snapped, "Are you quite done yet?"

Dragzel pulled on Lihn's robes in warning. Even Rivic wished she would hurry along and not evoke Cirvel's anger.

"I am. I'm leaving now. Thank you, Lord Cirvel," she said, rushing for the door with Dragzel just ahead of her. The door closed behind them.

Rivic remained quiet while he felt Cirvel continue to steam. Feeling like it was all Rivic's fault for disturbing them, Rivic still didn't know why Cirvel hadn't just sent him on his way. He didn't understand what purposed this all served for Cirvel, but Rivic was certain there was a point.

"Where was I?" Cirvel asked. "Ah, aye, I was trying to get you to reconsider your decision to stay with us. Alityka would miss you if you returned to your tribe, would she not? She could be yours, you know? It could be arranged."

Arranged? Rivic wondered what the Necroatheling had said to Cirvel about his kiss with Alityka the previous night. Was it already getting around that he and Alityka were more than just friends? Did he want to play along?

He attempted to scoot sideways in his chair. He wasn't sure if he wanted to fall out of it or get up. Either way, he didn't want to deal with the situation any longer. He didn't want anything arranged. He wanted to be done with Cirvel now.

"Or maybe," Cirvel uttered, seeming to pick up on Rivic's discomfort, "there's someone at the tribe who holds your thoughts? If there is someone else you would prefer –"

"'Tis not anyone else I would have," Rivic answered quickly. He momentarily felt the sharp taste of sickness in his mouth as he realized he'd chosen the lie with Alityka over letting Cirvel learn the truth about Ellonia.

"Are you certain? Or, is there another arrangement you would like to make? When one is powerful enough, others will always accommodate. 'Tis why I have amassed all this. Do you think that I train maeges and Necroathelings for my own amusement?"

Rivic's mouth felt dry. "Why have you done all this?"

"Because I am the most powerful man in the world. I am nearly as powerful as the gods themselves." He swept his arm out. "I hold the magic of this world. Since you have arrived here, have you wanted for a single thing?"

"Aye, I have. The power to help my sister when she needed it," he said flatly.

"Now, tell me why you didn't have that power?"

"Because the Necroatheling knew more than me."

Cirvel grinned as he nodded slowly. "That is correct. But if you were more powerful, if you had the secrets of the Necroathelings, they would not be able to stop you. What say you to that?"

"That I need to be stronger."

"Would you like to be formidable with your magic?"

Rivic paused, trying to discover anything in Cirvel's words which forebode of trickery. He found himself nodding. "Aye."

"Then let us begin. Maybe I can persuade you after all."

The world shifted around Rivic and he found himself transferred to another dimension. He glanced down and saw a silver thread leading out of his chest. He followed it, then saw Lord Cirvel standing back in the shadows, the thread hooked to a bracelet around Cirvel's wrist.

"What is this? What's going on?" Rivic asked.

"You fought in a Necroatheling training battle before. 'Twas intended on showing you how to focus a

Necroatheling's magic, allowing you to assimilate all you have learned. Now 'tis time for the real thing."

"That wasn't real before?"

"Not as real as this," Cirvel answered. "This time, I will not control you as the Necroatheling did. Taste the power I can offer, for this is the connection a Necroatheling has with me. Prepare yourself."

Rivic wasn't quite sure how he was supposed to do that.

Cirvel pointed to a black gap half the size of a normal doorway halfway up the wall of gray stone before them. "You need to go through the tunnel and grab the stone from the pedestal before another Necroatheling stops you or gets the stone first. In here, you may repeat spells. Do whatever it takes to win the stone."

"I'm not trained to go up against Necroathelings."

"But I am."

"Then you go after the stone."

"I have no need of the stone, but you do. Without it, you cannot advance. Now, lad, run!"

A short ledge in the stone provided the only way up to the gap in the wall. Rivic started jogging to the wall, searching for handholds that would allow him to get his feet on the ledge.

"Look sharp, lad," Cirvel yelled at Rivic.

Two Necroathelings stepped from the side walls, their faces remaining dark beneath their hoods as their cloaks changed from gray to heavy purple. The only difference between the two was that one had red stripes sewn to his cloak across each shoulder.

Seeing them, Rivic ran for the wall. The Necroathelings chased him, one on each side of Rivic. They fired spells. Rivic ducked and rolled, allowing the magic to bypass him. Explosions rocked the wall ahead of him.

He jumped for the ledge. His fingers scraped stone.

The Necroathelings seized him by the legs to pull him from the rock and tossed him to the ground. The impact knocked the air from Rivic's lungs.

"Malkibar," the Necroathelings shouted together.

A heavy, invisible weight slammed down into Rivic's chest as he lay on his back. He felt blood trickling down his throat. He gasped and choked. Blood sputtered from his mouth as he coughed. He was going to die here if he didn't escape them. He struck the ground with his flat palm. "Kil'-marc destiharye," he forced out. His blood spit from his mouth and splattered down over his face.

The stones shook as they rose beneath him, lifting him up.

"Shalish," Rivic heard one of the Necroathelings say, and a moment later the column lifting him wavered. He knew it would come down.

Already the rock at his back softened, beginning to wrap around him like sand as it began to fall.

Rivic rolled off the rock, coming down on top of the Necroatheling with the stripes. "Go'shay rocktardien."

They toppled to the ground and Rivic rolled to his feet, wondering if his spell had taken effect or not. The Necroatheling recovered in the same amount of time.

"Rok'shada tu-may vakara," the other Necroatheling said, aiming the spell toward the one Rivic had fallen on. He obviously didn't trust his buddy to be free of Rivic's spell.

Rivic raised his arms, palms outward, wondering if the striped Necroatheling was his to command or not. His opponent responded by lifting his hands in unison. "Practa be," the controlled Necroatheling recited, catching his companion in the beginnings of casting the next spell. A vine sprouted from the mouth of the dark maege, choking him.

"Talcor dun," Rivic said. He reappeared on the ledge to the gap. Knowing he couldn't expect his enchantment to hold onto the Necroatheling for much longer, Rivic looked down at the one he manipulated. "Shalish." The stone beneath both Necroathelings turned to quicksand and swallowed them more rapidly than he'd ever seen the magic do before.

Before Rivic turned to the black cavity behind him, he found a pleased look on Cirvel's face. Rivic wished he hadn't seen it, but now the satisfied look seemed etched on his memory.

Confronting the tunnel before him, Rivic raised his hand. "Laza'pre ren." A ball of light took flight from his palm and lit the short tunnel which opened into a larger cavern. Rivic scanned around him as he walked through the enormous open area, expecting an attack at any moment.

Heading deeper into the cave, he discovered a worn trail in the dust on the floor. Several people had been this way before.

The sides narrowed in as he went further and entered another passageway.

As he followed the path, he saw skeletons along the walls, piling in mounds as if someone had just tossed carcasses aside. Some newer bodies weren't completely decayed and they still wore purple robes.

He swore a hand reached out toward him.

Rivic jumped aside and didn't look back as he rushed forward.

The stone path tapered and the air felt too thick to breathe. His magical light sputtered and evaporated. In the darkness, the rocks glowed with an odd purple cast which wasn't quite enough to see clearly by.

"Laza'pre ren," Rivic said, creating another light.

"You fool," a Necroatheling said beside him. "Do you want everyone to see you? Malkibar!"

As Rivic slammed into the bumpy stone wall from the

invisible push of magic, he saw the Necroatheling seize and run off with his glowing orb. A moment later, the Necroatheling exploded after he was hit with at least five spells all at once. As Rivic picked himself up off the ground, he realized that the Necroatheling had saved him from those attacks. As much as the ball helped light the path ahead, it also created a signal for his exact position. He'd have to rethink this.

A Necroatheling phased through the wall. "Vendicus!"

Rivic felt the magic hit him and fall away. The Necroatheling, appearing shocked, tried the spell a second time with the same result. The man looked down at his hand as if it were actually his very body which had failed him rather than his magic.

"Malkibar," Rivic shouted while the Necroatheling was distracted.

Rivic didn't wait to see how badly the Necroatheling was hurt. He dashed into the next chamber and found it piled with more bodies. He'd have to crawl over them if he wanted to make it through. Was that why the previous Necroatheling had phased through the wall? Maybe there was another way. "Talcor dun," he said. The spell fizzled.

Wasn't Cirvel supposed to be helping him? Hadn't that been what the Lord of Gohaldinest had said, that he knew how to defeat the Necroathelings? Of course, so far they hadn't been anything too hard.

Rivic felt like he was missing something.

"Cazidor," Rivic said, his palm out toward the bodies and skeletons littering the floor ahead. They burned quickly, leaving only ash and bone fragments for Rivic to go through. He felt the heat on the bottoms of his boots, but he kept going.

In the other cavern chamber, Rivic saw the stone hanging in midair above a pedestal. He knew that stone. It was the blue teardrop gemstone Ellonia had given him to pass onto her sister.

He stopped. The sight of it shocked him. He'd given it to Alityka. What was it doing here?

A Necroatheling grabbed the stone.

More specifically, Kalt had seized it.

"Nay!" Rivic screamed, reaching out for the air where the gemstone had been hanging. There was no way he could let Kalt take that from him too. Rage exploded from him. "Wiklodia!"

Kalt's flesh tore off him in strips, blood splattering around the walls as the Necroatheling screamed. Kalt fell to his knees, his eyes seeming wide, but the eyelids had ripped away from his face along with half of his forehead.

Rivic wanted to take the spell back. He watched Kalt dropped forward onto his hands and knees, blood spilling off fleshless muscles. The pool of thick red spread over the floor faster than he could watch the macabre flood.

"I loved her," Kalt hollered through the pain of his shredding skin. "I never wanted it that way."

Rivic wasn't certain if he nodded in understanding or if his head merely bobbed from the tremors going through him. He hadn't wanted the spell to cause Kalt so much agony. It had simply happened.

Kalt crawled forward, first on his hands and knees, then falling and dragging himself over the stone while his legs slid behind in the chunky crimson ooze, until his body couldn't sustain any more. The Necroatheling stretched out, his face the last to come to rest on the cavern floor. The gemstone rolled out from his fingers and tumbled down the gentle rock slope toward Rivic, landing just inches away from him. Rivic slapped his hand on the ground, taking the stone up along in a grasp of other grit.

"Rivic, wake up."

Rivic felt a hand on his shoulder and he jumped at the touch. He found himself in a chair, leaning over the table in Cirvel's reading room. "Where are we?" he asked, wiping the drool from his mouth and cheek. Cirvel stood beside him.

"You fell asleep. I'm sorry to have left you alone for so long." Cirvel leaned a hip against the chair. "Had I known that you would be so tired from your studies, I wouldn't have called you."

"Wait. What?" Rivic looked at his hand. He still felt the stone and dirt against his palm, but when he opened his fingers, there was nothing there.

"You were dreaming," Cirvel repeated. "Had I known you were this tired, I would have had this discussion with you tomorrow. I merely wanted to tell you before I revealed this to your classmates."

Rivic pushed himself up in the chair, trying to shake the last remnants of slumber off of him. Where had reality ended and the dream begun? Had it been the relaxing of a stressed imagination or had Cirvel taken him to another dimension for training? When exactly had he gone to sleep? "Tell me what?" he asked, trying to remain present and focused.

Cirvel went to stand in the open door, a clear sign that Rivic was allowed to leave. But as Rivic rose to go, he watched the smile grow on Cirvel's lips before the Lord of Gohaldinest answered, "Tomorrow, I make you a Dominus."

CHAPTER 23

"*A* sacrifice?" Rivic overheard a young, terrified acolyte ask as he traversed through the hallways to class. Word had circulated at morning meal that Cirvel would be gathering all the acolyte in the amphitheater during the afternoon.

"Aye, to Azote, a terrifying demon that Cirvel has captive," said one of the older students. "Azote must be fed the blood of a human every year. 'Tis time for a sacrifice to be made. Have you proven yourself worthy to Lord Cirvel, Sempt?"

The boy, Sempt, seemed frightened, especially as the one telling the story raised clawed hands up and began to make scary faces.

Rivic pushed the troublemaker away. "'Tis time for Cirvel to announce who he is raising to become a Dominus."

"Really?" Sempt asked.

Rivic nodded as the older acolyte ran off. "Don't let them frighten you," he said to Sempt, watching the other boy join up with some friends further down the hall. "They tease because they are just as afraid as you."

Soon, it seemed that everyone knew it was time for the

best to move to the rank of Dominus. With that came the anticipation of potentially being chosen.

How fast emotions swayed from fear to excitement.

Rivic didn't feel the same enthusiasm. As he walked along with the others toward the amphitheater, he thought about going the other direction. How would Lord Cirvel feel when he called out Rivic's name before all his understudies and Rivic was nowhere to be found? He had the distinct feeling that if he did that, his life would magically end wherever he was standing.

"Good choice," Lord Cirvel whispered as Rivic walked by. The dark robes covering Cirvel's arm reached out and his fingers snatched onto Rivic, pulling him from the crowd. "You, of course, are coming with me." Cirvel turned toward a Necroatheling at his side, "Get the others."

"Aye, my lord."

"Now, let's come to a little arrangement, shall we?" Cirvel guided Rivic into a room a short distance down the gray hallway. "My other candidates for position of Dominus are exhilarated about the promotion. I need you to be as well. It does not look good if the other acolytes sense your displeasure. How are they to ever want to come up in the ranks if they have no good role models? They look to you, to your happiness, for their own growth."

"So you want me to go out there and be happy?" Rivic asked as he stared at the stone floor at the very edge of his boots. "Is that all?"

"That is all."

Rivic took a step away, but he locked his gaze with Cirvel's. "I have no displeasure or unhappiness over this promotion. Quite the opposite, in fact. I see becoming a Dominus as my true path. If I am to help those I care about, I must become as strong as I can. That has been made thoroughly clear to me." He hoped he put enough force behind his words so that Cirvel didn't detect the half-truths or fear behind them. He felt a little sickened even, knowing that Alityka had been right when she yelled at him about being scared of his power. Shouldn't he have it all under control now? Wasn't that one of the reasons he'd stayed in Gohaldinest, to learn to not be destructive with his magic?

"I am pleased that you have come to see it my way." Cirvel motioned Rivic forward toward the door. "'Tis time for the ceremony, and I have a rousing speech and one more guest I must gather before we start."

Rivic left the room ahead of Cirvel and saw that about two dozen other kids were lined up along the wall beneath sconces shaped like dragon heads. The lit candles inside the mouth made it appear as if the dragon were about to spit a fire ball.

A Necroatheling grabbed Rivic and positioned him toward the end of the line.

A boy two ahead reached around and poked Rivic's arm. "I'm excited, aren't you?" the boy asked.

"Melodin," Rivic said, a smile coming with a measured sense of relief. He'd seen so many faces that he hadn't actually taken a moment to see if he recognized anyone from the dormitory.

Melodin grinned. "I'm glad you were chosen too. Do you know if Alityka was? She's been waiting so long."

Rivic took a moment to look along the queue, firstly to see if he saw Alityka, but also for more familiar faces. He looked back to Melodin and shook his head.

Four Domini moved to block in the Lord of Gohaldinest between them. Cirvel walked along the queue looking down and smiling at each child as he passed. To a couple of them, he reached out and touched their face or their shoulder as he went by.

"You are my best and my brightest, my next generation.

You all have so much potential and beautiful energy," Cirvel said. "Today, you could go from being a mere acolyte to the next step of becoming a Dominus. Many of the classmates you are leaving behind will never ascend to the rank you are now. Be proud of your accomplishment."

As Cirvel walked along, his fingers twitched and made tiny circles in the air. Rivic sensed the magic sparkling off them and whispered a spell intent on deciphering it, but no answer came. Whatever Cirvel was up to, it was stronger than anything Rivic currently knew.

"Tonight, after the ceremony," Cirvel continued, "I request your presence at my table while we feast. After tonight, you will be sitting at the table for the Domini. I hope you all set your sights on going even further and choose to become Necroathelings. My elite guardsmen are made up of the best of the best. You must work hard if you seek to achieve that rank, but I guarantee you the rewards are well worth it." As if proving Cirvel's point, all the Necroathelings nodded in unison.

As Rivic watched the glances slide between the Necroathelings and knew that the rewards were sometimes painful for others, Rivic felt nauseous. As much as he wanted to decry the Necroathelings, he knew he had to appear anxious to become one. He had to show utter determination at reaching the next rank. Rivic stepped away from the wall and slammed a closed fist over his heart so loudly that his chest thumped. "All hail Lord Cirvel of Gohaldinest," Rivic yelled.

This action seemed to take Cirvel, the Domini, and the Necroathelings off guard. Each reached for their sword, but paused when they saw that Rivic meant no threat to them or to Cirvel.

"All hail Lord Cirvel of Gohaldinest," the remaining acolytes said, but without the same verve in their tone. In fact, it sounded more like a question coming from the others.

Rivic looked up and found Cirvel's delighted face staring back at him.

With a final nod of approval, Cirvel strode toward the amphitheater. Rivic saw two quick flashes of magic as Cirvel went through the door. For the moment in-between, Rivic knew that Cirvel had disappeared from this dimension. Had anyone else noticed the Lord of Gohaldinest's rapid departure and return all within a single step?

The puzzle gave him a lot to think about while Rivic waited along with the other acolytes, until the sound of cheers burst out from the amphitheater and broke through his thoughts. He could not see what was evoking such emotion from the crowd, but the fluctuating variations in the swells almost sounded like a game being played between sides.

Rivic and those in line with him stood there for what seemed like an awful long time.

"Maybe they started without us," someone down the processions said. "Do you think they forgot about us?"

"Or maybe we're being penalized," came another voice.

With the mention of punishment, several eyes slid in Rivic's direction. Certainly, since he'd been pulled aside by Lord Cirvel, not to mention his various visits from the Necroathelings over the last few weeks, Rivic was the one most in need of reprimand.

At last, a Dominus came into the hallway and waved for them to enter, admitting the acolytes one at a time. As Rivic drew closer he realized that it was so their names could be called out and cheering applause given.

The line inched toward the door, anticipation rising as the queue shortened.

The boy ahead of Rivic moved into the doorway and

when he looked out into the amphitheater, he gave a shudder. It made Rivic wonder what was coming. The boy didn't want to proceed, so the Dominus gave him a small, helpful shove. He went out with a whimper.

The Dominus rolled his eyes. Then he beckoned Rivic forward with the motion of his hand as he had done for every child before him. It was now Rivic's turn to move to the doorway.

With the steadying breath, Rivic lifted his foot in front of him and shifted his weight forward onto it. One small action to begin the next portion of his journey. Every step brought him closer to defeating Cirvel.

Rivic pivoted on the balls of his feet and looked out into the amphitheater. It seemed like all of Gohaldinest had turned out for this. This ceremony was a big deal. Bigger than he had imagined.

His attention turned to a man of significantly advanced age in white robes standing next to Cirvel. The color of their robes, black against white, seemed to juxtapose along with their stances. Cirvel stood straight and tall, while the elder hunched forward over his decrepit shoulders and clutched the little wooden table resting before him. The scent of magic reeked off of the old fellow in waves like a foul odor. Rivic knew now why the boy in front of them hadn't wanted to go out. He wasn't sure he wanted to proceed either, knowing that he had to walk over to that frail, shaking, putrid man. Rivic felt himself crouch low. He hissed low and deep.

"Acolyte, stand tall," the Dominus beside him spoke.

With a startle, Rivic looked up. He tried to fulfill the order but found his nose wrinkling in disgust. He couldn't wipe the feeling off of his face. That rancid man in the white robes was being kept alive unnaturally with the darkest magicks Rivic had ever seen in his life.

"Come forward, acolyte Rivic Taburath and take your place as Dominus Rivic Taburath."

For as long as Rivic could remember, he had never had a last name. As he heard it shouted out above him, he wondered if Cirvel had given it to him. Cirvel had never bothered to ask him his name.

The old man's head bobbed as he looked toward the doorway and leered at Rivic. In fact, the old man seemed so anxious for Rivic to come out that he tried to move forward with the table as support toward Rivic.

That scared Rivic even more.

Cirvel placed his hand on the table to hold it down.

The Dominus gave the customary helpful shove. At least Rivic managed to contain the whimper he felt, though his skin began to crawl as he walked toward the elder who death had forgotten.

Concentrating on getting this over, Rivic marched forward. He approached the table and the old man reached out to shake his hand. Swallowing his disgust, Rivic allowed the elder to clutch onto him and he felt a charge enter him. Involuntarily, he squeezed the man's hand.

Wide eyed, the elder opened his mouth, allowing Rivic to see the little yellow and black numbs which remained of his teeth. His chin quivered as he spoke. "Novi," the man said with a grotesque smile and a quavering voice.

Rivic withdrew his hand as fast as he could put it down at his side.

The elder looked at Cirvel and his grin widened. "Novi." He giggled as if he were a little girl rather than an old man. Stretching an aged, crooked finger toward Rivic, he continued to twitter while his tongue clicked against his gums.

Cirvel shook his head "Nay, just another up and coming Dominus. 'Tis nothing more, Sapere."

The old man looked about to protest, but Cirvel indicated that Rivic should move over with the other newly raised Domini. Rivic was more than pleased to get away. The old man tried to follow, but Cirvel prevented it with a sharp taint of magic in a spell intended to punish. Fighting back horrified curiosity, Rivic forced himself not to watch. Instead, he glanced to the reddish dust covering the compressed clay floor and how it clouded around his boots.

One more teen was announced to the status of Dominus before they were through. Cirvel moved to the center of the amphitheater and turned in a circle so that all the audience could get a glimpse of him. Then, with his arms raised, he called out, "Citizens of Gohaldinest, long has Sapere Berrik been announcing our new Domini. Please rise and thank him for his service."

The energy in the room raised as the crowd clapped and cheered. Streamers and confetti were thrown toward the pit. Once standing, people stomped their feet and called out as loudly as they could. Cirvel pivoted around again as if he were accepting the applause for himself.

Sapere Berrik clutched his table and looked to be in agony. A distorted smile smeared his face between pain and pride, and his eyes rolled as if he weren't really in his body.

Rivic sensed the magic streaming from Cirvel to Sapere Berrik. Cirvel used the audience's energy to fuel his spells over the man. Rivic wanted to cry out for everyone to stop. Couldn't they see how much pain Sapere Berrik was in? Before Rivic could step forward and yell, the audience began to settle.

Cirvel's fingers swayed with the rhythmic movement Rivic had seen him make in the hallway. A silver outline the size of a door raised up behind Sapere Berrik as Cirvel headed back the few steps toward him. Though Rivic couldn't see Cirvel's face, he imagined Cirvel with a happy leer. The elder looked none too pleased to have Cirvel approaching him, yet he didn't try to flee, maybe because he knew escaping was futile.

Cirvel put his arm around him and guided him toward the door. "Everyone say good-bye to Sapere Berrik for another cycle!"

Good-byes were screamed out from all around.

Cirvel and the elder crossed through the outline of the door and both vanished. Only Cirvel appeared back in the amphitheater another step later. It seemed as if he'd never disappeared.

Once more taking position in the middle of the ring, Cirvel raised his arms to bring the crowd to a hush. The Lord of Gohaldinest adored being the center of attention. Then his voice once again filled the amphitheater. "And now for the true moment you have all come here for. We have our Domini and now we shall see who gets weeded out and who among them rises to the top to earn their armor. Let the games begin." Cirvel's robes swirled about, seeming to wrap around him in a cloud of smoke. As it cleared, Cirvel had vanished off the field.

Rivic shuddered, realizing that Cirvel's disappearance hadn't been magic. No trace of a spell had been left behind. Or at least none he could detect. What ability had that been?

He had no time to ponder Cirvel's display any further as a new spell filled the air. Before each of the boys appeared an upright sword tied to a stand with a brightly colored ribbon, each of a different color. Rivic's was blue.

Unsure of the rules of this game, Rivic hesitated, watching as the other boys scrambled to untie their swords, and then fasten the ribbon around their bodies.

"You better get moving," the boy next to him said. "If you don't even get your ribbon on, you're going to be out as soon as I grab my sword."

Rivic tugged on his ribbon and the knot fell loose. The boy next to him glared as if realizing the same thing that Rivic did: his ribbon hadn't been tight on his securely as the other boys. Not knowing what else to do with it, Rivic wrapped the ribbon around his neck as if it were a scarf.

The boy chuckled. "That's a really stupid place to put it. Haven't your instructors been teaching you anything to prepare you for this?"

Before Rivic replied, the boy rushed with his sword for Rivic. His breath blew out as he awkwardly grabbed his sword and raise it to parry the attack. Rivic crashed awkwardly to the ground. His fingers smashed beneath his weight and pressed even deeper under the sword's hilt as he tumbled and rolled back up on his feet.

Another opponent charged him before Rivic could get a grip on his sword. Rivic caught that blow clumsily too. This time however, it felt like his sword had actually moved his arm rather than the other way around. As the first boy sent another thrust for Rivic, the sword did move of its own volition.

Somewhere in the pit, a youth screamed.

Using the distraction, Rivic turned his sword in his hand and gave a wide swing toward both boys attacking him. The second of his assailants jumped back avoiding it as the first boy got hit by the blow and fell to the ground. Rivic turned to the second boy, ready for another confrontation.

The kid gave him a questioning look. "Aren't you going to finish him off and take the prize?

Rivic didn't understand. He looked to the boy on the ground, who lay there bleeding and wondered if anyone was going to come help him. Should Rivic do something to help him?

The other kid stepped around him and reached down. "If

you're not going to take it, I will." He slid his sword under the ribbon, sliced it in two, and claimed his prize.

As Rivic looked around, he saw the other youths gathering up ribbons from fallen adversaries.

His rival stood with his arm outstretched, the sword pointing at him. "Why don't you just hand me your ribbon now, before I slice it off your throat?" For a moment, the kid's forehead creased as he realized Rivic still had no idea what was going on, then he sneered, "How did you make it to be a Dominus? You don't even understand what's happening, do you?" The tip of his sword lowered slightly.

"I can't say that I do." Rivic admitted.

The boy leveled the sword at Rivic's chest. "So, give me the ribbon." The boy reached his hand out as if to grab the ribbon.

Rivic ducked backwards, taking a step that carried him away from the boy. He sidestepped the thrust of another sword launched toward him. He hadn't seen it coming. He just knew to dodge. The boy engaged with the other combatant and was taken down quickly. The newcomer took the boy's ribbon plus the one he'd acquired. Rivic thought he might be starting to understand this game: hack down your opponents and take the ribbons.

He battled with the new foe, his sword striking swiftly and cleanly. It felt like he had barely moved, yet Rivic stepped with grace and precision.

A sight caught his eyes and Rivic turned to look. Cirvel, in his black and silver ropes, stood appraising him and nodded in approval. Rivic felt his energy rise. He charged forward into battle. It seemed as if no one saw him coming.

Then a sword caught him across his back, slicing through his tunic. Rivic dropped to his knees. His attacker reached for the ribbon. As Rivic felt the pressure tighten on his throat, anger overtook him. The arm that held the sword seemed to move on its own. Rivic turned sharply, led by the weapon. His hips cracked as they extended beyond their reach.

A woman screamed from somewhere in the amphitheater. "Rivic, nay!"

Rivic barely heard it. He twisted, the weapon still in control of itself. The blade sank into his attacker, driving right through his gut with an ample slice.

Rivic's eyes widened as he recognized his opponent and he released the sword. Melodin's blood and internal organs slid out over Rivic's hand. "Nay," he muttered breathlessly.

Melodin dropped to his knees before Rivic. Scared tears filling the boy's eyes, Melodin tried to say something, but nothing came out.

"Nay. Nay. Nay!" Rivic frantically reached for the sword as though he could take back the strike. His slick fingers just slid on the metal. He couldn't pull it from the boy.

Melodin toppled over.

Rivic watched as the life went right out of Melodin's eyes and flattened. "Nay. Nay."

Rivic couldn't even think. He felt so numb.

"The ribbons," the crowd cried out.

With the blood already drying on his fingers, Rivic's hands felt sticky. He didn't want to reach for the ribbons, but he didn't know what else to do. What would end this? He just wanted to be back in his bed. He didn't want to be here anymore.

The colored material seemed to find their way to his hand. A Dominus was there at his side yanking Rivic up to his feet and raising his arm in victory. Rivic knew this was not a triumphant moment.

"You have your champion," the Dominus called out to Cirvel.

It seemed as if Cirvel appeared at Rivic's side in a

moment. Rivic sensed the magic, but he didn't really understand what it meant until Cirvel appeared right beside him, leaning down toward Rivic. "Good job. Well done. You will now be the leader of those who have survived as their Knight Captain."

Had any of the boys survived his onslaught, Rivic wondered. He didn't see how they could have. It had been just a game, right? Nay, the blood in the air was far too real. "But... my sword..."

The amphitheater filled with cheers. Rivic had the distinct sense that his name had been called out again, but he didn't know why. Why was everyone cheering? Didn't they understand what it just happened here?

Rivic looked back at the sword that still protruded from Melodin's stomach. It seemed different now, as if it was no longer cast in sorcery. There had been powerful magicks on it, but Rivic had never noticed the dampening spell until now. Only residuals of the enchantments remained on it and were dissipating fast.

Rivic swept his glance around, quickly reaching out with his magic at other swords about the room, trying to feel anything. He sensed no spell on any of the other weapons in the room, only this one.

"Lord Cirvel, I can't accept the position. I had an unfair advantage, and I suspect you know that."

Cirvel feigned a look of disbelief at Rivic, but he continued to smile as he raised his head. "I have no idea what you're talking about."

"Aye, I think you do. There was magic on my sword." Rivic pointed to the weapon as if Lord Cirvel wouldn't know which one had been his. "We both know that I should not have this position. I didn't really earn it. I didn't even know what was going on."

Cirvel pulled him slightly aside and turned him so the

crowd on the other side of the amphitheater could view the champion. "I may have leveled the playing field myself. It gave you an advantage for your disadvantage." He emphasized the words with positivity on one and negativity on the other as if they brought a natural balance to one another.

"You could've just mentioned this when we were in the room together. You could've told me the rules of this game then."

A smile slowly opened on Cirvel's face as he looked down at the floor and began to nod. "Aye, I suppose I could have. But I did not."

"And so I killed Melodin, who should have been the rightful leader."

"I wish that you would look at it another way. Aye, the boy is dead and that is a terrible tragedy, but you looked your opponent in the eye, someone who would stand over you, and watched the life drain out of him. That is an experience that will serve you well and one that you will never forget."

Within Cirvel's harshness was also a true reality Rivic knew he would have to take to heart. He had watched the death of an opponent. And though Lord Cirvel did not know it, his own personal opponent stood face to face with him right now. Someday, Rivic would have to kill Cirvel. That was the only way to end this mission. In giving Rivic this lesson, Cirvel had prepared him in a way that Cirvel would never know.

The Lord of Gohaldinest had just primed Rivic to defeat him.

"Are you beginning to understand now what it means to serve me?" Cirvel asked.

Rivic snapped his feet together so fast that his boots sounded with a thud and he gave a bow. "I believe I'm beginning to understand." Rivic said. It sickened him.

"Good. Now go stand in line with the others." Cirvel went

back to the center of the ring, now being cleared of the injured youths who could no longer walk and the one dead.

Rivic cast another sharp look at Cirvel's back before returning to the line of eager-faced boys.

"These seventeen acolytes," Cirvel began, addressing the audience at large, "today rise in ranks to become honored Domini." Then he focused on the line before him. "Come forth as I call your name."

As each name was called out and the youngster approached, Cirvel placed his hand upon the person's head, and armor of red and black wrapped around them. When Rivic was called forward, Cirvel called him out as the Knight Captain. As Cirvel's magic settled over him, Rivic saw the armor was red and gold.

Rivic felt as if the crimson symbolized the blood of the boy he'd killed. He'd don this armor as a blood oath to end the darkness that had settled over Gohaldinest. Once Cirvel was gone, he'd never wear red again.

CHAPTER 24

*R*ivic's head spun as he walked out of the amphitheater. Knowing he was supposed to attend dinner with Cirvel, he followed along with the crowd as they moved through the hallways. He felt ill.

"Rivic," Nyree called out to him.

A whimper shuddered through him even as she called his name a second time. He tried to turn his head to look for her, but he couldn't even bring himself to do that much.

Then she was at his side, having fought her way through the flood of people toward him.

"Rivic, are you all right?" she asked.

"Nay, I'm not." He collapsed against the wall. Nyree crowded next to him, trying to stay out of the way as people buffeted around them. "Did you see?"

"I was watching."

He groaned. Why did she have to be there? Why had she seen him being a killer again?

"I'm always the observer."

Her flat voice startled him into looking up. Her eyes had taken on their black color with yellow torches. It lit her way through the darkness. He understood that now as his body rushed to take a deep breath filled with this new comprehension. "I have let Lord Cirvel and Gohaldinest come between us."

"'Twas always meant to be."

Why did she have to phrase it that way? Knowing she was half of his soul made his heart sink disparagingly? "What are we going to do?" he asked.

"Same as we have been doing."

Rivic couldn't say he grasped her statement. He was about to say that he didn't understand, but instead, "We're going to walk the path," came out of his mouth.

Rivic realized now that she had a hold of his hand. He squeezed her back, letting her know that he was right here with her and lucid.

"That's right." She leaned in and kissed him on the cheek. "Good-bye, Rivic."

He wanted to hold onto her as she drew away, but he knew there was nothing he could say to keep her there. As Nyree moved away, he saw Lihn coming toward him.

Something about Lihn's demeanor brought a fine calm to him that he welcomed. He wasn't sure, after all that had happened, if he deserved some reassuring comfort in his life. He could look back and see how much he'd changed. It wasn't all good. Maybe Gohaldinest transformed everyone.

"Congratulations, Rivic." The sorrow in her eyes reinforced the lie her voice held. Lihn knew just as much as he did that nothing about this had been a victory for him.

Seeing that Cirvel wasn't nearby, he accepted Lihn's outstretched hand and stepped closer to her. She clasped tighter onto him. They were two kindred spirits caught in the web Cirvel had around them.

"Let this not sway you. Alityka and I still need your help to defeat Cirvel. We cannot do this without you."

"I don't know if I can." Rivic felt empty inside, numb, but he didn't know how to put forth those words. "Nyree tells me to walk the path, but I get more beholden to Lord Cirvel every step I make."

"You cannot fight the magic that tangles between you and Cirvel. You must accept the fact all of our fates are intertwined."

"How do you do it, Lihn?" he asked, surprised that the words were coming out of his mouth. "Why do you share a bed with Cirvel when we are seeking to overthrow him?"

"My sole purpose is to try to make Cirvel want to be honorable and find hope in his heart again, so he will turn from this path of the Necronosti that he is walking. I would love to see him be the creature that the universe wanted him to be. If I can move Cirvel to do that, we have still won. I don't care how we acquire victory, as long as Cirvel, as the Necronosti, is defeated. Until then, he is a danger to the Onesong."

Realization came heavy to Rivic's already upset stomach. He swayed on his feet. "That's why my sister was so important to him, why he wanted to put a wedge between me and Nyree: he knew my sister was also connected to the Onesong and hoped that she would help him."

"Aye." Lihn smiled knowingly. "But in examining her, he found nothing that would aid him. 'Twas the same reason I didn't fear you going and giving him the secrets of the Onesong when you asked if I was scared about you doing just that. There is nothing that you could reveal which would restore his connection."

Restore the connection. "But you can help me?"

Lihn nodded slowly with a serene look on her face. "Whenever you are inclined."

He knew he wasn't ready now. "Soon," he whispered.

With a squeeze of her hand, he released her and began following the other Domini down the hallway.

In the main hall, the several rows of tables had been turned and a larger table added. Nearest the door, the table-cloths were gray, then red, and finally black on the longest. Behind that was an ornately carved pediment chair. Plates and goblets were already set.

Wondering who could have done this while all the acolytes were in the amphitheater, Rivic caught a glimpse of Necroathelings with red stripes across their shoulders sinking into the walls. He glanced around at the people nearby to see if they had noticed the dark maeges evaporating into the stone, but everyone else seemed to be in awe of the feast spread throughout the hall.

The acolytes filed off first to their place at the gray tables. Those who had previously held the rank of Dominus sat at the tables in red. Those who had just been elevated to that rank were shuffled off to the head table. The Necroatheling guiding them along indicated for Rivic to sit in the chair across from the ornate one.

Rivic remained standing beside the chair while the other new Domini took positions on this side of the table. A shuffle of black robes caught his attention and Cirvel moved to the ostentatious chair opposite Rivic. Necroathelings filled along the table to each side of Cirvel, each solemnly standing in their dark purple robes, hoods covering their faces.

Cirvel glanced along the Domini on the other side of the table and gave a long smile before his attention settled on Rivic. For what seemed like an eternal moment, Rivic felt shamefully weak and insignificant under the Lord of Gohaldinest's stare. Then Cirvel motioned for the Domini to turn around.

Rivic looked out over the sea of faces at the lower tables.

He tried to find Alityka, hoping that she would give him a moment of strength. What would she think of the horribly tortured look that had to be on his face?

"'Tis with great honor that I give you the new Domini of Gohaldinest," came Cirvel's voice from behind Rivic.

As claps rose around the room, Rivic sensed Cirvel standing on the other side of the table with his arms spread wide, his grand, black robes dangling like wings off his arms. Rivic could barely breathe. The Lord of Gohaldinest might very well be choking him.

Cirvel continued, "This is the last time they join me at this table until they become Necroathelings. I hope that you will continue to cheer them on toward that goal, for together we are all stronger."

A second round of applause went around the room, and Cirvel waited for it to quiet before adding, "With this feast, we also begin a period of reflection. We shall break from our training for a week's time. I hope you use this time to review what may be weaker aspects of your magical training and strengthen them. As I stand here looking out at all your shining faces, I know how far each one of you has come. You are the strength of Gohaldinest and the promise of a bright future for this world. I stand humbly before you to thank all of you for your service. Please be seated."

Hearing the shuffle of people taking their seats broke through Rivic's numbness and he found himself shaking as he turned. Those nearest him sat down, leaving Rivic standing for several seconds longer than anyone else. Cirvel subtly pointed with his finger for Rivic to sit. "Unless you want to do the honors, Knight Captain," Cirvel muttered.

Rivic dropped quickly into his chair. He already felt so sick that he wasn't certain he'd be able to eat. Just the thought of breathing in the scent of food was nearly too much for him.

"I know you all are anxious to eat, but I do have one more announcement I'd like to make." Cirvel paused while the room plummeted to silence. "I am pleased to say that the passes out of Gohaldinest are now clear enough for any acolyte or Dominus who wishes to leave to return to their tribe. If you wish to be released from your training here, please submit yourself to me during the next week."

Rivic's stomach gave another turn. As the new Knight Captain, would Cirvel discharge him if he asked? Would Cirvel let Nyree go? Was he safe to return to the tribe now? Did he have enough control of his magic?

What about his promise to Alityka and Lihn to help them overthrow Cirvel? Could he really say that he wanted to defeat the Lord of Gohaldinest? What Cirvel was accomplishing here didn't seem truly that bad. Some of his methods were extreme, but nothing going on in Gohaldinest seemed inherently evil.

Cirvel waved his arms and food appeared on the table. "Let us all feast to the Domini's success and their new journey."

The gasps behind him told him that the entire hall had received their feast. The others at the table began to hungrily reach for food.

Rivic found Cirvel merely staring at him.

A shiver pressed through his shoulders.

Mechanically forcing himself to receive a bowl being passed to his right, Rivic dumped a pile of potatoes on his plate. In the flow, Rivic noticed the Necroathelings to the right and left of Cirvel serving the Lord of Gohaldinest.

Rivic tried to eat. It was easier to keep his eyes on his own plate than to see Cirvel leaning close to speak with the Necroathelings at his side. Occasionally, there were calls from the Domini to get Cirvel's attention and add some remark to the conversation.

"Well, that sounds like something you'll have to run by your Knight Captain," Cirvel said, his voice cutting through Rivic's silent lamenting.

Rivic glanced up, unaware. "Um, get with me later and we'll discuss it." He tried to nod his head, but it felt more like mere inattentive flopping.

Cirvel grinned over his food. "Very diplomatic of you." He raised his gaze to look up at Rivic, who tried to ignore the pointed glance behind taking another bite.

"Stare at that plate any harder, boy, and it might break," the Necroatheling to Cirvel's right muttered just loud enough that those in the immediate vicinity could hear.

Rivic felt his magic heatedly rise and, in a moment of his own surprise, his cheeks didn't flush with embarrassment. He let the furiously feeling just swim around inside him, noticing how Cirvel watched him appraisingly.

The Necroatheling's own plate broke.

At the Necroatheling's gasp, Cirvel's eyes held a look of pleasure.

Controlled destruction.

Rivic began to eat in earnest now. He had what he'd come to Gohaldinest for.

CHAPTER 25

*R*ivic knocked at Cirvel's door and waited with his eyes closed until he was told to enter.

Cirvel didn't sit at the table as Rivic expected. The door to the bedchambers was slightly open and a Necroatheling stood guard there.

"I am here to see Lord Cirvel," Rivic announced, knowing that the Necroatheling had to sense the fear in his voice.

Surprisingly, the Necroatheling acquiesced and opened the door further. "He is on the balcony, Knight Captain."

Rivic hurried inside the room, afraid that the Necroatheling would close the door before him. Rather, the Necroatheling followed him inside, leaving the door open behind them. Two more Necroathelings stood beside the opening to the balcony. The day's cool breeze touched Rivic's cheeks. He hurried through the room, trying hard not to look at the spot on the wall where he'd hung in the painting for what seemed like an eternity, yet it was hard not to notice that there was nothing there now.

Cirvel leaned against the balcony railing as Rivic stepped out. Even though Cirvel held an open book before him, he wasn't reading, but rather looking over the edge to something down below.

"Look there," Cirvel said, pointing toward the courtyard where ten birds flickered between the flowers and drank of the nectar with their long beaks. It seemed amazing how the birds could hover there, completely still in the air, with their wings a blur. Before Rivic could overcome his awe and comment on their beauty, Cirvel continued, "The flutterbirds have returned early this cycle. I hope 'tis not to their detriment."

"How do you mean?" Rivic asked.

"It might still snow again. 'Twould be tragic for them to be trapped in the cold. Their little forms couldn't handle the drop in temperature."

"I still don't understand. I've never seen creatures like this before."

Cirvel leaned forward slightly, holding onto his book to keep it from dropping over the side. "Flutterbirds cannot remain still for more than a few moments. Their entire existence relies on the constant flapping of its wings, not only to keep up its body heat, but to process the rest of its internal functions properly. Its heart is so weak that the flapping of its wings squeezes the muscles in its chest, which applies pressure to the organ to make it beat. Digestion also depends upon that compression to push food through its system."

"Do they not sleep then?"

A slight grin accompanied Cirvel's sidelong glance. "Only for seconds at a time. Now let me ask you: how can such a beautiful creature like that be so cursed?"

Words felt like they were bubbling in Rivic's mouth, yet none came out. He really had no answer.

Cirvel looked toward Rivic, the Lord of Gohaldinest's dark eyes sharpening as if preparing to impale Rivic where he stood. "If it rests, it dies. The flutterbird is doomed to perish of exhaustion. In what universe is that just and right? What energy of the Onesong thought it would be funny to give an existence like that?"

Now his mouth felt dry and his tongue numb. Did Cirvel expect an answer, or was this question rhetorical in nature?

"I merely hope that these fluttebirds have not returned to the land they love so much only to wither and die in the harsh conditions," Cirvel added, and Rivic swallowed hard the knowledge that he'd probably seen a caring side of the Lord of Gohaldinest that very few ever witnessed.

Cirvel turned from watching the birds and closed the book, clasping the black leather cover in both hands before him in a casual fashion. "So, Dominus Rivic, my Knight Captain, what can I do for you?"

"My lord." He suddenly found his mouth sticky and dry. "I want to return to my tribe. Both me and Nyree."

"I see."

Rivic shifted his weight as if strengthening his stature would also harden his resolve. All it seemed to do was make his heart beat painfully in his chest. "Will you allow it?"

Cirvel turned and headed back inside. "I thought you were pleased about the promotion to Dominus, that you saw it as part of your path to becoming stronger, so that you could protect the people you love better."

Following Cirvel, Rivic hated having every word he'd said thrown back in his face. "I am honored, my lord, to have become a dominus so soon after arriving when others have waited many cycles for such a promotion. But I must think of what is best for my sister at this time."

"You believe returning your sister to life at the tribe is in the highest interest of her welfare?"

Rivic wondered if it might be too soon to return to the tribe, much like the flutterbirds outside, but he held his resolve. "Aye, my lord."

"I can tell you are resolute in this matter. You haven't addressed me as 'my lord' since our first meeting." Cirvel set the book atop his desk and turned. "What if your sister does not want to leave with you?"

"It doesn't matter. I have let Gohaldinest come between us, but once we are home, I shall repair the damage that has been done."

"Will you pull her kicking and screaming down the mountainside?"

"If I need to."

Cirvel nodded his head, his face unreadable. "I would certainly not like to lose you. Is there nothing I can do to keep you here?"

"Nay, my lord."

"Very well. Your mind has always been made up since you first arrived. I guess I shouldn't be surprised. I gave you my word then and I will remain true to it. You may return to your tribe, but do know that you will be welcome here any time."

Rivic hadn't expected his heart to sink so much. He started off nodding, but quickly bowed to Cirvel. "Thank you."

Walking back to the door, Rivic stopped and pivoted back to Cirvel. "I know that you like to have an inside man in order to keep a tribe safe from the attacks of the gargaxes. How would I become that person?"

Cirvel raised an eyebrow. "You would accept such a position?"

Rivic nodded. "I ask for it, if that is what is required."

Crossing his arms atop his chest, Cirvel headed out to the antechamber. "Ask for the station?" He shook his head. "I give the station; 'tis not one that can be acquired."

The tension in the air made Rivic hesitate, but he

followed anyway, dogging Cirvel's steps. "So, what do I need to do to gain your approval?"

"You can't."

It felt like Rivic's feet slid right out beneath him as he moved forward. "Why not?"

"I have specific requirements of those I choose." Cirvel sat down at the table and waved his hand. A book with a red cover appeared and he opened it to a place held by a golden tasseled marker. He looked down at the text, his fingers moving across the page as though seeking out the spot he'd left off. "You do not meet any of those conditions."

"But—"

Cirvel's head snapped up, his dark eyes narrowed. "I have said that you may take your twin and return to your tribe. That is all the disappointment I can take. Leave now and get yourself prepared."

CHAPTER 26

*R*ivic waited until the day of their departure before going to Nyree's room. He pounded upon the door until she opened it, and then pushed into her chambers, not letting her close the door in his face. "Get your things together."

Seeing a bag already packed on the sofa, he whirled around toward her. "You knew? Who told you?"

She blinked and her eyes changed to black with the gold torches. "As if I needed anyone to tell me."

He went to the bag and opened it to see what she'd put inside. The dress she'd arrived in and another he'd never seen before, a couple pairs of shoes, a thick blanket, and a box which looked like it held a few leftover sweets. "This is all you're taking?"

"What more will I need, out there, sleeping on the dirt, foraging for food, washing in the lake?"

The things that sounded so hateful from her lips were the ones he craved.

He mentally grabbed his tearing heart and held it together with resolve. This was why he'd waited. Slinging her pack over his shoulder, he reached out and took her wrist. "Then I hope you are happy with your selection. I've let this city come between us enough. Once we are back at Krithstand's tribe, you and I will work this out. We'll be close like we once were."

"Will we?" She tried to pull her arm away, but he held fast. "Do you really think that you can go back now that you've seen what's possible here?"

"If it means keeping you safe, aye!"

"But how much are you putting Krithstand's tribe in trouble by being there?"

"I've got control of my magic, Nyree."

Her next words came slowly. "But do you have control of Cirvel?"

"Nay, but—"

"Nay, Rivic! Do you really think that Cirvel will let you be? Do you think he won't send the gargaxes to attack in an attempt to bring you back to him?"

"He's allowing me to return. Aye, he tried to make me stay, but he knows that returning has always been my intent. Now let us be on our way before we are late."

"As if you think you can overcome him by simple will alone." She shook her head, but she let him pull her along.

The acolytes all dressed in gray were gathered in the courtyard, while the Domini stood positioned on streets of the inner castle of Gohaldinest around the grassy area.

An acolyte broke away from the group and jogged over to Rivic. He didn't notice who it was at first, and he slowly came to the recognition that it was Alityka. She stopped before him, her blue eyes harsh.

"Have you been avoiding me and Lihn? I keep trying to talk to you, but every time I see you, you look the other direction. Aren't you part of this plan anymore?" she asked.

Rivic felt totally taken back. He really just had never seen her in the crowds. Of course, he hadn't spent too much time looking for her either. "Nay. I'm leaving. Nyree and I are returning to the village."

Agonizing sadness filled her eyes. "I'm sorry to hear that. I'm sure Ellonia will be happy." Her words belied the statement.

"I am sorry. 'Twas never my intent to stay. I must see that my sister is cared for."

"Save it for my sister. She always believed you be the one to save us. Instead you run home rather than standing your ground." Alityka's blue eyes narrowed on Nyree, who merely looked back unconcerned. "Tell him what a fool you know he's being."

Nyree shrugged.

"She went to talk to Lihn last night," Alityka spat. "They were talking about you, Rivic."

Rivic continued pulling Nyree along toward the gathering where those leaving were assembling with their belongings. Alityka fell back.

"I thought you were here to help us," Alityka shouted behind him. "Traitor!"

"Aren't you going to ask what I said to Lihn?" Nyree asked.

Rivic shook his head. "Nay. I do not care. Soon, this place will be a distant memory."

"'Tis easy for you to say that. A part of me will always be trapped here."

Since they hadn't quite reached the group of those leaving, he stopped and whirled her around toward him. "I am so sorry for what happened to you. I regret the distance that has come between us. I miss you and I promise I will do everything within my power to make you forget this place."

"What will you do? Build me another city?"

He squeezed her hands. "If that's what it takes."

"Oh, Rivic." She shook her head and her shoulders sagged. "So much is beyond your understanding. Do you really think you are going to fit in out there in that world? Will the simple life of a hunter really satisfy all the needs that your magic now craves? Think about it, brother. Your magic is tangled within this city. You cannot separate yourself from it any more than you could cut off your leg."

"We'll see." He resumed his determined march toward the others. Once there, he watched Alityka stopping to speak with several of the acolytes, each in a hurry and seeming wary. The conversations generally ended with the acolyte nodding and Alityka patting the person's arm. He wished he didn't care what they were talking about, but he couldn't help wondering.

Cirvel appeared in the center of the courtyard with Lihn Harvestendale and two Necroathelings at his side. The tang of magic swirled through the air as if announcing his presence. Cirvel looked around at all the acolytes, raising his hand and waving at them in a gesture as though adoring all of them. A smile came to his face. "Look at all of you," he said warmly. "You all have learned so much in this last season and I am very proud of you."

He looked toward the Domini, his eyes narrowing for just a second as they fell upon Rivic. "For those acolytes and Domini who now wish to return to their tribes, please come forward." He waved his fingers, beckoning them closer.

Rivic's heart raced. Released. On his way back to see Ellonia. With several quick breaths, he held his position to keep from running now.

A number of the acolytes moved forward, some braver than others. It seemed as if not everyone trusted that they would be allowed to go home. One other Dominus stepped forward.

"Come, come," Cirvel urged. He drew them together in a tight little circle.

"'Tis been my pleasure to train you all. You have my welcome to return next snow season and continue your training. I hope to see you all again." Cirvel pointed toward one of the Necroathelings standing near the Domini who were remaining, then turned toward Lihn and began to speak quietly with her.

The Domini split to form two lines on the sides of those who were leaving as the Necroatheling took to the front.

"Let us walk to the gates," the Necroatheling said before leading the way.

There were a few people outside along the streets, having gathered to watch and see which students were leaving the castle. Everyone, spectators and travelers alike, seemed very somber.

If that wasn't enough, little swirls of magic swam around Rivic, plucking at his clothes as if wanting to hold him there. Tendrils of ancient spells reached from the cobblestone and tried to surround his feet and twist around his ankles. They had little power to actually retain him, but it felt as if Gohaldinest longed to keep him there.

Rivic's nerves grew as the massive gates of the outer wall lengthened before him and he found his footsteps slowing.

"You know I'm right," Nyree muttered.

All he had to do was walk through the gates and he'd be free. "I'm doing this for you."

She scoffed, but remained otherwise silent.

Ever step grew harder. The breath in his lungs felt like it no longer wanted to move in or out of him. He looked back over his shoulder to see where Cirvel walked behind them, Lihn demurely at his side and smiling at whatever story he was telling her. Rivic wondered why he couldn't be as pleasantly delighted as the Lord of Gohaldinest was.

He looked down the gray streets and wanted to smile at the kids he saw playing there. Even among their shouts and giggles, it seemed peaceful here.

"You are torn, aren't you?" Nyree asked, even though by the change in her eyes he knew she already perceived his answer.

"Is there a problem, Dominus Rivic?" Cirvel said behind them.

"Nay, my lord." He tried to pick up his pace. It felt more like slogging dismally through mud.

Nyree leaned close to him. "Rivic, you know what you must do. You need to walk that path."

"I don't want us to be separated. I've missed you."

"I should never have clung so tightly to you."

It felt like Rivic's heart broke.

She turned toward him and took both his hands. "Now, you must not cling so tightly to me. Let me go, Rivic, so you may do what you were born to do. 'Tis time and the way it must be."

Before Rivic could get a breath out from behind the constricting lump in his throat, Nyree put her fingers to Rivic's lips. "'Tis time for me to return to the tribe. I have much to teach Ellonia, everything I have learned here. We will be together again soon enough."

"Will we?"

She shook his hands. "Aye." She glanced back to Cirvel who, even at the leisurely pace, was coming up on them quickly. "Go."

Nyree's urging brought with it a sense of resigned calm. It sparked in his chest and flowed warmly over him. These were the footsteps he needed to take. He leaned forward and kissed his twin sister on her forehead before he departed.

Rivic walked over to where Cirvel stood and dropped onto bent knee before the Lord of Gohaldinest. "My lord?"

Cirvel broke from his conversation with Lihn to look down at him. "Now you have something to say, Dominus Rivic?"

"Aye."

"Rise and have it out." Cirvel's voice contained a high strain of irritation as if his happiness was a mask over the truth. Something in his tone made Rivic wonder if Cirvel felt disappointment in letting these trainees go, as if each one leaving were a little betrayal. How much of that had Rivic's request made?

Rivic stood, but he couldn't bring himself to look in Cirvel's dark eyes. "My lord, I felt conflicted about leaving. I believe my place is really here, training with you in Gohaldinest. I should like to stay, if I am truly welcome here as you stated earlier."

"Dominus Rivic, you are indeed welcome here. But what of your sister?"

"She wishes to return to the tribe."

"Really?" His gaze flickered to Nyree, who waited patiently several paces away. "Instruction resumes in just a couple of days and I doubt you are willing to let your sister proceed alone, but 'tis impossible for you to make the journey in that time without the use of magic."

Rivic knew full well that Cirvel could give him permission to teleport him and Nyree to the tribe and back, but had turned this to an unspoken challenge. What, indeed, would Rivic do?

Whether it was intentional to draw his attention or if Lihn was merely thinking the same thing that Rivic was, she took a subtle step, dragging her foot across the rocky ground.

Rivic found his idea bolstered. "Lord Cirvel, I would like your permission to take Nyree through the tower. I know the images in the column are different places. Certainly, there is one that is near my tribe. The Necroathelings that came for me there couldn't have gotten there so fast without me feeling it if there wasn't already a spot close by." Rivic paused. "They also couldn't have gotten away so quickly if they hadn't known of another location. It took me much longer to get to Gohaldinest."

A flashing smile broke Cirvel's austere stance. "That it did. I was beginning to wonder if you were coming."

"So, my lord, will you allow me to return Nyree to the tribe through the tower and then return the same way to Gohaldinest?"

Lihn drew Cirvel's attention with a hand on his arm. They exchanged only a look. "Aye," Cirvel said finally. "I will allow this."

"Thank you, my lord." Rivic bowed once more just for good measure. Then he returned to Nyree and gathered their belongings. They moved off to stand behind Cirvel, watching as the acolytes departed.

A moment of hesitation whispered through Rivic, but it was like the final sweep of a broom disposing of his doubts, leaving him optimistic that he was doing the right thing.

After those returning to their tribes had left and the gates were closed, Cirvel turned to them. "Let's get you home now," he said to Nyree, "if you are certain you want to leave. You are also welcome to stay."

Nyree curtsied, but her eyes never broke from Cirvel's. "I appreciate the offer, but Rivic has made me understand how much I mean to the tribe and my place right now is with them."

Rivic tried to hold his face emotionless, lest Cirvel read Nyree's lie off of him. Cirvel didn't seem pleased, but he didn't peruse Rivic in search of untruth. He merely nodded and turned.

The walk back to the castle didn't seem nearly as long or

heavy. They crossed through the grassy courtyard and came to the tower.

Cirvel entered and spoke a deeply toned word that rattled through Rivic with familiarity, but he couldn't place it. When Cirvel stepped upon the stairs, no question lit upon the stone for him to answer. Rivic realized that Cirvel had dispelled the challenge.

At the top of the stairs, Cirvel scrolled through the pictures until he found the one he searched for. "This will put you close. You may flash teleport from there to your tribe. As soon as she is safe with the people of Krithstand's tribe, return immediately."

Rivic nodded. "Aye, my lord."

"Vochey, Luminous." A melee weapon with several spiked balls dangling from chains came to Cirvel's hand. At first, Rivic thought to summon Honor, but Nyree squeezed his wrist. Submit, that was her weapon, and what she was calling him to do right now. Rivic stayed his actions. Cirvel placed Luminous into the column. "This will hold the way open for you. On the other side will be a similar column of blue. Find it and it will bring you back."

"Aye." Rivic stepped through. Nyree followed.

Behind Rivic stood the blue column much as Cirvel had said it would, and inside was the spiked ball and chain weapon.

"Sorry," Nyree said, staring at Luminous. "He had been planning on using his simple dagger and only changed his mind at the last moment. I think he wanted to make you afraid of not returning."

"As opposed to the fear of me returning to him?"

Nyree smiled. "You know that is meant to be. Come. If we hurry, you might have a moment with Ellonia before you need to depart."

Rivic saw the lake where he had bathed and Ellonia had

attempted to cut his hair. While he felt sorry there would be so little time, he knew that even a moment with Ellonia would be worth it. Hoisting the pack to adjust it on his shoulders, he hurried Nyree toward the camp. A few steps later, he placed his hand on her shoulder. "Talcor dun."

It took two spells to get them into camp. A cry of surprised alarm rose as they appeared. Several warriors raced forward, seizing and raising their weapons to attack.

Ellonia ran through the thickening crowd. "'Tis all right!"

Rivic held up his arms to catch her as she landed against him. He held her close, wishing this moment could become an eternity.

She sighed, nuzzling her cheek against him. "You've changed so much. I hardly recognized you."

Her voice broke through his thoughts and he realized that the warriors which had gathered quickly around them were now slowly backing away, though they were putting down their weapons with trepidation.

Rivic touched her face. "I don't have long. I must return to Gohaldinest. But Nyree needed to come back."

Ellonia gave a brave smile as she drew back from Rivic and turned toward Nyree. "'Tis good to see you." She stepped in to give a hug to Nyree, who looked less willing to accept the gesture than Rivic had. "You have much healing yet to be done."

"And far too little time," Nyree responded. "A moment, dear brother, for the safety of all."

Knowing she was correct, Rivic backed away, letting Ellonia reach out to him for one last touch. "I must go. I don't want Cirvel to send Necroathelings looking for me." Their fingers slowly slid apart, but Ellonia's eyes were strong and held no tears.

Rivic turned, heading out of the camp without looking back, though he could sense Nyree moving off with Ellonia.

He didn't want to leave, but he knew he must. Before he reached the edge of the camp, he whispered, "Talcor dun."

The mace with spiked metal balls still hung in the blue column. He reached inside and felt himself moved back to Gohaldinest.

Cirvel greeted him, but Lihn was no longer there. Had he taken a moment to send her back to her room?

Reaching into the column, Cirvel pulled the mace from inside. "Everything done that you needed to take care of? Ready to continue your training?"

This was the last place Rivic wanted to be. And yet...

Rivic nodded.

This was exactly where he needed to be.

He was here by choice, his choice, regardless of what Cirvel thought he held over Rivic. That returned his powers to him. It might, maybe, even make him more powerful.

Cirvel started down the stairs, the mace vanishing from his hand as he went.

Gathering his newfound strength, Rivic turned to follow the Lord of Gohaldinest and begin the next step of his journey, wherever it might lead.

RIVIC'S STORY CONTINUES

A ONESONG NOVEL
BOOK 2
Walk the Path

DAWN BLAIR
AUTHOR OF THE SACRED KNIGHT SERIES

COMING SOON!

The courage to become legendary:

Discover the magic in the epic fantasy adventure of Sacred Knight

The Missing Thread (book 5) coming soon!

READY FOR ANOTHER QUEST?

*S*ign up for Dawn Blair's newsletter to learn about new releases, get access to fun and free stuff, hear about events, and more!

It's easy.

*G*o to **www.dawnblair.com/newsletter** to join the adventure.

About the Author

Dawn Blair grew up on a ranch in a rural Nevada town. The old buildings provided inspiration for her imagination as she thrived on stories of unicorns, princesses, heroic knights, and hidden doors to other dimensions.

For as long as she can remember, Dawn has had a passion for storytelling. Though she started out writing, her creative life expanded into painting and illustration.

She loves creating worlds and spinning tales for people to enjoy. The best ones are the stories that surprise her as she's writing. She loves her characters doing the unexpected. She'll gladly tell you that the most exciting part about being a writer is being the first one on the journey.

Thank you for taking the time to join her on these adventures.

Find more about Dawn and read free fiction on her blog at:
www.toursofimagination.com

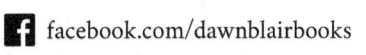

facebook.com/dawnblairbooks

twitter.com/dawnblair

instagram.com/dawn.blair